COSME'S THIN, DARK HAND SHOT ACROSS THE TABLE AND GRIPPED THE FELLOW'S WRIST (*page* 102)

HIDDEN CREEK

BY
KATHARINE NEWLIN BURT
AUTHOR OF "THE BRANDING IRON" AND "THE RED LADY"

With Illustrations by
GEORGE GIGUÈRE

BOSTON AND NEW YORK
HOUGHTON MIFFLIN COMPANY
The Riverside Press Cambridge
1920

COPYRIGHT, 1920, BY THE RIDGWAY COMPANY
COPYRIGHT, 1920, BY KATHARINE NEWLIN BURT

ALL RIGHTS RESERVED

TO
MAXWELL STRUTHERS BURT
WHO BLAZED THE TRAIL

CONTENTS

PART ONE: THE GOOD OLD WORLD

I.	SHEILA'S LEGACY	3
II.	SYLVESTER HUDSON COMES FOR HIS PICTURE	5
III.	THE FINEST CITY IN THE WORLD	14
IV.	MOONSHINE	24
V.	INTERCESSION	37
VI.	THE BAWLING-OUT	50
VII.	DISH-WASHING	60
VIII.	ARTISTS	72
IX.	A SINGEING OF WINGS	82
X.	THE BEACON LIGHT	98
XI.	IN THE PUBLIC EYE	110
XII.	HUDSON'S QUEEN	123
XIII.	SYLVESTER CELEBRATES	137
XIV.	THE LIGHT OF DAWN	146
XV.	FLAMES	152

PART TWO: THE STARS

I.	THE HILL	161
II.	ADVENTURE	172
III.	JOURNEY'S END	187
IV.	BEASTS	196
V.	NEIGHBOR NEIGHBOR	201

CONTENTS

VI.	A History and a Letter	213
VII.	Sanctuary	221
VIII.	Desertion	234
IX.	Work and a Song	247
X.	Winter	251
XI.	The Pack	262
XII.	The Good Old World Again	274
XIII.	Loneliness	284
XIV.	Sheila and the Stars	295

ILLUSTRATIONS

Cosme's thin, dark hand shot across the table and gripped the fellow's wrist *Frontispiece*

So Sheila Arundel left the garret where the stars pressed close, and went with Sylvester Hudson out into the world   14

The only car in sight was Hudson's own, which wriggled and slipped its way courageously along   22

Then "Pap's" voice cracked out at him   52

It was not easy, even with Babe's good-humored help, to go down and submit to Mrs. Hudson's hectoring   62

It was an indulgent and forgiving smile, but, meeting Dickie's look, it went out   96

A man kneeling over the water lifted a white and startled face   176

For an instant his look went beyond her and remembered troubling things   206

HIDDEN CREEK

PART ONE
THE GOOD OLD WORLD

HIDDEN CREEK

CHAPTER I
SHEILA'S LEGACY

JUST before his death, Marcus Arundel, artist and father of Sheila, bore witness to his faith in God and man. He had been lying apparently unconscious, his slow, difficult breath drawn at longer and longer intervals. Sheila was huddled on the floor beside his bed, her hand pressing his urgently in the pitiful attempt, common to human love, to hold back the resolute soul from the next step in its adventure. The nurse, who came in by the day, had left a paper of instructions on the table. Here a candle burned under a yellow shade, throwing a circle of warm, unsteady light on the head of the girl, on the two hands, on the rumpled coverlet, on the dying face. This circle of light seemed to collect these things, to choose them, as though for the expression of some meaning. It felt for them as an artist feels for his composition and gave to them a symbolic value. The two hands were in the center of the glow — the long, pale, slack one, the small, desperate, clinging one. The conscious and the unconscious, life and death, humanity and God — all that is mysterious and tragic seemed to find expression there in the two hands.

So they had been for six hours, and it would soon be morning. The large, bare room, however, was still possessed by night, and the city outside was at its lowest ebb of life, almost soundless. Against the skylight the winter stars seemed to be pressing; the sky was laid across the panes of glass like a purple cloth in which sparks burned.

Suddenly and with strength Arundel sat up. Sheila rose with him, drawing up his hand in hers to her heart.

"Keep looking at the stars, Sheila," he said with thrilling emphasis, and widened his eyes at the visible host of them. Then he looked down at her; his eyes shone as though they had caught a reflection from the myriad lights. "It is a good old world," he said heartily in a warm and human voice, and he smiled his smile of everyday good-fellowship.

Sheila thanked God for his return, and on the very instant he was gone. He dropped back, and there were no more difficult breaths.

Sheila, alone there in the garret studio above the city, cried to her father and shook him, till, in very terror of her own frenzy in the face of his stillness, she grew calm and laid herself down beside him, put his dead arm around her, nestled her head against his shoulder. She was seventeen years old, left alone and penniless in the old world that he had just pronounced so good. She lay there staring at the stars till they faded, and the cold, clear eye of day looked down into the room.

CHAPTER II

SYLVESTER HUDSON COMES FOR HIS PICTURE

BACK of his sallow, lantern-jawed face, Sylvester Hudson hid successfully, though without intention, all that was in him whether of good or ill. Certainly he did not look his history. He was stoop-shouldered, pensive-eyed, with long hands on which he was always turning and twisting a big emerald. He dressed quietly, almost correctly, but there was always something a little wrong in the color or pattern of his tie, and he was too fond of brown and green mixtures which did not become his sallowness. He smiled very rarely, and when he did smile, his long upper lip unfastened itself with an effort and showed a horizontal wrinkle halfway between the pointed end of his nose and the irregular, nicked row of his teeth.

Altogether, he was a gentle, bilious-looking sort of man, who might have been anything from a country gentleman to a moderately prosperous clerk. As a matter of fact, he was the owner of a dozen small, not too respectable, hotels through the West, and had an income of nearly half a million dollars. He lived in Millings, a town in a certain Far-Western State, where flourished the most pretentious and respectable of his hotels. It had a famous bar, to which rode the sheep-herders, the cowboys, the ranchers, the dry-farmers of the surrounding country — yes, and sometimes, thirstiest of all, the workmen from more distant oil-fields, a dangerous crew. Millings at that time had not yielded to the generally increasing "dryness" of the West. It was "wet," notwithstanding its choking alkali dust; and the deep pool of its wetness lay in Hudson's bar, The Aura. It was named for a woman who had become his wife.

When Hudson came to New York he looked up his Eastern patrons, and it was one of these who, knowing Arundel's need, encouraged the hotel-keeper in his desire to secure a "jim-dandy picture" for the lobby of The Aura and took him for the purpose to Marcus's studio. On that morning, hardly a fortnight before the artist's death, Sheila was not at home.

Marcus, in spite of himself, was managed into a sale. It was of an enormous canvas, covered weakly enough by a thin reproduction of a range of the Rockies and a sagebrush flat. Mr. Hudson in his hollow voice pronounced it "classy." "Say," he said, "put a little life into the foreground and that would please *me*. It's what I'm seekin'. Put in an automobile meetin' one of these old-time prairie schooners — the old West sayin' howdy to the noo. That will tickle the trade." Mark, who was feeling weak and ill, consented wearily. He sketched in the proposed amendment and Hudson approved with one of his wrinkled smiles. He offered a small price, at which Arundel leapt like a famished hound.

HUDSON COMES FOR HIS PICTURE 7

When his visitors had gone, the painter went feverishly to work. The day before his death, Sheila, under his whispered directions, put the last touches to the body of the "automobile."

"It's ghastly," sighed the sick man, "but it will do — for Millings." He turned his back sadly enough to the canvas, which stood for him like a monument to fallen hope. Sheila praised it with a faltering voice, but he did not turn nor speak. So she carried the huge picture out of his sight.

The next day, at about eleven o'clock in the morning, Hudson called. He came with stiff, angular motions of his long, thin legs, up the four steep, shabby flights and stopped at the top to get his breath.

"The picture ain't worth the climb," he thought; and then, struck by the peculiar stillness of the garret floor, he frowned. "Damned if the feller ain't out!" He took a stride forward and knocked at Arundel's door. There was no answer. He turned the knob and stepped into the studio.

A screen stood between him and one half of the room. The other half was empty. The place was very cold and still. It was deplorably bare and shabby in the wintry morning light. Some one had eaten a meager breakfast from a tray on the little table near the stove. Hudson's canvas stood against the wall facing him, and its presence gave him a feeling of ownership, of a right to be there. He put his long, stiff hands into his pockets and strolled forward. He came round the corner of the screen and found himself looking at the dead body of his host.

The nurse, that morning, had come and gone. With Sheila's help she had prepared Arundel for his burial. He lay in all the formal detachment of death, his eyelids drawn decently down over his eyes, his lips put carefully together, his hands, below their white cuffs and black sleeves, laid carefully upon the clean smooth sheet.

Hudson drew in a hissing breath, and at the sound Sheila, crumpled up in exhausted slumber on the floor beside the bed, awoke and lifted her face.

It was a heart-shaped face, a thin, white heart, the peak of her hair cutting into the center of her forehead. The mouth struck a note of life with its dull, soft red. There was not lacking in this young face the slight exaggerations necessary to romantic beauty. Sheila had a strange, arresting sort of jaw, a trifle over-accentuated and out of drawing. Her eyes were long, flattened, narrow, the color of bubbles filled with smoke, of a surface brilliance and an inner mistiness — indescribable eyes, clear, very melting, wistful and beautiful under sooty lashes and slender, arched black brows.

Sheila lifted this strange, romantic face on its long, romantic throat and looked at Hudson. Then she got to her feet. She was soft and silken, smooth and tender, gleaming white of skin. She had put on an old black dress, just a scrap of a flimsy, little worn-out

HUDSON COMES FOR HIS PICTURE 9

gown. A certain slim, crushable quality of her body was accentuated by this flimsiness of covering. She looked as though she could be drawn through a ring — as though, between your hands, you could fold her to nothing. A thin little kitten of silky fur and small bones might have the same feel as Sheila.

She stood up now and looked tragically and helplessly at Hudson and tried to speak.

He backed away from the bed, beckoned to her, and met her in the other half of the room so that the leather screen stood between them and the dead man. They spoke in hushed voices.

"I had no notion, Miss Arundel, that — that — of — this," Hudson began in a dry, jerky whisper. "Believe *me*, I would n't 'a' thought of intrudin'. I ordered the picture there from your father a fortnight ago, and this was the day I was to come and give it a last looking-over before I came through with the cash, see? I had n't heard he was sick even, much less" — he cleared his throat — "gone beyond," he ended, quoting from the "Millings Gazette" obituary column. "You get me?"

"Yes," said Sheila, in her voice that in some mysterious way was another expression of the clear mistiness of her eyes and the suppleness of her body. "You are Mr. Hudson." She twisted her hands together behind her back. She was shivering with cold and nervousness. "It's done, you see. Father finished it."

Hudson gave the canvas an absent glance and motioned Sheila to a chair with a stiff gesture of his arm.

"You set down," he said.

She obeyed, and he walked to and fro before her.

"Say, now," he said, "I'll take the picture all right. But I'd like to know, Miss Arundel, if you'll excuse me, how you're fixed?"

"Fixed?" Sheila faltered.

"Why, yes, ma'am — as to finances, I mean. You've got some funds, or some re-lations or some friends to call upon —?"

Sheila drew up her head a trifle, lowered her eyes, and began to plait her thin skirt across her knee with small, delicate fingers. Hudson stopped in his walk to watch this mechanical occupation. She struggled dumbly with her emotion and managed to answer him at last.

"No, Mr. Hudson. Father is very poor. I have n't any relations. We have no friends here nor anywhere near. We lived in Europe till quite lately — a fishing village in Normandy. I — I shall have to get some work."

"Say!" It was an ejaculation of pity, but there was a note of triumph in it, too; perhaps the joy of the gratified philanthropist.

"Now, look-a-here, little girl, the price of that picture will just about cover your expenses, eh? — board and — er — funeral?"

Sheila nodded, her throat working, her lids pressing down tears.

HUDSON COMES FOR HIS PICTURE 11

"Well, now, look-a-here. I've got a missus at home."

Sheila looked up and the tears fell. She brushed them from her cheeks. "A missus?"

"Yes'm — my wife. And a couple of gels about your age. Well, say, we've got a job for you."

Sheila put her hand to her head as though she would stop a whirling sensation there.

"You mean you have some work for me in your home?"

"You've got it first time. Yes, *ma'am*. Sure thing. At Millings, finest city in the world. After you're through here, you pack up your duds and you come West with me. Make a fresh start, eh? Why, it'll make me plumb cheerful to have a gel with me on that journey . . . seem like I'd Girlie or Babe along. They just cried to come, but, say, Noo York's no place for the young."

"But, Mr. Hudson, my ticket? I'm sure I won't have the money — ?"

"Advance it to you on your pay, Miss Arundel."

"But what is the work?" Sheila still held her hand against her forehead.

Hudson laughed his short, cracked cackle. "Jest old-fashioned house-work, dish-washing and such. 'Help' can't be had in Millings, and Girlie and Babe kick like steers when Momma leads 'em to the dish-pan. Not that you'd have to do it all, you know, just lend a hand to Momma. Maybe you're too fine for that?"

"Oh, no. I have done all the work here. I'd be glad. Only —"

He came closer to her and held up a long, threatening forefinger. It was a playful gesture, but Sheila had a distinct little tremor of fear. She looked up into his small, brown, pensive eyes, and her own were held as though their look had been fastened to his with rivets.

"Now, look-a-here, Miss Arundel, don't you say 'only' to me. Nor 'but.' Nor 'if.' Nary one of those words, if you please. Say, I've got daughters of my own and I can manage gels. I know *how*. Do you know my nickname? Well — say — it's 'Pap.' Pap Hudson. I'm the adopting kind. Sort of paternal, I guess. Kids and dogs follow me in the streets. You want a recommend? Just call up Mr. Hazeldean on the telephone. He's the man that fetched me here to buy that picture off Poppa."

"Oh," said Sheila, daughter of Mark who looked at stars, "of course I should n't think of asking for a recommendation. You've been only too kind —"

He put his hand on her shoulder in its thin covering and patted it, wondering at the silken, cool feeling against his palm.

"Kind, Miss Arundel? Pshaw! My middle name's 'Kind' and that's the truth. Why, how does the song go — ''T is love, 't is love that makes the world go round' — love's just another word for kindness, ain't it? And it's not such a bad old world either, eh?"

HUDSON COMES FOR HIS PICTURE

Without knowing it, with the sort of good luck that often attends the enterprises of such men, Hudson had used a spell. He had quoted, almost literally, her father's last words and she felt that it was a message from the other side of death.

She twisted about in her chair, took his hand from her shoulder, and drew it, stiff and sallow, to her young lips.

"Oh," she sobbed, "you're kind! It *is* a good world if there are such men as you!"

When Sylvester Hudson went down the stairs a minute or two after Sheila's impetuous outbreak, his sallow face was deeply flushed. He stopped to tell the Irishwoman who rented the garret floor to the Arundels, that Sheila's future was in his care. During this colloquy, pure business on his side and mixed business and sentiment on Mrs. Halligan's, Sylvester did not once look the landlady in the eye. His own eyes skipped hers, now across, now under, now over. There are some philanthropists who are overcome with such bashfulness in the face of their own good deeds. But, sitting back alone in his taxicab on his way to the station to buy Sheila's ticket to Millings, Sylvester turned his emerald rapidly about on his finger and whistled to himself. And cryptically he expressed his glow of gratified fatherliness.

"As smooth as silk," said Sylvester aloud.

CHAPTER III

THE FINEST CITY IN THE WORLD

So Sheila Arundel left the garret where the stars pressed close, and went with Sylvester Hudson out into the world. It was, that morning, a world of sawing wind, of flying papers and dust-dervishes, a world, to meet which people bent their shrinking faces and drew their bodies together as against the lashing of a whip. Sheila thought she had never seen New York so drab and soulless; it hurt her to leave it under so desolate an aspect.

"Cheery little old town, is n't it?" said Sylvester. "Gee! Millings is God's country all right."

On the journey he put Sheila into a compartment, supplied her with magazines and left her for the most part to herself — for which isolation she was grateful. With her compartment door ajar, she could see him in his section, when he was not in the smoking-car, or rather she could see his lean legs, his long, dark hands, and the top of his sleek head. The rest was an outspread newspaper. Occasionally he would come into the compartment to read aloud some bit of information which he thought might interest her. Once it was the prowess of a record-breaking hen; again it was a joke about a mother-in-law; another time it was the Hilliard murder case, a scandal of New York

SO SHEILA ARUNDEL LEFT THE GARRET WHERE THE STARS PRESSED CLOSE
AND WENT WITH SYLVESTER HUDSON OUT INTO THE WORLD

THE FINEST CITY IN THE WORLD 15

high-life, the psychology of which intrigued Sylvester.

"Is n't it queer, though, Miss Arundel, that such things happen in the slums and they happen in the smart set, but they don't happen near so often with just plain folks like you and me! Is n't this, now, a real Tenderloin Tale — South American wife and American husband and all their love affairs, and then one day her up and shooting him! Money," quoth Sylvester, "sure makes love popular. Now for that little ro-mance, poor folks would hardly stop a day's work, but just because the Hilliards here have po-sition and spon-dulix, why, they'll run a couple of columns about 'em for a week. What's your opinion on the subject, Miss Arundel?"

He was continually asking this, and poor Sheila, strange, bewildered, oppressed by his intrusion into her uprooted life, would grope wildly through her odds and ends of thought and find that on most of the subjects that interested him, she had no opinions at all.

"You must think I'm dreadfully stupid, Mr. Hudson," she faltered once after a particularly deplorable failure.

"Oh, you're a kid, Miss Sheila, that's all your trouble. And I reckon you're half asleep, eh? Kind of brought up on pictures and country walks, in — what's the name of the foreign part? — Normandy? No friends of your own age? No beaux?"

Sheila shook her head, smiling. Her flexible smile was as charming as a child's. It dawned on the gravity of her face with an effect of spring moonlight. In it there was some of the mischief of fairyland.

"What *you* need is — Millings," prescribed Sylvester. "Girlie and Babe will wake you up. Yes, and the boys. You'll make a hit in Millings." He contemplated her for an instant with his head on one side. "We ain't got anything like you in Millings."

Sheila, looking out at the wide Nebraskan prairies that slipped endlessly past her window hour by hour that day, felt that she would not make a hit at Millings. She was afraid of Millings. Her terror of Babe and Girlie was profound. She had lived and grown up, as it were, under her father's elbow. Her adoration of him had stood between her and experience. She knew nothing of humanity except Marcus Arundel. And he was hardly typical — a shy, proud, head-in-the-air sort of man, who would have been greatly loved if he had not shrunk morbidly from human contacts. Sheila's Irish mother had wooed and won him and had made a merry midsummer madness in his life, as brief as a dream. Sheila was all that remained of it. But, for all her quietness, the shadow of his broken heart upon her spirit, she was a Puck. She could make laughter and mischief for him and for herself — not for any one else yet; she was too shy. But that might come. Only, Puck laughter is a little unearthly, a little delicate. The ear of Millings might

THE FINEST CITY IN THE WORLD 17

not be attuned.... Just now, Sheila felt that she would never laugh again. Sylvester's humor certainly did not move her. She almost choked trying to swallow becomingly the mother-in-law anecdote.

But Sylvester's talk, his questions, even his jokes, were not what most oppressed her. Sometimes, looking up, she would find him staring at her over the top of his newspaper as though he were speculating about something, weighing her, judging her by some inner measurement. It was rather like the way her father had looked a model over to see if she would fit his dream.

At such moments Sylvester's small brown eyes were the eyes of an artist, of a visionary. They embarrassed her painfully. What was it, after all, that he expected of her? For an expectation of some kind he most certainly had, and it could hardly have to do with her skill in washing dishes.

She asked him a few small questions as they drew near to Millings. The strangeness of the country they were now running through excited her and fired her courage — these orange-colored cliffs, these purple buttes, these strange twisting cañons with their fierce green streams.

"Please tell me about Mrs. Hudson and your daughters?" she asked.

This was a few hours before they were to come to Millings. They had changed trains at a big, bare, glaring city several hours before and were now in a small, gritty car with imitation-leather seats. They were running through a gorge, and below and ahead Sheila could see the brown plain with its patches of snow and, like a large group of red toy houses, the town of Millings, far away but astonishingly distinct in the clear air.

Sylvester, considering her question, turned his emerald slowly.

"The girls are all *right*, Miss Sheila. They're lookers. I guess I've spoiled 'em some. They'll be crazy over you — sort of a noo pet in the house, eh? I've wired to 'em. They must be hoppin' up and down like a popper full of corn."

"And Mrs. Hudson?"

Sylvester grinned — the wrinkle cutting long and deep across his lip. "Well, ma'am, she ain't the hoppin' kind."

A few minutes later Sheila discovered that emphatically she was not the hopping kind. A great, bony woman with a wide, flat, handsome face, she came along the station platform, kissed Sylvester with hard lips and stared at Sheila . . . the stony stare of her kind.

"Babe ran the Ford down, Sylly," she said in the harshest voice Sheila had ever heard. "Where's the girl's trunk?"

Sylvester's sallow face reddened. He turned quickly to Sheila.

"Run over to the car yonder, Miss Sheila, and get

used to Babe, while I kind of take the edge off Momma."

Sheila did not run. She walked in a peculiar light-footed manner which gave her the look of a proud deer.

"Momma" was taken firmly to the baggage-room, where, it would seem, the edge was removed with difficulty, for Sheila waited in the motor with Babe for half an hour.

Babe hopped. She hopped out of her seat at the wheel and shook Sheila's hand and told her to "jump right in."

"Sit by me on the way home, Sheila." Babe had a tremendous voice. "And leave the old folks to gossip on the back seat. Gee! you're different from what I thought you'd be. Ain't you small, though? You've got no form. Say, Millings will do lots for you. Is n't Pap a character, though? Were n't you tickled the way he took you up? Your Poppa was a painter, was n't he? Can you make a picture of me? I've got a steady that would be just wild if you could."

Sheila sat with hands clenched in her shabby muff and smiled her moonlight smile. She was giddy with the intoxicating, heady air, with the brilliant sunset light, with Babe's loud cordiality. She wanted desperately to like Babe; she wanted even more desperately to be liked. She was in an unimaginable panic, now.

Babe was a splendid young animal, handsome and

round and rosy, her body crowded into a bright-blue braided, fur-trimmed coat, her face crowded into a tight, much-ornamented veil, her head with heavy chestnut hair, crowded into a cherry-colored, velvet turban round which seemed to be wrapped the tail of some large wild beast. Her hands were ready to burst from yellow buckskin gloves; her feet, with high, thick insteps, from their tight, thin, buttoned boots, even her legs shone pink and plump below her short skirt, through silk stockings that were threatened at the seams. And the blue of her eyes, the red of her cheeks, the white of her teeth, had the look of being uncontainable, too brilliant and full to stay where they belonged. The whole creature flashed and glowed and distended herself. Her voice was a riot of uncontrolled vitality, and, as though to use up a little of all this superfluous energy, she was violently chewing gum. Except for an occasional slight smacking sound, it did not materially interfere with speech.

"There's Poppa now," she said at last. "Say, Poppa, you two sit in the back, will you? Sheila and I are having a fine time. But, Poppa, you old tin-horn, what did you mean by saying in your wire that she was a husky girl? Why, she's got the build of a sage-brush mosquito! Look-a-here, Sheila." Babe by a miracle got her plump hand in and out of a pocket and handed a telegram to her new friend. "Read that and learn to know Poppa!"

THE FINEST CITY IN THE WORLD 21

Sylvester laughed rather sheepishly as Sheila read:

Am bringing home artist's A1 picture for The Aura and artist's A1 daughter. Husky girl. Will help Momma.

"Well," said Sylvester apologetically, "she's one of the wiry kind, are n't you, Miss Sheila?"

Sheila was struggling with an attack of hysterical mirth. She nodded and put her muff before her mouth to hide an uncontrollable quivering of her lips.

"Momma" had not spoken. Her face was all one even tone of red, her nostrils opened and shut, her lips were tight. Sylvester, however, was in a genial humor. He leaned forward with his arms folded along the back of the front seat and pointed out the beauties of Millings. He showed Sheila the Garage, the Post-Office, and the Trading Company, and suddenly pressing her shoulder with his hand, he cracked out sharply:

"There's The Aura, girl!"

His eyes were again those of the artist and the visionary. They glowed.

Sheila turned her head. They were passing the double door of the saloon and went slowly along the front of the hotel.

It stood on that corner where the main business street intersects with the Best Residence Street. Its main entrance opened into the flattened corner of the building where the roof rose to a fantastic façade. For the rest, the hotel was of yellowish-brick, half-surrounded by a wooden porch where at milder seasons of the year in deep wicker chairs men and women were always rocking with the air of people engaged in serious and not unimportant work. At such friendlier seasons, too, by the curb was always a weary-looking Ford car from which grotesquely arrayed "travelers" from near-by towns and cities were descending covered with alkali dust — faces, chiffon veils, spotted silk dresses, high white kid boots, dangling purses and all, their men dust-powdered to a wrinkled sameness of aspect. At this time of the year the porch was deserted, and the only car in sight was Hudson's own, which wriggled and slipped its way courageously along the rutted, dirty snow.

Around the corner next to the hotel stood Hudson's home. It was a large house of tortured architecture, cupolas and twisted supports and strange, overlapping scallops of wood, painted wavy green, pinkish red and yellow. Its windows were of every size and shape and appeared in unreasonable, impossible places — opening enormous mouths on tiny balconies with twisted posts and scalloped railings, like embroidery patterns, one on top of the other up to a final absurdity of a bird cage which found room for itself between two cupolas under the roof.

Up the steps of the porch Mrs. Hudson mounted grimly, followed by Babe. Sylvester stayed to tinker with the car, and Sheila, after a doubtful, tremulous moment, went slowly up the icy path after the two women.

THE ONLY CAR IN SIGHT WAS HUDSON'S OWN, WHICH WRIGGLED AND
SLIPPED ITS WAY COURAGEOUSLY ALONG

She stumbled a little on the lowest step and, in recovering herself, she happened to turn her head. And so, between two slender aspen trees that grew side by side like white, captive nymphs in Hudson's yard, she saw a mountain-top. The sun had set. There was a crystal, turquoise translucency behind the exquisite snowy peak, which seemed to stand there facing God, forgetful of the world behind it, remote and reverent and most serene in the light of His glory. And just above where the turquoise faded to pure pale green, a big white star trembled. Sheila's heart stopped in her breast. She stood on the step and drew breath, throwing back her veil. A flush crept up into her face. She felt that she had been traveling all her life toward her meeting with this mountain and this star. She felt radiant and comforted.

"How beautiful!" she whispered.

Sylvester had joined her.

"Finest city in the world!" he said.

CHAPTER IV

MOONSHINE

DICKIE HUDSON pushed from him to the full length of his arm the ledger of The Aura Hotel, tilted his chair back from the desk, and, leaning far over to one side, set the needle on a phonograph record, pressed the starter, and absorbed himself in rolling and lighting a cigarette. This accomplished, he put his hands behind his head and, wreathed in aromatic, bluish smoke, gave himself up to complete enjoyment of the music.

It was a song from some popular light opera. A very high soprano and a musical tenor duet, sentimental, humoresque:

> "There, dry your eyes,
> I sympathize
> Just as a mother would —
> Give me your hand,
> I understand, we're off to slumber land
> Like a father, like a mother, like a sister,
>   like a brother."

Listening to this melody, Dickie Hudson's face under the gaslight expressed a rapt and spiritual delight, tender, romantic, melancholy.

He was a slight, undersized youth, very pale, very fair, with the face of a delicate boy. He had large, near-sighted blue eyes in which lurked a wistful, deprecatory smile, a small chin running from wide cheek-bones to a point. His lips were sensitive and undecided, his nose unformed, his hair soft and easily ruffled. There were hard blue marks under the long-lashed eyes, an unhealthy pallor to his cheeks, a slight unsteadiness of his fingers.

Dickie held a position of minor importance in the hotel, and his pale, innocent face was almost as familiar to its patrons as to those of the saloon next door — more familiar to both than it was to Hudson's "residence." Sometimes for weeks Dickie did not strain the scant welcome of his "folks." To-night, however, he was resolved to tempt it. After listening to the record, he strolled over to the saloon.

Dickie was curious. He shared Millings's interest in the "young lady from Noo York." Shyness fought with a sense of adventure, until to-night, a night fully ten nights after Sheila's arrival, the courage he imbibed at the bar of The Aura gave him the necessary impetus. He pulled himself up from his elbow, removed his foot from the rail, straightened his spotted tie, and pushed through the swinging doors out into the night.

It was a moonlit night, as still and pure as an angel of annunciation — a night that carried tall, silver lilies in its hands. Above the small, sleepy town were lifted the circling rim of mountains and the web of blazing stars. Sylvester's son, after a few crunching steps along the icy pavement, stopped with his hand against the wall, and stood, not quite steadily, his face lifted. The whiteness sank through his tainted body and brain to the undefiled child-soul. The stars blazed awfully for Dickie, and the mountains were awfully white and high, and the air shattered against his spirit like a crystal sword. He stood for an instant as though on a single point of solid earth and looked giddily beyond earthly barriers.

His lips began to move. He was trying to put that mystery, that emotion, into words . . . "It's white," he murmured, "and sharp — burning — like — like" — his fancy fumbled — "like the inside of a cold flame." He shook his head. That did not describe the marvelous quality of the night. And yet — if the world had gone up to heaven in a single, streaming point of icy fire and a fellow stood in it, frozen, swept up out of a fellow's body . . . Again he shook his head and his eyes were possessed by the wistful, apologetic smile. He wished he were not tormented by this queer need of describing his sensations. He remembered very vividly one of the many occasions when it had roused his father's anger. Dickie, standing with his hand against the cold bricks of The Aura, smiled with his lips, not happily, but with a certain amusement, thinking of how Sylvester's hand had cracked against his cheek and sent all his thoughts flying like broken china. He had been apologizing for his slowness over an errand — something about leaves, it had been — the leaves of those aspens in the yard — he had told his father that they had been little green flames — he had stopped to look at them. "You damn fool!" Sylvester had said as he struck. "You damn fool!" Once, when a stranger asked five-year-old Dickie his name, he had answered innocently "Dickie-damn-fool!"

"They'll probably put it on my tombstone," Dickie concluded, and, stung by the cold, he shrank into his coat and stumbled round the corner of the street. The reek of spirits trailed behind him through the purity like a soiled rag.

Number 18 Cottonwood Avenue was brilliantly lighted. Girlie was playing the piano, Babe's voice, "sassing Poppa," was audible from one end to the other of the empty street. Her laughter slapped the air. Dickie hesitated. He was afraid of them all — of Sylvester's pensive, small, brown eyes and hard, long hands, of Babe's bodily vigor, of Girlie's mild contemptuous look, of his mother's gloomy, furtive tenderness. Dickie felt a sort of aching and compassionate dread of the rough, awkward caress of her big red hand against his cheek. As he hesitated, the door opened — a blaze of light, yellow as old gold, streamed into the blue brilliance of the moon. It was blotted out and a figure came quickly down the steps. It had an air of hurry and escape. A small, slim figure, it came along the path and through the gate; then, after just an instant of hesitation, it turned away from Dickie and sped up the wide street.

Dickie named it at once. "That's the girl," he said;

and possessed by his curiosity and by the sense of adventure which whiskey had fortified, he began to walk rapidly in the same direction. Out there, where the short street ended, began the steep side of a mesa. The snow on the road that was graded along its front was packed by the runners of freighting sleighs, but it was rough. He could not believe the girl meant to go for a walk alone. And yet, would she be out visiting already, she, a stranger? At the end of the street the small, determined figure did not stop; it went on, a little more slowly, but as decidedly as ever, up the slope. On the hard, frozen crust, her feet made hardly a sound. Above the level top of the white hill, the peak that looked remote from Hudson's yard became immediate. It seemed to peer — to lean forward, bright as a silver helmet against the purple sky. Dickie could see that "the girl" walked with her head tilted back as though she were looking at the sky. Perhaps it was the sheer beauty of the winter night that had brought her out. Following slowly up the hill, he felt a sense of nearness, of warmth; his aching, lifelong loneliness was remotely comforted because a girl, skimming ahead of him, had tilted her chin up so that she could see the stars. She reached the top of the mesa several minutes before he did and disappeared. She was now, he knew, on the edge of a great plateau, in summer covered with the greenish silver of sagebrush, now an unbroken, glittering expanse. He stood still to get his breath and listen to the very light crunch of her steps. He could hear a coyote wailing off there in the foothills, and the rushing noise of the small mountain river that hurled itself down upon Millings, ran through it at frenzied speed, and made for the cañon on the other side of the valley. Below him Millings twinkled with a few sparse lights, and he could, even from here, distinguish the clatter of Babe's voice. But when he came to the top, Millings dropped away from the reach of his senses. Here was dazzling space, the amazing presence of the mountains, the pressure of the starry sky. Far off already across the flat, that small, dark figure moved. She had left the road, which ran parallel with the mountain range, and was walking over the hard, sparkling crust. It supported her weight, but Dickie was not sure that it would do the same for his. He tried it carefully. It held, and he followed the faint track of small feet. It did not occur to him, dazed as he was by the fumes of whiskey and the heady air, that the sight of a man in swift pursuit of her loneliness might frighten Sheila. For some reason he imagined that she would know that he was Sylvester's son, and that he was possessed only by the most sociable and protective impulses.

He was, besides, possessed by a fateful feeling that it was intended that out here in the brilliant night he should meet her and talk to her. The adventurous heart of Dickie was aflame.

When the hurrying figure stopped and turned

quickly, he did not pause, but rather hastened his steps. He saw her lift her muff up to her heart, saw her waver, then move resolutely toward him. She came thus two or three steps, when a treacherous pitfall in the snow opened under her frightened feet and she went down almost shoulder deep. Dickie ran forward.

Bending over her, he saw her white, heart-shaped face, and its red mouth as startling as a June rose out here in the snow. And he saw, too, the panic of her shining eyes.

"Miss Arundel" — his voice came thin and tender, feeling its way doubtfully as though it was too heavy a reality — "let me help you. You *are* Miss Arundel, are n't you? I'm Dickie — Dickie Hudson, Pap Hudson's son. You had n't ought to be scared. I saw you coming out alone and took after you. I thought you might find it kind of lonesome up here on the flat at night in all the moonlight — hearing the coyotes and all. And, look-a-here, you might have had a time getting out of the snow. Oncet a fellow breaks through it sure means a floundering time before a fellow pulls himself out — "

She had given him a hand, and he had pulled her up beside him. Her smile of relief seemed very beautiful to Dickie.

"I came out," she said, "because it looked so wonderful — and I wanted to see — " She stopped, looking at him doubtfully, as though she expected him

MOONSHINE 31

not to understand, to think her rather mad. But he finished her sentence.

"— To see the mountains, was n't it?"

"Yes." She was again relieved, almost as much so, it seemed, as at the knowledge of his friendliness. "Especially that big one." She waved her muff toward the towering peak. "I never did see such a night! It's like — it's like — " She widened her eyes, as though, by taking into her brain an immense picture of the night, she might find out its likeness.

Dickie, moving uncertainly beside her, murmured, "Like the inside of a cold flame, a very white flame."

Sheila turned her chin, pointed above the fur collar of her coat, and included him in the searching and astonished wideness of her look.

"You work at The Aura, don't you?" she asked with childlike *brusquerie*.

Dickie's sensitive, undecided mouth settled into mournfulness. He looked away.

"Yes, ma'am," he said plaintively.

Sheila's widened eyes, still fixed upon him, began to embarrass him. A flush came up into his face.

She moved her look across him and away to the range.

"It *is* like that," she said — "like a cold flame, going up — how did you think of that?"

Dickie looked quickly, gratefully at her. "I kind of felt," he said lamely, "that I had got to find out what it was like. But " — he shook his head with his deprecatory smile — "but that don't tell it, Miss Arundel. It's more than that." He smiled again. "I bet you, you could think of somethin' better to say about it, could n't you?"

Sheila laughed. "What a funny boy you are! Not like the others. You don't even look like them. How old are you? When I first saw you I thought you were quite grown up. But you can't be much more than nineteen."

"Just that," he said, "but I'll be twenty next month."

"You've always lived here in Millings?"

"Yes, ma'am. Do you like it? I mean, do you like Millings? I hope you do."

Sheila pressed her muff against her mouth and looked at him over it. Her eyes were shining as though the moonlight had got into their misty grayness. She shook her head; then, as his face fell, she began to apologize.

"Your father has been so awfully kind to me. I am so grateful. And the girls are awfully good to me. But, Millings, you know? — I would n't have told you," she said half-angrily, "if I had n't been so sure you hated it."

They had come to the edge of the mesa, and there below shone the small, scattered lights of the town. The graphophone was playing in the saloon. Its music — some raucous, comic song — insulted the night.

"Why, no," said Dickie, "I don't hate Millings. I

never thought about it that way. It's not such a bad place. Honest, it is n't. There's lots of fine folks in it. Have you met Jim Greely?"

"Why, no, but I've seen him. Is n't that Girlie's — 'fellow'?"

Dickie made round, respectful eyes. He was evidently very much impressed.

"Say!" he ejaculated. "Is that the truth? Girlie's aiming kind of high."

It was not easy to walk side by side on the rutted snow of the road. Sheila here slipped ahead of him and went on quickly along the middle rut where the horses' hoofs had beaten a pitted path.

She looked back at him over her shoulder with a sort of malice.

"Is it aiming high?" she said. "Girlie is much more beautiful than Jim Greely."

"Oh, but he's some looker — Jim."

"Do you think so?" she said indifferently, with a dainty touch of scorn.

Dickie staggered physically from the shock of her speech. She had been speaking — was it possible? — of Jim Greely . . .

"I mean Mr. James Greely, the son of the president of the Millings National Bank," he said painstakingly, and a queer confusion came to him that the words were his feet and that neither were under his control. Also, he was not sure that he had said "Natural," or "National."

"I do mean Mr. James Greely," Sheila's clear voice came back to him. "He is, I should think, a very great hero of yours."

"Yes, ma'am," said Dickie.

Astonished at the abject humility of his tone, Sheila stopped and turned quite around to look at him. He seemed to be floundering in and out of invisible holes in the snow. He stepped very high, plunged, put out his hand, and righted himself by her shoulder. And he stayed there, lurched against her for a moment. She shook him off and began to run down the hill. His breath had struck her face. She knew that he was drunk.

Dickie followed her as fast as he could. Several times he fell, but, on the whole, he made fairly rapid progress, so that, by the time she dashed into the Hudsons' gate, he was only a few steps behind her and caught the gate before it shut. Sheila fled up the steps and beat at the door with her fist. Dickie was just behind her.

Sylvester himself opened the door. Back of him pressed Babe.

"Why, say," she said, "it's Sheila and she's got a beau already. You're some girl — "

"Please let me in," begged Sheila; "I — I am frightened. It's your brother, Dickie — but I think — there's something wrong — "

Sylvester put his hand on her and pushed her to one side.

He strode out on the small porch. Dickie wavered before him on the top step.

"I thought I'd make the ac-acquaintance of the young lady," he began doubtfully. "I saw her admiring at the stars and I — "

"Oh, you did!" snarled Hudson. "All right. Now go and make acquaintance with the bottom step." He thrust a long, hard hand at Dickie's chest, and the boy fell backward, clattering ruefully down the steps with a rattle of thin knees and elbows. At the bottom he lay for a minute, painfully huddled in the snow.

"Go in, Miss Sheila," said Sylvester. "I'm sorry my son came home to-night and frightened you. He usually has more sense. He'll have more sense next time."

He ran down the steps, but before he could reach the huddled figure it gathered itself fearfully together and fled, limping and staggering across the yard, through the gate and around the corner of the street.

Hudson came up, breathing hard.

"Where's Sheila?" he asked sharply.

"She ran upstairs," said Babe. "Ain't it a shame? What got into Dick?"

"Something that will get kicked out of him good and proper to-morrow," said his father grimly.

He stood at the bottom of the steep, narrow stairs, looking up, his hands thrust into his pockets, his under lip stuck out. His eyes were unusually gentle and pensive.

"I would n't 'a' had her scared that way for anything," he said, "not for anything. That's likely to spoil all my plans."

He swore under his breath, wheeled about, and going into the parlor he shut the door and began walking to and fro. Babe crept rather quietly up the stairs. There were times when even Babe was afraid of "Poppa."

CHAPTER V

INTERCESSION

BABE tiptoed up the first flight, walked solidly and boldly up the second, and ran up the third. She had decided to have a talk with Sheila, to soothe her indignation, and, if possible, to explain Dickie. It seemed to Babe that Dickie needed explanation.

Sheila's room was at the top of the house — the very room, in fact, whose door opened on the bird cage of a balcony between two cupolas. Babe came to the door and knocked. A voice answered sharply: "Come in," and Babe, entering, shut the door and leaned against it.

It was a small, bare, whitewashed room, with a narrow cot, a washstand, a bureau, and two extraordinary chairs — a huge one that rocked on damaged springs, enclosed in plaited leather like the case of an accordion, and one that had been a rocker, but stood unevenly on its diminished legs. Babe had protested against Momma's disposal of the "girl from Noo York," and had begged that Sheila be allowed to share her own red, white, and blue boudoir below. But Sheila had preferred her small room. It was red as a rose at sunset, still and high, remote from Millings, and it faced The Hill.

Now, the gaslight flared against the bare walls and

ceiling. Sheila's hat and coat and muff lay on the bed where she had thrown them. She stood, looking at Babe. Her face was flushed, her eyes gleamed, that slight exaggeration of her chin was more pronounced than usual.

Babe put her head on one side. "Oh, say, Sheila, why bother about Dickie. Nobody cares about Dickie. He'll get a proper bawlin'-out from Poppa to-morrow. But I'd think myself simple to be scared by him. He's harmless. The poor kid can't half help himself now. He got started when he was awful young."

"Oh," said Sheila, as sharply as before, stopping before Babe, "I'm not frightened. I'm angry — angry at myself. I *like* Dickie. I like him!"

Babe's lips fell apart. She sat down in the accordion-plaited chair and rocked. A squealing, shaking noise accompanied the motion. Her fingers sought and found against the chair-back a piece of chewing-gum which she had stuck there during her last visit to Sheila. Babe hid and resurrected chewing-gum as instinctively as a dog hides and resurrects his bones.

"I can *see* you likin' Dickie," she remarked ironically.

"But I do, I tell you! He was sweet. He did n't say a word or do a thing to frighten me — "

"But he was full, Shee, you know he was."

"Yes. He'd been drinking. I smelt it. And he did n't walk very straight, and he was a little mixed in his

INTERCESSION

speech. But, all the same, he was as good as gold. And friendly and nice. I might have walked home quietly with him and sent him away at the door. And he would n't have been seen by his father." Sheila's eyes filled. "It was dreadful — to — to knock him down the steps!"

"Say, if you'd had as much to put up with from Dickie as Poppa's had — "

"Oh," said Sheila in a tone that welled up as from under a weight, "if I had always lived in Millings, I'd drink myself!"

Babe looked red and resentful, but Sheila's voice rushed on.

"That saloon is the only interesting and attractive place in town. The only thrilling people that ever come here go in through those doors. I've seen some wonderful-looking men. I'd like to paint them. I've made some drawings of them — men from over there back of the mountains."

"You mean the cowboys from over The Hill, I guess," drawled Babe contemptuously. "Those sagebrush fellows from Hidden Creek. I don't think a whole lot of them. Put one of them alongside of one of our town boys! Why, they don't speak good, Sheila, and they're rough as a hill trail. You'd be scared to death of them if you knew them better."

"They look like real men to me," said Sheila. "And I never did like towns."

"But you're a town girl."

"I am not. I've been in cities and I've been in the country. I've never lived in a town."

"Well, there'll be a dance one of these days next summer in the Town Hall, and maybe you'll meet some of those rough-necks. You'll change your mind about them. Why, I'd sooner dance with a sheep-herder from beyond the bad-lands, or with one of the hands from the oil-fields, than with those Hidden Creek fellows. Horse-thieves and hold-ups and Lord knows what-all they are. No account runaways. Nothing solid or respectable about them. Take a boy like Robert, now, or Jim — "

Sheila put her hands to her ears. Her face, between the hands, looked rather wicked in a sprite-like fashion.

"Don't mention to me Mr. James Greely of the Millings National Bank!"

Babe rose pompously. "I think you're kind of off your bat to-night, Sheila Arundel," she said, chewing noisily. "First you run out at night with the mercury at 4 below and come dashing back scared to death, banging at the door, and then you tell me you like Dickie and ask me not to mention the finest fellow in Millings!"

"The finest fellow in the finest city in the world!" cried Sheila and laughed. Her laugh was like a torrent of silver coins, but it had the right maliceful ring of a brownie's "Ho! Ho! Ho!"

Babe stopped in the doorway and spoke heavily.

INTERCESSION 41

"You're short on sense, Sheila," she said. "You're kind of dippy . . . going out to look at the stars and drawing pictures of that Hidden Creek trash. But you'll learn better, maybe."

"Wait a minute, Babe!" Sheila was sober again and not unpenitent. "I'm coming down with you. I want to tell your father that Dickie was sweet to me. I don't want him to — to — what was it he was going to do to-morrow?"

"Bawl Dickie out."

"Yes. I don't want him to do that. It sounds awful."

"Well, it is. But it won't hurt Dickie any. He's used to it."

Babe, forgiving and demonstrative, here forgot the insult to Millings and Jim Greely, put her arm round Sheila, and went down the stairs, squeezing the smaller girl against the wall.

"I guess I won't go with you to see Poppa," she said, stopping at the top of the last flight. "Poppa's kind of a rough talker sometimes."

Sheila looked rather alarmed. "You mean you think he — he will bawl me out?"

"I wouldn't wonder." Babe smiled, showing a lump of putty-colored chewing-gum between her flashing teeth.

Sheila stood halfway down the stairs. She had not yet quite admitted to herself that she was afraid of Sylvester Hudson and now she did admit it. But with a forlorn memory of Dickie, she braced herself and went slowly down the six remaining steps. The parlor door was shut and back of it to and fro prowled Sylvester. Sheila opened the door.

Hudson's face, ready with a scowl, changed. He came quickly toward her.

"Well, say, Miss Sheila, I am sure-ly sorry — "

Sheila shook her head. "Not half so sorry as I am, Mr. Hudson. I came down to apologize."

He pulled out a chair and Sheila sat down. Sylvester placed himself opposite to her and lighted a huge black cigar, watching her meanwhile curiously, even anxiously. His face was as quiet and sallow and gentle as usual. Sheila's fear subsided.

"*You* came down to apologize?" repeated Hudson. "Well, ma'am, that sounds kind of upside down to me."

"I behaved like a goose. Your son had n't done or said anything to frighten me. He was sweet. I like him so much. He was coming home and saw me walking off alone, and he thought that I might be lonely or frightened or fall into the snow — which I did" — Sheila smiled coaxingly; "I went down up to my neck and Dickie pulled me out and was — lovely to me. It was n't till I was halfway down the hill that I — that it came to me, all of a sudden, that — perhaps — he'd been drinking — "

"Perhaps," said Sylvester dryly. "It's never perhaps with Dickie."

INTERCESSION

Sheila's eyes filled. For a seventeen-year-old girl the situation was difficult. It was not easy to discuss Dickie's habit with his father.

"I am so — sorry," she faltered. "I behaved absurdly. Just because I saw that he was n't quite himself I ran away from him and made a scene. Truly, Mr. Hudson, he had not said or done anything the least bit horrid. He'd been sensible and nice and friendly — Oh, dear!" For she saw before her a relentless and incredulous face. "You won't believe me now, I suppose!"

"I can't altogether, Miss Sheila, for I reckon you would n't have run away from a true-blue, friendly fellow, would you?"

"Yes, Mr. Hudson, I would. Because, you see, I did. It was just a sort of panic. Too much moonshine."

"Yes, ma'am. Too much moonshine inside of Dickie. I hope" — he leaned toward her, and Sheila, the child, could not help but be flattered by his deference — "I hope you're not thinking that Dickie's unfortunate habit is my fault. I'm his father and I own that saloon. But, all the same, it's not my fault nor The Aura's fault either. I never did spoil Dickie. And I'm a sober man myself. He's just naturally ornery, no account. He always was. I believe he's kind of lacking in the upper story."

"Oh, *no*, Mr. Hudson!"

The protest was so emphatic that Sylvester pulled

his cigar out of his mouth, brushed away the smoke, and looked searchingly at Sheila. She was sitting very straight. Against the crimson plush of an enormous chair-back her small figure looked extravagantly delicate and her little pointed fingers on the arms, startlingly white and fine. A color flamed in her cheeks, her eyes and lips were possessed by the remorseful earnestness of her appeal.

"Well, say, if *you* think not!" Sylvester narrowed his eyes and thrust the cigar back into a hole made by his mouth for its reception; "you're the first person that has n't kind of agreed with me on that point. I can't see why he took to the whiskey, anyway. Moderation's my motto and always was. It's the motto of The Aura. There ain't a bar east nor west of the Rockies, Miss Sheila, believe *me*, that has the reputation for decency and moderation that my Aura has. She's classy, she's stylish — well, sir — she's exquisite" — he pronounced it ex-*squis*it — "I don't mind sayin' so. She's a saloon in a million. And she's famous. You can hear talk of The Aura in the best clubs, the most se-lect bars of Chicago and Noo York and San Francisco. She's mighty near perfect. Well, say, there was an Englishman in there one night two summers ago. He was some Englishman, too, an earl, that was him. Been all over the world, east, west, and in between. Had a glass in his eye — one of those fellers. Do you know what he told me, Miss Sheila? Can you guess?"

INTERCESSION

"That The Aura was classy?" suggested Sheila bravely.

"More'n that," Sylvester leaned farther toward her and emphasized his words with the long forefinger.

"'It's all but perfect' — that's what he said — 'it only needs one thing to make it quite perfect!'"

"What was the thing?"

But Hudson did not heed her question. "Believe me or not, Miss Sheila, that saloon — "

"But I do believe you," said Sheila with her enchanting smile. "And that's just the trouble with Dickie, isn't it? Your saloon is — must be — the most fascinating place in Millings. Why, Mr. Hudson, ever since I came here, I've been longing to go into it myself!"

She got up after this speech and went to stand near the stove. Not that she was cold — the small room, which looked even smaller on account of its huge flaming furniture and the enormous roses on its carpet and wall-paper, was as hot as a furnace — but because she was abashed by her own speech and by his curious reception of it. The dark blood of his body had risen to his face; he had opened his eyes wide upon her, had sunk back again and begun to smoke with short, excited puffs.

Sheila thought that he was shocked and she was very close to tears. She blinked at the stove and moved her fingers uncertainly. "Nice girls," she thought, "never want to go into saloons!"

Then Sylvester spoke. "You're a girl in a million, Miss Sheila!" he said. His voice was more cracked than usual. Sheila transferred her blinking, almost tearful look from the stove to him. "You're a heap too good for dish-washing," said Sylvester.

For some reason the girl's heart began to beat unevenly. She had a feeling of excitement and suspense. It was as if, after walking for many hours through a wood where there was a lurking presence of danger, she had heard a nearing step. She kept her eyes upon Sylvester. In his there was that mysterious look of appraisal, of vision. He seemed nervous, rolled his cigar and moved his feet.

"Are you satisfied with your work, Miss Sheila?"

Sheila assembled her courage. "I know you'll think me a beast, Mr. Hudson, after all your kindness — and it is n't that I don't like the work. But I've a feeling — no, it's more than a feeling! — I *know* that your wife does n't need me. And I know she does n't want me. She does n't like to have me here. I've been unhappy about that ever since I came. And it's been getting worse. Yesterday she said she could n't bear to have me whistling round her kitchen. Mr. Hudson" — Sheila's voice broke childishly — "I can't help whistling. It's a habit. I could n't work at all if I did n't whistle. I would n't have told you, but since you asked me — "

Sylvester held up his long hand. Its emerald glittered.

INTERCESSION

"That's all right," he said. "I wanted to learn the truth about it. Perhaps you've noticed, Miss Sheila, that I'm not a very happy man at home."

"You mean — ?"

"I mean," said Sylvester heavily — "*Momma*."

Sheila overcame a horrible inclination to laugh.

"I'm so sorry," she said uncertainly. She was acutely embarrassed, but did not know how to escape. And she *was* sorry for him, for certainly it seemed to her that a man married to Momma had just cause for unhappiness.

"I ought to be ashamed of myself for bringing you here, Miss Sheila. You see, that's me. I'm so all-fired soft-hearted that I just don't think. I'm all feelings. My heart's stronger than my head, as the palmists say." He rose and came over to Sheila; standing beside her and smiling so that the wrinkle stood out sharply across his unwilling lip. "Did you ever go to one of those fellows?" he asked.

"Palmists?"

"Yes, ma'am. Well, now, say, did they ever tell you that you were going to be the pride and joy of old Pap Hudson? Give me your little paw, girl!"

Sheila's hand obeyed rather unwillingly her irresolute, polite will. Hudson's came quickly to meet it, spread it out flat in his own long palm, and examined the small rigid surface.

"Well, now, Miss Sheila, I can read something there."

"What can you read?"

"You're goin' to be famous. You're goin' to make Millings famous. Girl, you're goin' to be a picture that will live in the hearts of fellows and keep 'em warm when they're herding winter nights. The thought of you is goin' to keep 'em straight and pull 'em back here. You're goin' to be a — a sort of a beacon light."

He was holding her slim hand with its small, crushable bones in an excited grip. He was bending forward, not looking at the palm, but at her. Sheila pulled back, wincing a little.

"What do you mean, Mr. Hudson? How could I be all that?"

Sylvester let her go. He began to pace the room. He stopped and looked at her, almost wistfully.

"You really think that I've been kind of nice to you?" he asked.

"Indeed, you have!"

"I'm not a happy man and I've got to be sort of distrustful. I haven't got much faith in the thankfulness of people. I've got fooled too often."

"Try me," said Sheila quickly.

He looked at her with a long and searching look. Then he sighed.

"Some day maybe I will. Run away to bed now."

Sheila felt as if she had been pushed away from a half-opened door. She drew herself up and walked across the huge flowers of the carpet. But before

INTERCESSION

going out she turned back. Sylvester quickly banished a sly smile.

"You won't be angry with Dickie?" she asked.

"Not if it's going to deal you any misery, little girl."

"You're *very* kind to me."

He put up his hand. "That's all right, Miss Sheila," he said. "That's all right. It's a real pleasure and comfort to me to have you here and I'll try to shape things so they'll suit you — and Momma too. Trust *me*. But don't you ask me to put any faith in Dickie's upper story. I've climbed up there too often. I'll give up my plan to go round there to-morrow and — " He paused grimly.

"And bawl him out?" suggested Sheila with one of her Puckish impulses.

"Hump! I was going a little further than that. He would likely have done the bawlin'. But don't you worry yourself about Dickie. He's safe for this time — so long's you don't blame me, or — The Aura."

His voice on the last word suffered from one of its cracks. It was as though it had broken under a load of pride and tenderness.

Sheila saw for a moment how it was with him. To every man his passion and his dream: to Sylvester Hudson, his Aura. More than wife or child, he loved his bar. It was a fetish, an idol. To Sheila's fancy Dickie suddenly appeared the sacrifice.

CHAPTER VI

THE BAWLING-OUT

DICKIE'S room in The Aura Hotel was fitted in between the Men's Lavatory and the Linen Room. It smelt of soiled linen and defective plumbing. Also, into its single narrow window rose the dust of ashes, of old rags and other refuse thrown light-heartedly into the back yard, which not being visible from the street supplied the typical housewife of a frontier town with that relaxation from any necessity to keep up an appearance of economy and cleanliness so desirable to her liberty-loving soul. The housekeeper at The Aura was not Mrs. Hudson, but an enormously stout young woman with blonde hair, named Amelia Plecks. She was so tightly laced and booted that her hard breathing and creaking were audible all over the hotel. When Dickie woke in his narrow room after his moonlight adventure, he heard this heavy breathing in the linen room and, groaning, thrust his head under the pillow. With whatever bitterness his kindly heart could entertain, he loathed Amelia. She took advantage of the favor of Sylvester and of her own exalted position in the hotel to taunt and to humiliate him. His plunge under the pillow did not escape her notice.

"Ain't you up yet, lazybones?" she cried, rapping

THE BAWLING-OUT 51

on the wall. "You won't get no breakfast. It's half-past seven. Who's at the desk to see them Duluth folks off? Pap's not going to be pleased with you."

"I don't want any breakfast," muttered Dickie.

Amelia laughed. "No. I'll be bound you don't. Tongue like a kitten and a head like a cracked stove!"

She slapped down some clean sheets on a shelf and creaked toward the hall, but stopped at the open door. Sylvester Hudson was coming down the passage and she was in no mind to miss the "bawling-out" of Dickie which this visit must portend. She shut the linen-room door softly, therefore, and controlled her breathing.

But Dickie knew that she was there and, when his father rapped, he knew why she was there.

He tumbled wretchedly from his bed, swore at his injured ankle, hopped to the door, unlocked it, and hopped back with panic swiftness before his father's entrance. He sat in his crumpled pajamas amidst his crumpled, dingy bedclothes, his hair scattered over his forehead, his large, heavy eyes fixed anxiously upon Sylvester.

"Say, Poppa — " he began.

Then "Pap's" voice cracked out at him.

"You hold your tongue," snapped Sylvester, "or you'll get what's comin' to you!" He jerked Dickie's single chair from against the wall, threw the clothing from it, and sat down, crossing his legs, and holding up at his son the long finger that had frightened Sheila. Dickie blinked at it.

"You know what I was plannin' to do to you after last night? I meant to come round here and pull you out of your covers and onto the floor there" — he pointed to a spot on the boards to which Dickie fearfully directed his own eyes — "and kick the stuffin' out of you." Dickie contemplated the long, pointed russet shoes of his parent and shuddered visibly. Nevertheless in the slow look he lifted from the boot to his father's face, there was a faint gleam of irony.

"What made you change your mind?" he asked impersonally.

It was this curious detachment of Dickie's, this imperturbability, that most infuriated Hudson. He flushed.

"Just a little sass from you will bring me back to the idea," he said sharply.

Dickie lowered his eyes.

"What made me change was — Miss Arundel's kindness. She came and begged you off. She said you had n't done anything or said anything to frighten her, that you'd been" — Sylvester drawled out the two words in the sing-song of Western mockery — "'sweet and love-ly.'"

Dickie's face was pink. He began to tie a knot in the corner of one of his thin gray sheet-blankets.

"I don't know how sweet and lovely you can be, Dickie, when you're lit up, but I guess you were

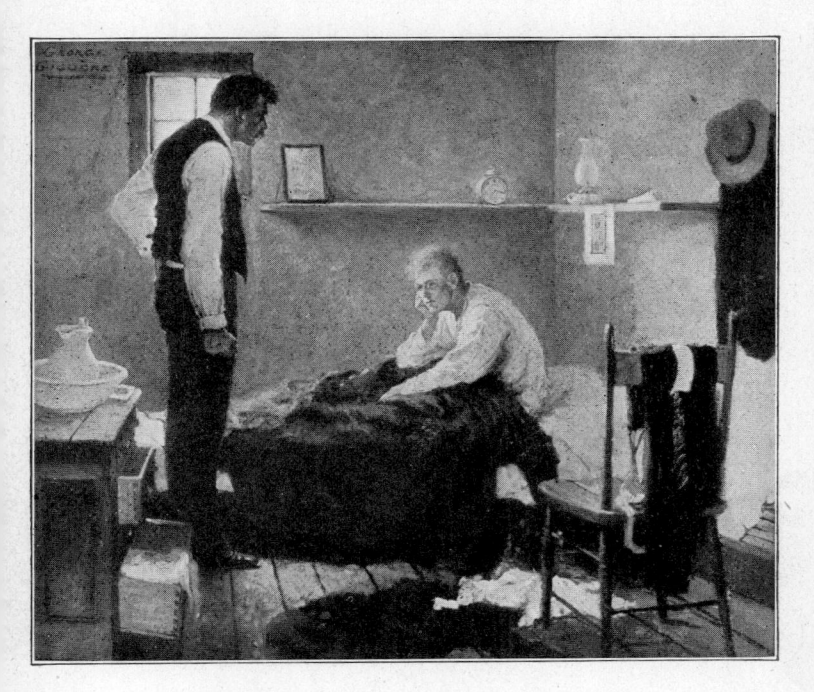

THEN "PAP'S" VOICE CRACKED OUT AT HIM

THE BAWLING-OUT 53

awful sweet. Anyway, if you did n't say anything or do anything to scare her, you don't deserve a kickin'. But, just the same, I've a mind to turn you out of Millings."

This time, Dickie's look was not ironical. It was terrified. "Oh, Poppa, say! I'll try not to do it again."

"I never heard that before, did I?" sneered Sylvester. "You put shame on me and my bar. And I'm not goin' to stand it. If you want to get drunk buy a bottle and come up here in your room. God damn you! You're a nice son for the owner of The Aura!"

He stood up and looked with frank disgust at the thin, huddled figure. Under this look, Dickie grew slowly redder and his eyes watered.

Sylvester lifted his upper lip. "Faugh!" he said. He walked over to the door. "Get up and go down to your job and don't you bother Miss Sheila — hear me? Keep away from her. She's not used to your sort and you'll disgust her. She's here under my protection and I've got my plans for her. I'm her guardian — that's what I am." Sylvester was pleased like a man that has made a discovery. "Her guardian," he repeated as though the word had a fine taste.

Dickie watched him. There was no expression whatever in his face and his lips stood vacantly apart. He might have been seven years old.

"Keep away from her — hear me?"

"Yes, sir," said Dickie meekly.

After his father had gone out, Dickie sat for an instant with his head on one side, listening intently. Then he got up, limped quietly and quickly on his bare feet out into the hall, and locked the linen-room door on the outside.

"Amelia's clean forgot to lock it," he said aloud. "Ain't she careless, though, this morning!"

He went back. There was certainly a sound now behind the partition, a sound of hard breathing that could no longer be controlled.

"I'll hand the key over to Mary," soliloquized Dickie in the hollow and unnatural voice of stage confidences. "She'll be goin' in for the towels about noon."

Then he fell on his bed and smothered a fit of chuckling.

Suddenly the mirth died out of him. He lay still, conscious of a pain in his head and in his ankle and somewhere else — an indeterminate spot deep in his being. He had been forbidden to see the girl who ran away out into the night to look at the stars, the girl who had not laughed at his attempt to describe the white ecstasy of the winter moon. He had frightened her — disgusted her. He must have been more drunk than he imagined. It *was* disgusting — and so hopeless. Perhaps it would be better to leave Millings.

He sat up on the edge of his bed and let his hands hang limply down between his knees. It seemed to him that his thoughts were like a wheel, half-sub-

THE BAWLING-OUT 55

merged in running water. The wheel went round rapidly, plunging in and out of his consciousness. Hardly had he grasped the meaning of one half when it went under and another blur of moving spokes emerged. Something his father had said, for instance, now began to pass through his mind . . . "I've got my plans for her" . . . Dickie tried to stop the turning wheel because this speech gave him a distinct feeling of anger and alarm. By an effort of his will, he held it before his contemplation . . . What possible plans could Sylvester have for Sheila? Did she understand his plans? Did she approve of them? She was so young and small, with that sad, soft mouth and those shining, misty eyes. Dickie, with almost a paternal air, shook his ruffled head. He shut his eyes so that the long lashes stood out in little points. A vision of those two faces — Sheila's so gleaming fair and open, Sylvester's so dark and shut — stood there to be compared. Her guardian, indeed!

Dickie dressed slowly and dragged himself down to the desk, where very soberly and sadly he gave the key of the linen room to Mary. Then he sat down, turned on the Victor, and lit a cigarette. The "Duluth folks" had gone without any assistance from him. There was nothing to do. It occurred to Dickie, all at once, that in Millings there was always nothing to do. Nothing, that is, for him to do. Perhaps, after all, he did n't like Millings. Perhaps that was what was wrong with him.

The Victor was playing:

> "Here comes Tootsie,
> Play a little music on the band.
> Here comes Tootsie,
> Tootsie, you are looking simply grand.
> Play a little tune on the piccolo and flutes,
> The man who wrote the rag wrote it especially for Toots.
> Here comes Tootsie — play a little music on the band."

On the last nasal note, the door of The Aura flew open and a resplendent figure crossed the chocolate-colored varnish of the floor. Tootsie herself was not more "simply grand." This was a young man, perhaps it would be more descriptive to say *the* young man that accompanies *the* young woman on the cover of the average American magazine. He had — a nose, a chin, a beautiful mouth, large brown eyes, wavy chestnut hair, a ruddy complexion, and, what is not always given to the young man on the cover, a deep and generous dimple in the ruddiest part of his right cheek. He was dressed in the latest suit produced by Schaffner and Marx; he wore a tie of variegated silk which, like Browning's star, "dartled" now red, now blue. The silk handkerchief, which protruded carefully from his breast pocket, also "dartled." So did the socks. One felt that the heart of this young man matched his tie and socks. It was resplendent with the vanity and hopefulness and illusions of twenty-two years.

The large, dingy, chocolate-colored lobby became suddenly a background to Mr. James Greely, cashier

THE BAWLING-OUT 57

of the Millings National Bank, and the only child of its president.

Upon the ruffled and rumpled Dickie he smiled pleasantly, made a curious gesture with his hand — they both belonged to the Knights of Sagittarius and the Fire Brigade — and came to lean upon the desk.

"Holiday at the bank this morning," he said, "in honor of Dad's wedding-anniversary. We're giving a dance to-night in the Hall. Want to come, Dickie?"

"No," said Dickie, "I hurt my ankle last night on the icy pavement. And anyhow I can't dance. And I sort of find girls kind of tiresome."

"That's too bad. I'm sure sorry for you, Hudson. Particularly as I came here just for the purpose of handing you over the cutest little billy-doo you ever saw."

He drew out of his pocket an envelope and held it away from Dickie.

"You're trying to job me, Jim," — but Dickie had his head coaxingly on one side and his face was pink.

"I'll give it to you if you can guess the sender."

"Babe?"

"Wrong."

"Girlie?"

"Well, sir, it ain't Girlie's fist — not the fist she uses when she drops *me* billy-doos."

Dickie's eyes fell. He turned aside in his chair and stopped the grinding of the graphophone. He made no further guess. Jim, with his dimple deepening, tossed the small paper into the air and caught it again deftly.

"It's from the young lady from Noo York who's helping Mrs. Hudson," he said. "I guess she's kind of wishful for a beau. She's not much of a looker Girlie tells me."

"Haven't you met her yet, Jim?" Dickie's hands were in his pockets, but his eyes followed the gyrations of the paper.

"No. Ain't that a funny thing, too? Seems like I never get round to it. I just saw her peeping at me one day through the parlor curtains while I was saying sweet nothings to Girlie on the porch. I guess she was kind of in-ter-ested. She's skinny and pale, Girlie says. Your mother hasn't got any use for her. I bet you, it won't be long before she makes tracks back to Noo York, Dickie. Girlie says she won't be lingering on here much longer. Too much competition."

Jim handed the note to Dickie, who had listened to this speech with his seven-year-old expression. He made no comment, but silently unfolded Sheila's note.

The writing itself was like her, slender and fine and straight, a little reckless, daintily desperate. That "I," now, on the white paper might be Sheila skimming across the snow.

My dear Dickie — somehow I can't call you "Mr. Hudson" — I am so terribly sorry about the way I acted to

THE BAWLING-OUT

you last night. I don't know why I was so foolish. I have tried to explain to your father that you did nothing and said nothing to frighten me, that you were very polite and kind, but I am afraid he does n't quite understand. I hope he won't be very cross with you, because it was all my fault — no, not quite all, because I think you ought n't to have followed me. I'm sure you're sorry that you did. But it was a great deal my fault, so I'm writing this to tell you that I was n't really frightened nor very angry. Just sorry and disappointed. Because I thought you were so very nice. And not like Millings. And you liked the mountains better than the town. I wanted — I still want — you to be my friend. For I do need a friend here, dreadfully. Will you come to see me some afternoon? I hope you did n't hurt yourself when you slipped on those icy steps.

Sincerely
SHEILA ARUNDEL

Dickie put the note into his pocket and looked unseeingly at Jim. Jim was turning up the bottoms of his trousers preparing to go.

"So you won't come to our dance?" he asked straightening himself, more ruddy than ever.

"Well, sir," said Dickie slowly and indifferently, "I would n't wonder if I would."

CHAPTER VII
Dish-Washing

On that night, while all Millings was preparing itself for the Greelys' dance, while Dickie, bent close to his cracked mirror, was tying his least crumpled tie with not too steady fingers, while Jim was applying to his brown crest a pomade sent to him by a girl in Cheyenne, while Babe was wondering anxiously whether green slippers could be considered a match or a foil to a dress of turquoise blue, while Girlie touched her cream-gold hair with cream-padded finger-tips, Sheila Arundel prowled about her room with hot anger and cold fear in her heart.

Nothing, perhaps, in all this mysterious world is so inscrutable a mystery as the mind of early youth. It crawls, the beetle creature, in a hard shell, hiding the dim, inner struggle of its growing wings, moving numbly as if in a torpid dream. It has forgotten the lively grub stage of childhood, and it cannot foresee the dragon-fly adventure just ahead. This blind, dumb, numb, imprisoned thing, an irritation to the nerves of every one who has to deal with it, suffers. First it suffers darkly and dimly the pain growth, and then it suffers the sharp agony of a splitting shell, the dazzling wounds of light, the torture of first moving its feeble wings. It drags itself from its shell, it

DISH-WASHING

clings to its perch, it finds itself born anew into the world.

When Sheila had left the studio with Sylvester, she was not yet possessed of wings. Now, the shell was cracking, the dragon-fly adventure about to begin. To a changed world, changed stars — the heavens above and the earth beneath were strange to her that night.

It had begun, this first piercing contact of reality, rudely enough. Mrs. Hudson had helped to split the protecting shell which had saved Sheila's growing dreams. Perhaps "Momma" had her instructions, perhaps it was only her own disposition left by her knowing husband to do his trick for him. Sheila had not overstated the unhappiness that Mrs. Hudson's evident dislike had caused her. In fact, she had greatly understated it. From the first moment at the station, when the hard eyes had looked her over and the harsh voice had asked about "the girl's trunk," Sheila's sensitiveness had begun to suffer. It was not easy, even with Babe's good-humored help, to go down into the kitchen and submit to Mrs. Hudson's hectoring. "Momma" had all the insolence of the underdog. Of her daughters, as of her husband, she was very much afraid. They all bullied her, Babe with noisy, cheerful effrontery — "sass" Sylvester called it — and Girlie with a soft, unyielding tyranny that had the smothering pressure of a large silk pillow. Girlie was tall and serious and beautiful, the proud possessor of what Millings called "a perfect form." She was inexpressibly slow and untidy, vain and ignorant and self-absorbed. At this time her whole being was centered upon the attentions of Jim Greely, with whom she was "keeping company." With Jim Greely in her mind, she had looked Sheila over, thin and weary Sheila in her shabby black dress, and had decided that here no danger threatened. Nevertheless she did not take chances. Sheila had been in Millings a fortnight and had not met the admirable Jim. Her attempt that morning to send the note to Dickie by Jim was exactly the action that led to the painful splitting of her shell.

She had seen from her window Sylvester's departure after breakfast. There was something in his grim, angular figure, moving carefully over the icy pavement in the direction of the hotel, that gave her a pang for Dickie. She was sure that Hudson was going to be very disagreeable in spite of her attempt to soften his anger. And she was sorry that Dickie, with his odd, wistful, friendly face and his eyes so wide and youthful and apologetic for their visions, should think that she was angry or disgusted. She wrote her letter in a little glow of rescue, and was proud of the tact of that reference to his "fall down the steps" — for she reasoned that the self-esteem of any boy of nineteen must suffer poignantly over the memory of being knocked down by his father before the eyes of a strange girl. She wrote her note and ran down the

IT WAS NOT EASY, EVEN WITH BABE'S GOOD-HUMORED HELP, TO GO DOWN AND SUBMIT TO MRS. HUDSON'S HECTORING

DISH-WASHING

stairs, then stopped to wonder how she could get it promptly to Dickie. It was intended as a poultice to be applied after the "bawling-out," and she could not very well take it to him herself. She knew that he worked in the hotel, and the hotel was just around the corner. All that was needed was a messenger.

She was standing, pink of cheek and vague of eye, fingering her apron like a cottage child and nibbling at the corner of her envelope, the light from a window on the stairs falling on the jewel-like polish of her hair, when Girlie opened the door of the "parlor" and came out into the hall. Girlie saw her and half-closed the door. Her lazy eyes, as reflective and receptive and inexpressive as small meadow pools under a summer sky, rested upon Sheila. In the parlor a pleasant baritone voice was singing,

> "Treat me nice, Miss Mandy Jane,
> Treat me nice.
> Don't you know I'se not to blame,
> Lovers all act just the same,
> Treat me nice . . ."

Girlie's fingers tightened on the doorknob.

"What do you want, Sheila?" she asked, and into the slow, gentle tones of her voice something had crept, something sinuous and subtle, something that slid into the world with Lilith for the eternal torment of earth's daughters.

"I want to send this note to your brother," said Sheila with the simplicity of the aristocrat. "Is that Mr. Greely? Is he going past the hotel?"

She took a step toward Jim, but Girlie held out her soft long hand.

"Give it to me. I'll ask him."

Sheila surrendered the note.

"You'd better get back to the dishes," said Girlie over her shoulder. "Momma's kind of rushed this morning. She's helping Babe with her party dress. I would n't 'a' put in my time writing notes to Dickie to-day if I'd 'a' been you. Sort of risky."

She slid in through the jealous door and Sheila hurried along the hall to the kitchen where there was an angry clash and clack of crockery.

The kitchen was furnished almost entirely with blue-flowered oilcloth; the tables were covered with it, the floor was covered with it, the shelves were draped in it. Cold struck up through the shining, clammy surface underfoot so that while Sheila's face burned from the heat of the stove her feet were icy. The back door was warped and let in a current of frosty air over its sill, a draught that circled her ankles like cold metal. On the table in the middle of the room, "Momma" had placed an enormous tin dishpan piled high with dirty dishes, over which she was pouring the contents of the kettle. Steam rose in clouds, half-veiling her big, fierce face which, seen through holes in the vapor, was like that of a handsome, vulgar witch.

Through the steam she shot at Sheila a cruel look. "Are n't you planning to do any work to-day,

DISH-WASHING

Sheila?" she asked in her voice of harsh, monotonous accents. "Here it's nine o'clock and I ain't been able to do a stroke to Babe's dress. I dunno what you was designed for in this house — an ornament on the parlor mantel, I guess."

Sheila's heart suffered one of the terrible swift enlargements of angry youth. It seemed to fill her chest and stop her breath, forcing water into her eyes. She could not speak, went quickly up and took the kettle from "Momma's" red hand.

The table at which dish-washing was done, was inconveniently high. When the big dishpan with its piled dishes topped it, Sheila's arms and back were strained over her work. She usually pulled up a box on which she stood, but now she went to work blindly, her teeth clenched, her flexible red lips set close to cover them. The Celtic fire of her Irish blood gave her eyes a sort of phosphorescent glitter. "Momma" looked at her.

"Don't show temper!" she said. "What were you doin'? Upstairs work?"

"I was writing a letter," said Sheila in a low voice, beginning to wash the plates and shrinking at the pain of scalding water.

"Hmp! Writing letters at this hour! One of your friends back East? I thought it was about time somebody was looking you up. What do your acquaintance think of you comin' West with Sylly?"

Now that she was at liberty to put a "stroke" of

work on Babe's dress, "Momma" seemed in no particular hurry to do so. She stood in the middle of the kitchen wrapping her great bony arms in her checked apron and staring at Sheila. Her eyes were like Girlie's turned to stone, as blank and blind as living eyes can be.

Sheila did not answer. She was white and her hands shook.

"Hmp!" said "Momma" again. "We are n't goin' to talk about our acquaintance, are we? Well, some folks' acquaintance don't bear talkin' about; they're either too fine or they ain't the kind that gets into decent conversation." She walked away.

Sheila did her work, holding her anger and her misery away from her, refusing to look at them, to analyze their cause. It was a very busy day. The help Babe usually gave, and "Momma's" more effectual assistance, were not to be had. Sheila cleaned up the kitchen, swept the dining-room, set the table and cooked the supper. Her exquisite French omelette and savory baked tomatoes were reviled. The West knows no cooking but its own, and, like all victims of uneducated taste, it prefers the familiar bad to the unfamiliar good.

"You've spoiled a whole can of tomatoes," said Babe.

Sylvester laughed good-humoredly: "Oh, well, Miss Sheila, you'll learn!" This, to Sheila, whose omelette had been taught her by Mimi Lolotte and whose

DISH-WASHING

baked tomatoes, delicately flavored with onion, were something to dream about. And she had toasted the bread golden brown and buttered it, and she had made a delectable vegetable soup! She had never before been asked to cook a meal at Number 18 Cottonwood Avenue and she was eager to please Sylvester. His comment, "You'll learn," fairly took her breath. She would not sit down with them at the table, but hurried back into the kitchen, put her scorched cheek against some cold linoleum, and cried.

By the time dinner was over and more dishes ready to be washed, the cook's wounded pride was under control. Her few tears had left no marks on her face. Babe, helping her, did not even know that there had been a shower.

Babe was excited; her chewing was more energetic even than usual. It smacked audibly.

"Say, Sheila, wot'll you wear to-night?" she yelled above the clatter.

"Wear?" repeated Sheila.

"To the dance, you silly! What did you think I meant — to bed?"

Sheila's tired pallor deepened a little. "I am not going to the dance."

"Not going?" Babe put down a plate. "What do you mean? Of course you're going! You've gotta go. Say — Momma, Pap, Girlie" — she ran, at a sort of sliding gallop across the oilcloth through the swinging door into the dining-room — "will you listen to this? Sheila says she's not going to the dance!"

"Well," said "Momma" audibly, "she'd better. I'm agoin' to put out the fires, and the house'll be about 12 below."

Sylvester murmured, "Oh, we must change that."

And Girlie said nothing.

"Well," vociferated Babe. "I call it too mean for words. I've just set my heart on her meeting some of the folks and getting to know Millings. She's been here a whole two weeks and she hasn't met a single fellow but Dickie, and he don't count, and she hasn't even got friendly with any of the girls. And I wanted her to see one of our real swell affairs. Why — just for the credit of Millings, she's gotta go."

"Why fuss her about it, if she don't want to?" Girlie's soft voice was poured like oil on the troubled billows of Babe's outburst.

"I'll see to her," Sylvester's chair scraped the floor as he rose. "I know how to manage girls. Trust Poppa!"

He pushed through the door, followed by Babe. Sheila looked up at him helplessly. She had her box under her feet, and so was not entirely hidden by the dishpan. She drew up her head and faced him.

"Mr. Hudson," she began — "please! I can't go to a dance. You know I can't — "

"Nonsense!" said Pap. "In the bright lexicon of youth there's no such word as 'can't.' Say, girl, you

DISH-WASHING

can and you must. I won't have Babe crying her eyes out and myself the most unpopular man in Millings. Say, leave your dishes and go up and put on your best duds."

"That's talking," commented Babe.

In the dining-room "Momma" said, "Hmp!" and Girlie was silent.

Sheila looked at her protector. "But, you see, Mr. Hudson, I — I — it was only a month ago — " She made a gesture with her hands to show him her black dress, and her lips trembled.

Pap walked round to her and patted her shoulder. "I know," he said. "I savvy. I get you, little girl. But, say, it won't do. You've got to begin to live again and brighten up. You're only seventeen and that's no age for mourning, no, nor moping. You must learn to forget, at least, that is" — for he saw the horrified pain of her eyes — "that is, to be happy again. Yes'm. Happiness — that's got to be your middle name. Now, Miss Sheila, as a favor to me!"

Sheila put up both her hands and pushed his from her shoulder. She ran from him past Babe into the dining-room, where, as she would have sped by, "Momma" caught her by the arm.

"If you're not aimin' to please *him*," said "Momma" harshly, "wot are you here for?"

Sheila looked at her unseeingly, pulled herself away, and went upstairs on wings. In her room the tumult, held down all through the ugly, cluttered, drudging day, broke out and had its violent course. She flew about the room or tossed on the bed, sobbing and whispering to herself. Her wound bled freely for the first time since it had been given her by death. She called to her father, and her heart writhed in the grim talons of its loneliness. That was her first agony and then came the lesser stings of "Momma's" insults, and at last, a fear. An incomprehensible fear. She began to doubt the wisdom of her Western venture. She began to be terrified at her situation. All about her lay a frozen world, a wilderness, so many thousand miles from anything that she and her father had ever known. And in her pocket there was no penny for rescue or escape. Over her life brooded powerfully Sylvester Hudson, with his sallow face and gentle, contemplative eyes. He had brought her to his home. Surely that was an honorable and generous deed. He had given her over to the care and protection of his wife and daughters. But why did n't Mrs. Hudson like it? Why did she tighten her lips and pull her nostrils when she looked at her helper? And what was the sinister, inner meaning of those two speeches . . . about the purpose of her being in the house at all? "An ornament on the parlor mantel" . . . "aiming to please him . . ." Of the existence of a sinister, inner meaning, "Momma's" voice and look left no doubt.

Something was wrong. Something was hideously wrong. And to whom might she go for help or for advice? As though to answer her question came a footstep on the stair. It was a slow, not very heavy step. It came to her door and there followed a sharp but gentle rap.

"Who is it?" asked Sheila. And suddenly she felt very weak.

"It's Pap. Open your door, girl."

She hesitated. Her head seemed to go round. Then she obeyed his gentle request.

Pap walked into the room.

CHAPTER VIII

Artists

Pap closed the door carefully behind him before he looked at Sheila. At once his face changed to one of deep concern.

"Why, girl! What's happened to you? You got no call to feel like that!"

He went over to her and took her limp hand. She half turned away. He patted the hand.

"Why, girl! This is n't very pleasant for me. I aimed to make you happy when I brought you out to Millings. I kind of wanted to work myself into your Poppa's place, kind of meant to make it up to you some way. I aimed to give you a home. 'Home, sweet home, there's no place like home' — that was my motto. And here you are, all pale around the gills and tears all over your face — and, say, there's a regular pool there on your pillow. Now, now — " he clicked with his tongue. "You're a bad girl, a regular bad, ungrateful girl, hanged if you are n't! You know what I'd do to you if you were as young as you are little and foolish? Smack you — good and plenty. But I'm not agoin' to do it, no, ma'am. Don't pull your hand away. Smacking's not in my line. I never smacked my own children in their lives, except Dickie. There was no other way with him. He was

ARTISTS

ornery. You come and set down here in the big chair and I'll pull up the little one and we'll talk things over. Put your trust in me, Miss Sheila. I'm all heart. I was n't called 'Pap' for nothing. You know what I am? I'm your guardian. Yes'm. And you just got to make up your mind to cast your care upon me, as the hymn says. Nary worry must you keep to yourself. Come on now, kid, out with it. Get it off your chest."

Sheila had let him put her into the big creaking leather chair. She sat with a handkerchief clenched in both her hands, upon which he, drawing up the other chair, now placed one of his. She kept her head down, for she was ashamed of the pale, stained, and distorted little face which she could not yet control.

"Now, then, girl . . . Well, if you won't talk to me, I'll just light up and wait. I'm a patient man, I am. Don't hurry yourself any."

He withdrew his hand and took out a cigar. In a moment he was sitting on the middle of his spine, his long legs sprawled half across the room, his hands in his pockets, his head on the chair-back so that his chin pointed up to the ceiling. Smoke rose from him as from a volcano.

Sheila presently laughed uncertainly.

"That's better," he mumbled around his cigar.

"I've had a dreadful day," said Sheila.

"You won't have any more of them, my dear," Sylvester promised quietly.

She looked at him with faint hope.

"Yes'm, dish-washing's dead."

"But what can I do, then?"

Hudson nodded his head slowly, or, rather, he sawed the air up and down with his chin. He was still looking at the ceiling so that Sheila could see only the triangle beneath his jaw and the dark, stringy neck above his collar.

"I've got a job for you, girl — a real one."

He pulled out his cigar and sat up. "You remember what I told you the other night?"

"About my being a — a — beacon?" Sheila's voice was delicately tinged with mockery. So was her doubtful smile.

"Yes'm," he said seriously. "Well, that's it."

"What does a beacon do?" she asked.

"It burns. It shines. It looks bright. It wears the neatest little black dress with a frilly apron and deep frilly cuffs. Say, do you recollect something else I told you?"

"I remember everything you told me."

"Well, ma'am, I remember everything you told *me*. Somebody said she was grateful. Somebody said she'd do anything for Pap. Somebody said — 'Try me.'"

"I meant it, Mr. Hudson. I did mean it."

"Do you mean it now?"

"Yes. I — I owe you so much. You're always so very kind to me. And I behave very badly. I was hateful to you this evening. And, when you came to my door, just now, I was — I was *scared*."

ARTISTS

Pap opened his eyes at her, held his cigar away from him and laughed. The laugh was both bitter and amused.

"Scared of Pap Hudson? *You* scared? But, look-a-here, girl, what've I done to deserve that?"

He sat forward, rested his chin in his hand, supported by an elbow on his crossed knees and fixed her with gentle and reproachful eyes.

"Honest, you kind of make me feel bad, Miss Sheila."

"I am dreadfully sorry. It was horrid of me. I only told you because I wanted you to know that I'm not worth helping. I don't deserve you to be so kind to me. I — I must be disgustingly suspicious."

"Well!" Sylvester sighed. "Very few folks get me. I'm kind of mis-understood. I'm a real lonesome sort of man. But, honest, Miss Sheila, I thought you were my friend. I don't mind telling you, you've hurt my feelings. That shot kind of got me. It's stuck into me."

"I'm horrid!" Sheila's eyes were wounded with remorse.

"Oh, well, I'm not expecting understanding any more."

"Oh, but I do — I do understand!" she said eagerly and she put her hand shyly on his arm. "I think I do understand you. I'm very grateful. I'm very fond of you."

"Ah!" said Sylvester softly. "That's a good hearing!" He lifted his arm with Sheila's hand on it and touched it with his lips. "You got me plumb stirred up," he said with a certain huskiness. "Well!" She took away her hand and he made a great show of returning to common sense. "I reckon we are a pretty good pair of friends, after all. But you must n't be scared of me, Miss Sheila. That does hurt. Let's forget you told me that."

"Yes — please!"

"Well, then — to get back to business. Do you recollect a story I told you?"

"A story? Oh, yes — about an Englishman — ?"

"Yes, ma'am. That Englishman put his foot on the rail and stuck his glass in his eye and set his tumbler down empty. And he looked round that bar of mine, Miss Sheila. You savvy, he'd been all over the globe, that feller, and I should say his ex-perience of bars was — some — and he said, 'Hudson, it's all but perfect. It only needs one thing.'"

This time Sheila did not ask. She waited.

"'And that's something we have in our country,' said he." Hudson cleared his throat. He also moistened his lips. He was very apparently excited. He leaned even farther forward, tilting on the front legs of his chair and thrusting his face close to Sheila's "'*A pretty barmaid!*' said he."

There was a profound silence in the small room. The runners of a sleigh scraped the icy street below, its horses' hoofs cracked noisily. The music of a fiddle

ARTISTS

sounded in the distance. Babe's voice humming a waltz tune rose from the second story.

"A barmaid?" asked Sheila breathlessly. She got up from her chair and walked over to the window. The moon was already high. Over there, beckoning, stood her mountain and her star. It was all so shining and pure and still.

"That's what you want me to be — your barmaid?"

"Yes'm," said Sylvester humbly. "Don't make up your mind in a hurry, Miss Sheila. Wait till I tell you more about it. It's — it's a kind of dream of mine. I think it'd come close to breaking me up if you turned down the proposition. The Aura's not an ordin-ar-y bar and I'm not an ordin-ar-y man, and, say, Miss Sheila, you're not an ordin-ar-y girl."

"Is that why you want me to work in your saloon?" said Sheila, staring at the star.

"Yes'm. That's why. Let me tell you that I've searched this continent for a girl to fit my ideal. That's what it is, girl — my ideal. That bar of mine has got to be perfect. It's near to perfect now. I want when that Englishman comes back to Millings to hear him say, 'It's perfect' ... no 'all but,' you notice. Why, miss, I could 'a' got a hundred ordin-ar-y girls, lookers too. The world's full of lookers."

"Why did n't you offer your — 'job' to Babe or Girlie?"

Sylvester laughed. "Well, girl, as a matter of fact, I did."

"You did?" Sheila turned back and faced him. There was plenty of color in her cheeks now. Her narrow eyes were widely opened. Astonishingly large and clear they were, when she so opened them.

"Yes'm." Sylvester glanced aside for an instant.

"And what did they say?"

"They balked," Sylvester admitted calmly. "They're fine girls, Miss Sheila. And they're lookers. But they just are n't quite fine enough. They're not artists, like your Poppa and like you — and like me."

Sheila put a hand up to her cheek. Her eyes came back to their accustomed narrowness and a look of doubt stole into her face.

"Artists?"

"Yes'm." Sylvester had begun to walk about. "Artists. Why, what's an artist but a person with a dream he wants to make real? My dream's — The Aura, girl. For three years now" — he half-shut his eyes and moved his arm in front of him as though he were putting in the broad first lines of a picture — "I've seen that girl there back of my bar — shining and *good* and fine — not the sort of a girl a man'd be lookin' for, mind you, just *not* that! A girl that would sort of take your breath. Say, picture it, Sheila!" He stood by her and pointed it out as though he showed her a view. "You're a cowboy. And you come ridin' in, bone-tired, dusty, with a *thirst.* Well, sir, a thirst in your throat and a thirst in your heart and a thirst in your soul. You're wantin' re-freshment. For your body and your eyes and your mind. Well, ma'am, you tie your pony up there and you push open those doors and you push 'em open and step plumb into Paradise. It's cool in there — I'm picturin' a July evenin', Miss Sheila — and it's quiet and it's shining clean. And there's a big man in white who's servin' drinks — cold drinks with a grand smell. That's my man Carthy. He keeps order. You bet you, he does keep it too. And beside him stands a girl. Well, she's the kind of girl you — the cowboy — would 'a' dreamed about, lyin' out in your blanket under the stars, if you'd 'a' knowed enough to be able to dream about her. After you've set eyes on her, you don't dream about any other kind of girl. And just seein' her there so sweet and bright and dainty-like, makes a different fellow of you. Say, goin' into that bar is like goin' into church and havin' a jim-dandy time when you get there — which is something the churches have n't got round to offerin' yet to my way of thinkin'. Now, I want to ask you, Miss Sheila, if you've got red blood in your veins and a love of adventure and a wish to see that real entertaining show we call 'life' — and mighty few females ever get a glimpse of it — and if you've acquired a feeling of gratitude for Pap and if you've got any real religion, or any ambition to play a part, if you're a real woman that wants to be an in-spire-ation to men, well, ma'am, I ask you, could you turn down a chance like that?"

He stood away a pace and put his question with a lifted forefinger.

Sheila's eyes were caught and held by his. Again her mind seemed to be fastened to his will. And the blood ran quickly in her veins. Her heart beat. She was excited, stirred. He had seen through her shell unerringly as no one else in all her life had seen. He had mysteriously guessed that she had the dangerous gift of adventure, that under the shyness and uncertainty of inexperience there was no fear in her, that she was one of those that would rather play with fire than warm herself before it. Sheila stood there, discovered and betrayed. He had played upon her as upon a flexible young reed: that stop, her ambition, this, her romanticism, that, her vanity, the fourth, her gratitude, the fifth, her idealism, the sixth, her recklessness. And there was this added urge — she must stay here and drudge under the lash of "Momma's" tongue or she must accept this strange, this unimaginable offer. Again she opened her eyes wider and wider. The pupils swallowed up the misty gray. Her lips parted.

"I'll do it," she said, narrowed her eyes and shut her mouth tight. With such a look she might have thrown a fateful toss of dice.

Sylvester caught her hands, pressed them up to his chest.

"It's a promise, girl?"

"Yes."

ARTISTS 81

"God bless you!"

He let her go. He walked on air. He threw open the door.

There on the threshold — stood "Momma."

"I kind of see," she drawled, "why Sheila don't take no interest in dancin'!"

"You're wrong," said Sheila very clearly. "I have been persuaded. I am going to the dance."

Sylvester laughed aloud. "One for you, Momma!" he said. "Come on down, old girl, while Miss Sheila gets into her party dress. Say, Aura, are n't you goin' to give me a dance to-night?"

His wife looked curiously at his red, excited face. She followed him in silence down the stairs.

Sheila stood still listening to their descending steps, then she knelt down beside her little trunk and opened the lid. The sound of the fiddle stole hauntingly, beseechingly, tauntingly into her consciousness. There in the top tray of her trunk wrapped in tissue paper lay the only evening frock she had, a filmy French dress of white tulle, a Christmas present from her father, a breath-taking, intoxicating extravagance. She had worn it only once.

It was with the strangest feeling that she took it out. It seemed to her that the Sheila that had worn that dress was dead.

CHAPTER IX

A Singeing of Wings

ALL the vitality of Millings — and whatever its deficiencies the town lacked nothing of the splendor and vigor of its youth — throbbed and stamped and shook the walls of the Town Hall that night. To understand that dance, it is necessary to remember that it took place on a February night with the thermometer at zero and with the ground five feet beneath the surface of the snow. There were men and women and children, too, who had come on skis and in toboggans for twenty miles from distant ranches to do honor to the wedding-anniversary of Greely and his wife.

A room near the ballroom was reserved for babies, and here, early in the evening, lay small bundles in helpless, more or less protesting, rows, their needs attended to between waltzes and polkas by father or mother according to the leisure of the parent and the nature of the need. One infant, whose home discipline was not up to the requirements of this event, refused to accommodate himself to loneliness and so spent the evening being dandled, first by father, then by mother, in a chair immediately beside the big drum. Whether the spot was chosen for the purpose of smothering his cries or enlivening his spirits nobody cared to inquire. Infants in the Millings and Hidden Creek communities, where certified milk and scientific feeding were unknown, were treated rather like family parasites to be attended to only when the irritation they caused became acute. They were not taken very seriously. That they grew up at all was largely due to their being turned out as soon as they could walk into an air that buoyed the entire nervous and circulatory systems almost above the need of any other stimulant.

The dance began when the first guests arrived, which on this occasion was at about six o'clock, and went on till the last guest left, at about ten the next morning. In the meantime the Greelys' hospitality provided every variety of refreshment.

When Sheila reached the Town Hall, crowded between Sylvester and joyous Babe in her turquoise blue on the front seat of the Ford, while the back seat was occupied by Girlie in scarlet and "Momma" in purple velveteen, the dance was well under way. The Hudsons came in upon the tumult of a quadrille. The directions, chanted above the din, were not very exactly heeded; there was as much confusion as there was mirth. Sheila, standing near Girlie's elbow, felt the exhilaration which youth does feel at the impact of explosive noise and motion, the stamping of feet, the shouting, the loud laughter, the music, the bounding, prancing bodies: savagery in a good humor, childhood again, but without the painful intensity of childhood. Sheila wondered just as any *débutante* in a city ballroom wonders, whether she would have partners, whether she would have "a good time." Color came into her face. She forgot everything except the immediate prospect of flattery and rhythmic motion.

Babe pounced upon a young man who was shouldering his way toward Girlie.

"Say, Jim, meet Miss Arundel! Gee! I've been wanting you two to get acquainted."

Sheila held out her hand to Mr. James Greely, who took it with a surprised and dazzled look.

"Pleased to meet you," he murmured, and the dimple deepened in his ruddy right cheek.

He turned his blushing face to Girlie. "Gee! You look great!" he said.

She was, in fact, very beautiful — a long, firm, round body, youthful and strong, sheathed in a skin of cream and roses, lips that looked as though they had been used for nothing but the tranquil eating of ripe fruit, eyes of unfathomable serenity, and hair almost as soft and creamy as her shoulders and her finger-tips. Her beauty was not marred to Jim Greely's eyes by the fact that she was chewing gum. Amongst animals the only social poise, the only true self-possession and absence of shyness is shown by the cud-chewing cow. She is diverted from fear and soothed from self-consciousness by having her nervous attention distracted. The smoking man has this

A SINGEING OF WINGS 85

release, the knitting woman has it. Girlie and Babe had it from the continual labor of their jaws. Every hope and longing and ambition in Girlie's heart centered upon this young man now complimenting her, but as he turned to her, she just stood there and looked up at him. Her jaws kept on moving slightly. There was in her eyes the minimum of human intelligence and the maximum of unconscious animal invitation — a blank, defenseless expression of — "Here I am. Take me." As Jim Greely expressed the look: "Girlie makes everything easy. She don't give a fellow any discomfort like some of these skittish girls do. She's kind of home folks at once."

"We can't get into the quadrille now," said Jim, "but you'll give me the next, won't you, Girlie?"

"Sure, Jim," said the unsmiling, rosy mouth.

Jim moved uneasily on his patent-leather feet. He shot a sidelong glance at Sheila.

"Say, Miss Arundel, may I have the next after . . . Meet Mr. Gates," he added spasmodically, as the hand of a gigantic friend crushed his elbow.

Sheila looked up a yard or two of youth and accepted Mr. Gates's invitation for "the next."

The head at the top of the tower bent itself down to her with a snakelike motion.

"Us fellows," it said, "have been aiming to give you a good time to-night."

Sheila was relieved to find him within hearing. Her

smile dawned enchantingly. It had all the inevitability of some sweet natural event.

"That's very good of — you fellows. I did n't know you knew that there was such a person as — as me in Millings."

"You bet you, we knew. Here goes the waltz. Do you want to Castle it? I worked in a Yellowstone Park Hotel last summer, and I'm wise on dancing."

Sheila found herself stretched ceilingwards. She must hold one arm straight in the air, one elbow as high as she could make it go, and she must dance on her very tip-toes. Like every girl whose life has taken her in and out of Continental hotels, she could dance, and she had the gift of intuitive rhythm and of yielding to her partner's intentions almost before they were muscularly expressed. Mr. Gates felt that he was dancing with moonlight, only the figure of speech is not his own.

Girlie in the arms of Jim spoke to him above her rigid chin. Girlie had the haughty manner of dancing.

"She's not much of a looker, is she, Jim?" But the pain in her heart gave the speech an audible edge.

"She's not much of anything," said Jim, who had not looked like the young man on the magazine cover for several busy years in vain. "She's just a scrap."

But Girlie could not be deceived. Sheila's delicate, crystalline beauty pierced her senses like the frosty beauty of a winter star: her dress of white mist, her

A SINGEING OF WINGS 87

slender young arms, her long, slim, romantic throat, the finish and polish of her, every detail done lovingly as if by a master's silver-pointed pencil, her hair so artlessly simple and shining, smooth and rippled under the lights, the strangeness of her face! Girlie told herself again that it was an irregular face, that the chin was not right, that the eyes were not well-opened and lacked color, that the nose was odd, defying classification; she knew, in spite of the rigid ignorance of her ideals, that these things mysteriously spelled enchantment. Sheila was as much more beautiful than anything Millings had ever seen as her white gown was more exquisite than anything Millings had ever worn. It was a work of art, and Sheila was, also, in some strange sense, a work of art, something shaped and fashioned through generations, something tinted and polished and retouched by race, something mellowed and restrained, something bred. Girlie did not know why the white tulle frock, absolutely plain, shamed her elaborate red satin with its exaggerated lines. But she did know. She did not know why Sheila's subtle beauty was greater than her obvious own. But she did know. And so great and bewildering a fear did this knowledge give her that, for an instant, it confused her wits.

"She's going back East soon," she said sharply.

"Is she?" Jim's question was indifferent, but from that instant his attention wandered.

When he took the small, crushable silken partner

into his arms for "the next after," a one-step, he was troubled by a sense of hurry, by that desire to make the most of his opportunity that torments the reader of a "best-seller" from the circulating library.

"Say, Miss Arundel," he began, looking down at the smooth, jewel-bright head, "you have n't given Millings a square deal."

Sheila looked at him quizzically.

"You see," went on Jim, "it's winter now."

"Yes, Mr. Greely. It *is* winter."

"And that's not our best season. When summer comes, it's awfully pretty and it's good fun. We have all sorts of larks — us fellows and the girls. You'd like a motor ride, would n't you?"

"Not especially, thank you," said Sheila, who really at times deserved the Western condemnation of "ornery." "I don't like motors. In fact, I hate motors."

Jim swallowed a nervous lump. This girl was not "home folks." She made him feel awkward and uncouth. He tried to remember that he was Mr. James Greely, of the Millings National Bank, and, remembering at the same time something that the girl from Cheyenne had said about his smile, he caught Sheila's eye deliberately and made use of his dimple.

"What do you like?" he asked. "If you tell me what you like, I — I'll see that you get it."

"You're very powerful, are n't you? You sound like a fairy godmother."

A SINGEING OF WINGS 89

"You look like a fairy. That's just what you do look like."

"I like horses much better than motors," said Sheila. "I thought the West would be full of adorable little ponies. I thought you'd ride like wizards, bucking — you know."

"Well, I can ride. But, I guess you've been going to the movies or the Wild West shows. This town *must* seem kind of dead after Noo York."

"I hate the movies," said Sheila sweetly.

"Say, it would be easy to get a pony for you as soon as the snow goes. I sold my horse when Dad bought me my Ford."

"Sold him? Sold your own special horse!"

"Well, yes, Miss Arundel. Does that make you think awfully bad of me?"

"Yes. It does. It makes me think *awfully* 'bad' of you. If I had a horse, I'd — I'd tie him to my bedpost at night and feed him on rose-leaves and tie ribbons in his mane."

Jim laughed, delighted at her childishness. It brought back something of his own assurance.

"I don't think Pap Hudson would quite stand for that, would he? Seems to me as if — "

But here his partner stopped short, turned against his arm, and her face shone with a sudden friendly sweetness of surprise. "There's Dickie!"

She left Jim, she slipped across the floor. Dickie limped toward her. His face was white.

"Dickie! I'm so glad you came. Somehow I did n't expect you to be here. But you're lame! Then you can't dance. What a shame. After Mr. Greely and I have finished this, could you sit one out with me?"

"Yes'm," whispered Dickie.

He was not as inexpressive as it might seem however. His face, a rather startling face here in this crowded, boisterous room, a face that seemed to have come in out of the night bringing with it a quality of eternal childhood, of quaint, half-forgotten dreams — his face was very expressive. So much so, that Sheila, embarrassed, went back almost abruptly to Jim. Her smile was left to bewilder Dickie. He began to describe it to himself. And this was the first time a woman had stirred that mysterious trouble in his brain.

"It's not like a smile at all," thought Dickie, the dancing crowd invisible to him; "it's like something — it's — what is it? It's as if the wind blew it into her face and blew it out again. It does n't come from anywhere, it does n't seem to be going anywhere, at least not anywhere a fellow knows . . ." Here he was rudely joggled by a passing elbow and the pain of his ankle brought a sharp "Damn!" out of him. He found a niche to lean in, and he watched Sheila and Jim. He found himself not quite so overwhelmed as usual by admiration of his friend. His mood was even very faintly critical. But, as the dance came to an end, Dickie fell a prey to base anxiety. How would

A SINGEING OF WINGS 91

"Poppa" take it if he, Dickie, should be seen sitting out a dance with Miss Arundel? Dickie was profoundly afraid of his father. It was a fear that he had never been allowed the leisure to outgrow. Sylvester with torture of hand and foot and tongue had fostered it. And Dickie's childhood had lingered painfully upon him. He could not outgrow all sorts of feelings that other fellows seemed to shed with their short trousers. He was afraid of his father, physically and morally; his very nerves quivered under the look of the small brown eyes.

Nevertheless, as Sheila thanked Jim for her waltz, her elbow was touched by a cold finger.

"Here I am," said Dickie. He had a demure and startled look. "Let's sit it out in the room between the babies and the dancin'-room — two kinds of a b-a-w-l, ain't it? But I guess we can hear ourselves speak in there. There's a sort of a bench, kind of a hard one . . ."

Sheila followed and found herself presently in a half-dark place under a row of dangling coats. An iron stove near by glowed with red sides and a round red mouth. It gave a flush to Dickie's pale face. Sheila thought she had never seen such a wistful and untidy lad.

Yet, poor Dickie at the moment appeared to himself rather a dashing and heroic figure. He had certainly shown courage and had done his deed with jauntiness. Besides, he had on his only good suit of dark-blue serge, very thin serge. It was one that he had bought second-hand from Jim, and he was sure, therefore, of its perfection. He thought, too, that he had mastered, by the stern use of a wet brush, a cowlick which usually disgraced the crown of his head. He had n't. It had long ago risen to its wispish height.

"Jim dances fine, don't he?" Dickie said. "I kind of wish I liked to dance. Seems like athletic stunts don't appeal to me some way."

"Would you call dancing an athletic stunt?" Sheila leaned back against a coat that smelled strongly of hay and tobacco and caught up her knees in her two hands so that the small white slippers pointed daintily, clear of the floor.

Dickie looked at them. It seemed to him suddenly that a giant's hand had laid itself upon his heart and turned it backwards as a pilot turns his wheel to change the course of a ship. The contrary movement made him catch his breath. He wanted to put the two white silken feet against his breast, to button them inside his coat, to keep them in his care.

"Ain't it, though?" he managed to say. "Ain't it an athletic stunt?"

"I've always heard it called an accomplishment."

"God!" said Dickie gently. "I'd 'a' never thought of that. I do like ski-ing, though. Have you tried it, Miss Arundel?"

"No. If I call you Dickie, you might call me Sheila, I think."

A SINGEING OF WINGS

Dickie lifted his eyes from the feet. "Sheila," he said.

He was curiously eloquent. Again Sheila felt the confusion that had sent her abruptly back to Jim. She smoothed out the tulle on her knee.

"I think I'd love to ski. Is it awfully hard to learn?"

"No, ma'am. It's just dandy. Especially on a moonlight night, like night before last. And if you'd 'a' had skis on you wouldn't 'a' broke through. You go along so quiet and easy, pushing yourself a little with your pole. There's a kind of a swing to it — "

He stood up and threw his light, thin body gracefully into the ski-er's pose. "See? You slide on one foot, then on the other. It's as easy as dreaming, and as still."

"It's like a gondola — " suggested Sheila.

Dickie put his head on one side and Sheila explained. She also sang a snatch of a Gondel-lied to show him the motion.

"Yes'm," said Dickie. "It's like that. It kind of has a — has a — "

"Rhythm?"

"I guess that's the word. So's riding. I like to do the things that have that."

"Well, then, you ought to like dancing."

"Yes'm. Maybe I would if it wasn't for havin' to pull a girl round about with me. It kind of takes my mind off the pleasure."

Sheila laughed. Then, "Did you get my note?" she asked.

"Yes'm." Her laughter had embarrassed him, and he had suddenly a hunted look.

"And are you going to be my friend?"

The sliding of feet on a floor none too smooth, the music, the wailing of a baby accompanied Dickie's silence. He was very silent and sat very still, his hands hanging between his knees, his head bent. He stared at Sheila's feet. His face, what she could see of it, was, even beyond the help of firelight, pale.

"Why, Dickie, I believe you're going to say No!"

"Some fellows would say Yes," Dickie answered. "But I sort of promised not to be your friend. Poppa said I'd kind of dis-gust you. And I figure that I would — "

Sheila hesitated.

"You mean because you — you — ?"

"Yes'm."

"Can't you stop?"

He shook his head and gave her a tormented look.

"Oh, Dickie! Of course you can! At your age!"

"Seems like it means more to me than anything else."

"Dickie! Dickie!"

"Yes'm. It kind of takes the awful edge off things."

"What *do* you mean? I don't understand."

"Things are so sort of — sharp to me. I mean, I don't know if I can tell you. I feel like I had to put something between me and — and things. Oh, damn! I can't make you see — "

"No," said Sheila, distressed.

"It's always that-a-way," Dickie went on. "I mean, everything's kind of — too much. I used to run miles when I was a kid. And sometimes now when I can get out and walk or ski, the feeling goes. But other times — well, ma'am, whiskey sort of takes the edge off and lets something kind of slack down that gets sort of screwed up. Oh, I don't know . . ."

"Did you ever go to a doctor about it?"

Dickie looked up at her and smiled. It was the sweetest smile — so patient of this misunderstanding of hers. "No, ma'am."

"Then you don't care to be my friend enough to — to try — "

"I would n't be a good friend to you," said Dickie. And he spoke now almost sullenly. "Because I would n't want you to have any other friends. I hate it to see you with any other fellow."

"How absurd!"

"Maybe it is absurd. I guess it seems awful foolish to you." He moved his cracked patent-leather pump in a sort of pattern on the floor. Again he looked up, this time with a freakish, an almost elfin flicker of his extravagant eyelashes. "There's something I could be real well," he said. "Only, I guess Poppa's got there ahead of me. I could be a dandy guardian to you — Sheila."

Again Sheila laughed. But the ringing of her silver coins was not quite true. There was a false note. She shut her eyes involuntarily. She was remembering that instant an hour or two before when Sylvester's look had held hers to his will. The thought of what she had promised crushed down upon her consciousness with the smothering, sudden weight of its reality. She could not tell Dickie. She could not — though this she did not admit — bear that he should know.

"Very well," she said, in a hard and weary voice. "Be my guardian. That ought to sober any one. I think I shall need as many guardians as possible. And — here comes your father. I have this dance with him."

Dickie got hurriedly to his feet. "Oh, gosh!" said he. He was obviously and vividly a victim of panic. Sheila's small and very expressive face showed a little gleam of amused contempt. "My guardian!" she seemed to mock. To shorten the embarrassment of the moment she stepped quickly into the elder Hudson's arm. He took her hand and began to pump it up and down, keeping time to the music and counting audibly. "One, two, three." To Dickie he gave neither a word nor look.

Sheila lifted her chin so that she could smile at Dickie over Pap's shoulder. It was an indulgent and forgiving smile, but, meeting Dickie's look, it went out.

The boy's face was scarlet, his body rigid, his lips

IT WAS AN INDULGENT AND FORGIVING SMILE, BUT, MEETING DICKIE'S LOOK IT WENT OUT

A SINGEING OF WINGS

tight. The eyes with which he had overcome her smile were the hard eyes of a man. Sheila's contempt had fallen upon him like a flame. In a few dreadful minutes as he stood there it burnt up a part of his childishness.

Sheila went on, dancing like a mist in Hudson's arms. She knew that she had done something to Dickie. But she did not know what it was that she had done . . .

CHAPTER X

THE BEACON LIGHT

OUT of the Wyoming Bad Lands — orange, turquoise-green, and murky blue, of outlandish ridges, of streaked rock, of sudden, twisted cañons, a country like a dream of the far side of the moon — rode Cosme Hilliard in a choking cloud of alkali dust. He rode down Crazy Woman's Hill toward the sagebrush flat, where, in a half-circle of cloudless, snow-streaked mountains, lay the town of Millings on its rapid glacier river.

Hilliard's black hair was powdered with dust; his olive face was gray; dust lay thick in the folds of his neck-handkerchief; his pony matched the gray-white road and plodded wearily, coughing and tossing his head in misery from the nose-flies, the horse-flies, the mosquitoes, a swarm of small, tormenting presences. His rider seemed to be charmed into patience, and yet his aquiline face was not the face of a patient man. It was young in a keen, hard fashion; the mouth and eyes were those of a Spanish-American mother, golden eyes and a mouth originally beautiful, soft, and cruel, which had been tightened and straightened by a man's will and experience. It had been used so often for careless, humorous smiling that the cruelty had been almost worked out of it. Almost, not altogether. His mother's blood kept its talons on him. He was Latin and dangerous to look at, for all the big white Anglo-Saxon teeth, the slow, slack, Western American carriage, the guarded and amused expression of the golden eyes. Here was a bundle of racial contradictions, not yet welded, not yet attuned. Perhaps the one consistent, the one solvent, expression was that of alert restlessness. Cosme Hilliard was not happy, was not content, but he was eternally entertained. He was not uplifted by the hopeful illusions proper to his age, but he loved adventure. It was a bitter face, bitter and impatient and unschooled. It seemed to laugh, to expect the worst from life, and not to care greatly if the worst should come. But for such minor matters of dust and thirst and weariness, he had patience. Physically the young man was hard and well-schooled. He rode like a cowboy and carried a cowboy's rope tied to his saddle. And the rope looked as though it had been used.

Millings, that seemed so close below there through the clear, high atmosphere, was far to reach. The sun had slipped down like a thin, bright coin back of an iron rock before the traveler rode into the town. His pony shied wearily at an automobile and tried to make up his mind to buck, but a light pressure of the spur and a smiling word was enough to change his mind.

"Don't be a fool, Dusty! You know it's not worth the trouble. Remember that fifty miles you've come to-day!"

The occupants of the motor snapped a camera and hummed away. They had no prevision of being stuck halfway up Crazy Woman's Hill with no water within fifteen miles, or they would n't have exclaimed so gayly at the beauty and picturesqueness of the tired cowboy.

"He looks like a movie hero, does n't he?" said a girl.

"No, ma'am," protested the Western driver, who had been a chauffeur only for a fortnight and knew considerably less about the insides of his Ford than he did about the insides of Hilliard's cow-pony. "He ain't no show. He's the real thing. Seems like you dudes got things kinder twisted. Things ain't like shows. Shows is sometimes like things."

"The real thing" certainly behaved as the real thing would. He rode straight to the nearest saloon and swung out of his saddle. He licked the dust off his lips, looked wistfully at the swinging door, and turned back to his pony.

"You first, Dusty — damn you!" and led the stumbling beast into the yard of The Aura. In an hour or more he came back. He had dined at the hotel and he had bathed. His naturally vivid coloring glowed under the street-light. He was shaved and brushed and sleek. He pushed quickly through the swinging doors of the bar and stepped into the saloon. It was truly a famous bar — The Aura — and it deserved its fame. It shone bright and cool and polished.

THE BEACON LIGHT

There was a cheerful clink of glasses, a subdued, comfortable sound of talk. Men drank at the bar, and drank and played cards at the small tables. A giant in a white apron stood to serve the newcomer.

Hilliard ordered his drink, sipped it leisurely, then wandered off to a near-by table. There he stood, watching the game. Not long after, he accepted an invitation and joined the players. From then till midnight he was oblivious of everything but the magic squares of pasteboard, the shifting pile of dirty silver at his elbow, the faces — vacant, clever, or rascally — of his opponents. But at about midnight, trouble came. For some time Hilliard had been subconsciously irritated by the divided attention of a player opposite to him across the table. This man, with a long, thin face, was constantly squinting past Cosme's shoulder, squinting and leering and stretching his great fulllipped mouth into a queer half-smile. At last, abruptly, the irritation came to consciousness and Cosme threw an angry glance over his own shoulder.

Beside the giant who had served him his drink a girl stood: a thin, straight girl in black and white who held herself so still that she seemed painted there against the mirror on the wall. Her hands rested on her slight hips, the fine, pointed, ringless fingers white against the black stuff of her dress. Her neck, too, was white and her face, the pure unpowdered whiteness of childhood. Her chin was lifted, her lips laid together, her eyes, brilliant and clear, of no definite color, looked through her surroundings. She was very young, not more than seventeen. The mere presence of a girl was startling enough. Barmaids are unknown to the experience of the average cowboy. But this girl was trebly startling. For her face was rare. It was not Western, not even American. It was a fine-drawn, finished, Old-World face, with long, arched eyebrows, large lids, shadowed eyes, nostrils a little pinched, a sad and tender mouth. It was a face whose lines might have followed the pencil of Botticelli — those little hollows in the cheeks, that slight exaggeration of the pointed chin, that silky, rippling brown hair. There was no touch of artifice; it was an unpainted young face; hair brushed and knotted simply; the very carriage of the body was alien; supple, unconscious, restrained.

Cosme Hilliard's look lasted for a minute. Returning to his opponent it met an ugly grimace. He flushed and the game went on.

But the incident had roused Hilliard's antagonism. He disliked that man with the grimacing mouth. He began to watch him. An hour or two later Cosme's thin, dark hand shot across the table and gripped the fellow's wrist.

"Caught you that time, you tin-horn," he said quietly.

Instantly, almost before the speech was out, the giant in the apron had hurled himself across the room and gripped the cheat, who stood, a hand arrested

THE BEACON LIGHT 103

on its way to his pocket, snarling helplessly. But the other players, his fellow sheep-herders, fell away from Hilliard dangerously.

"No shootin'," said the giant harshly. "No shootin' in The Aura. It ain't allowed."

"No callin' names either," growled the prisoner. "Me and my friends would like to settle with the youthful stranger."

"Settle with him, then, but somewheres else. No fightin' in The Aura."

There was an acquiescent murmur from the other table and the sheep-herder gave in. He exchanged a look with his friends, and Carthy, seeing them disposed to return quietly to the game, left them and took up his usual position behind the bar. The barmaid moved a little closer to his elbow. Hilliard noticed that her eyes had widened in her pale face. He made a brief, contemptuous excuse to his opponents, settled his account with them, and strolled over to the bar. From Carthy he ordered another drink. He saw the girl's eyes studying the hand he put out for his glass and he smiled a little to himself. When she looked up he was ready with his golden eyes to catch her glance. Both pairs of eyes smiled. She came a step toward him.

"I believe I've heard of you, miss," he said.

A delicate pink stained her face and throat and he wondered if she could possibly be shy.

"Some fellows I met over in the Big Horn country

lately told me to look you up if I came to Millings. They said something about Hudson's Queen. It's the Hudson Hotel is n't it? — "

A puzzled, rather worried look crept into her eyes, but she avoided his question. "You were working in the Big Horn country? I hoped you were from Hidden Creek."

"I 'm on my way there," he said. "I know that country well. You come from over there?"

"No." She smiled faintly. "But" — and here her breast lifted on a deep, spasmodic sigh — "some day I'm going there."

"It's not like any other country," he said, turning his glass in his supple fingers. "It's wonderful. But wild and lonesome. You would n't be caring for it — not for longer than a sunny day or two, I reckon."

He used the native phrases with sure familiarity, and yet in his speaking of them there was something unfamiliar. Evidently she was puzzled by him, and Cosme was not sorry that he had so roused her curiosity. He was very curious himself, so much so that he had forgotten the explosive moment of a few short minutes back.

The occupants of the second table pushed away their chairs and came over to the bar. For a while the barmaid was busy, making their change, answering their jests, bidding them good-night. It was, "Well, good-night, Miss Arundel, and thank you."

THE BEACON LIGHT

"See you next Saturday, Miss Arundel, if I'm alive —"

Hilliard drummed on the counter with his fingertips and frowned. His puzzled eyes wove a pattern of inquiry from the men to the girl and back. One of them, a ruddy-faced, town boy, lingered. He had had a drop too much of The Aura's hospitality. He rested rather top-heavily against the bar and stretched out his hand.

"Are n't you going to say me a real good-night, Miss Sheila," he besought, and a tipsy dimple cut itself into his cheek.

"Do go home, Jim," murmured the barmaid. "You've broken your promise again. It's two o'clock."

He made great ox-eyes at her, his hand still begging, its blunt fingers curled upward like a thirsty cup.

His face was emptied of everything but its desire.

It was perfectly evident that "Miss Sheila" was tormented by the look, by the eyes, by the hand, by the very presence of the boy. She pressed her lips tight, drew her fine arched brows together, and twisted her fingers.

"I'll go home," he asserted obstinately, "when you tell me a proper goo'-night — not before."

Her eyes glittered. "Shall I tell Carthy to turn you out, Jim?"

He smiled triumphantly. "Uh," said he, "your

watch-dog went out. Dickie called him to answer the telephone. Now, will you tell me good-night, Sheila?"

Cosme hoped that the girl would glance at him for help, he had his long steel muscles braced; but, after a moment's thought — "And she can think. She's as cool as she's shy," commented the observer — she put her hand on Jim's. He grabbed it, pressed his lips upon it.

"Goo'-night," he said, "Goo'-night. I'll go now." He swaggered out as though she had given him a rose.

The barmaid put her hand beneath her apron and rubbed it. Cosme laughed a little at the quaint action.

"Do they give you lots of trouble, Miss Arundel?" he asked her sympathetically.

She looked at him. But her attitude was not so simple and friendly as it had been. Evidently her little conflict with Jim had jarred her humor. She looked distressed, angry. Cosme felt that, unfairly enough, she lumped him with The Enemy. He wondered pitifully if she had given The Enemy its name, if her experience had given her the knowledge of such names. He had a vision of the pretty, delicate little thing standing there night after night as though divided by the bar from prowling beasts. And yet she was known over the whole wide, wild country as "Hudson's Queen." Her crystal, childlike look must be one of those extraordinary survivals, a piteous sort of accident. Cosme called himself a sentimentalist. Spurred by this reaction against his more

THE BEACON LIGHT 107

romantic tendencies, he leaned forward. He too was going to ask the barmaid for a good-night or a greeting or a good-bye. His hand was out, when he saw her face stiffen, her lips open to an "Oh!" of warning or of fear. He wheeled and flung up his arm against a hurricane of blows.

His late opponents had decided to take advantage of Carthy's absence, and inflict chastisement prompt and merciless upon the "youthful stranger." If it had not been for that small frightened "Oh" Cosme would have been down at once.

With that moment's advantage he fought like a tiger, his golden eyes ablaze. Swift and dangerous anger was one of his gifts. He was against the wall, he was torn from it. One of his opponents staggered across the room and fell, another crumpled up against the bar. Hilliard wheeled and jabbed, plunged, was down, was up, bleeding and laughing. He was whirled this way and that, the men from whom he had struck himself free recovered themselves, closed in upon him. A blow between the eyes half stunned him, another on his mouth silenced his laughter. The room was getting blurred. He was forced back against the bar, fighting, but not effectively. The snarling laughter was not his now, but that of the cheat.

Something gave way behind him; it was as if the bar, against which he was bent backwards, had melted to him and hardened against his foes. For an instant he was free from blows and tearing hands.

He saw that a door in the bar had opened and shut. There was a small pressure on his arm, a pressure which he blindly obeyed. In front of him another door opened, and closed. He heard the shooting of a bolt. He was in the dark. The small pressure, cold through the torn silk sleeve of his white shirt, continued to urge him swiftly along a passage. He was allowed to rest an instant against a wall. A light was turned on with a little click above his head. He found himself at the end of the open hallway. Before him lay the brilliant velvet night.

Hilliard pressed his hands upon his eyes trying to clear his vision. He felt sick and giddy. The little barmaid's face, all terrified and urgent eyes, danced up and down.

"Don't waste any time!" she said. "Get out of Millings! Where's your pony?"

At that he looked at her and smiled.

"I'm not leaving Millings till to-morrow," he said uncertainly with wounded lips. "Don't look like that, girl. I'm not much hurt. If I'm not mistaken, your watch-dog is back and very much on his job. I reckon that our friends will leave Millings considerably before I do."

In fact, behind them at the end of the passage there was a sort of roar. Carthy had returned to avenge The Aura.

"You're sure you're not hurt? You're sure they won't try to hurt you again?"

THE BEACON LIGHT 109

He shook his head. "Not they . . ." He stood looking at her and the mist slowly cleared, his vision of her steadied. "Shall I see you to-morrow?"

She drew back from him a little. "No," she said. "I sleep all the morning. And, afterwards, I don't see any one except a few old friends. I go riding . . ."

He puckered his eyelids inquiringly. Then, with a sudden reckless fling of his shoulders, he put out his hand boldly and caught her small pointed chin in his palm. He bent down his head.

She stood there quite still and white, looking straight up into his face. The exquisite smoothness of her little cool chin photographed itself upon his memory. As he bent down closer to the grave and tender lips, he was suddenly, unaccountably frightened and ashamed. His hand dropped, sought for her small limp hand. His lips shifted from their course and went lower, just brushing her fingers.

"I beg your pardon," he said confusedly. He was painfully embarrassed, stammered, "I — I wanted to thank you. Good-bye . . ."

She said good-bye in the smallest sweet voice he had ever heard. It followed his memory like some weary, pitiful little ghost.

CHAPTER XI

IN THE PUBLIC EYE

No sight more familiar to the corner of Main and Resident Streets than that of Sylvester Hudson's Ford car sliding up to the curb in front of his hotel at two o'clock in a summer afternoon. He would slip out from under his steering-wheel, his linen duster flapping about his long legs, and he would stalk through the rocking, meditative observers on the piazza and through the lobby past Dickie's frozen stare, upstairs to the door of Miss Arundel's "suite." There he was bidden to come in. A few minutes later they would come down together, Sheila, too, passing Dickie wordlessly, and they would hum away from Millings leaving a veil of golden dust to smother the comments in their wake. There were days when Sheila's pony, a gift from Jim Greely, was led up earlier than the hour of Hudson's arrival, on which days Sheila, in a short skirt and a boy's shirt and a small felt Stetson, would ride away alone toward the mountain of her dreams. Sometimes Jim rode with her. It was not always possible to forbid him.

The day after Cosme Hilliard's spectacular passage was one of Hudson's days. The pony did not appear, but Sylvester did and came down with his prize. The lobby was crowded. Sheila threaded her way amongst

IN THE PUBLIC EYE 111

the medley of tourists, paused and deliberately drew near to the desk. At sight of her Dickie's whiteness dyed itself scarlet. He rose and with an apparent effort lifted his eyes to her look.

They did not smile at each other. Sheila spoke sharply, each word a little soft lash.

"I want to speak to you. Will you come to my sitting-room when I get back?"

"Yes'm," said Dickie. It was the tone of an unwincing pride. Under the desk, hidden from sight, his hand was a white-knuckled fist.

Sheila passed on, trailed by Hudson, who was smiling not agreeably to himself. Over the smile he gave his son a cruel look. It was as though an enemy had said, "Hurts you, does n't it?" Dickie returned the look with level eyes.

The rockers on the piazza stopped rocking, stopped talking, stopped breathing, it would seem, to watch Sylvester help Sheila into his car; not that he helped her greatly — she had an appearance of melting through his hands and getting into her place beside his by a sort of sleight of body. He made a series of angular movements, smiled at her, and started the car.

"Well, little girl," said he, "where to this afternoon?"

When Sheila rode her pony she always rode toward The Hill. But in that direction she had never allowed Sylvester to take her. She looked vaguely through the wind-shield now and said, "Anywhere — that cañon, the one we came home by last week. It was so queer."

"It'll be dern dusty, I'm afraid."

"I don't care." Sheila wrapped her gray veil over her small hat which fitted close about her face. "I'm getting used to the dust. Does it ever rain around Millings? And does it ever stop blowing?"

"We don't like Millings to-day, do we?"

Sylvester was bending his head to peer through the gray mist of her veil. She held herself stiffly beside him, showing the profile of a small Sphinx. Suddenly it turned slightly, seemed to wince back. Girlie, at the gate of Number 18 Cottonwood Avenue, had stopped to watch them pass. Girlie did not speak. Her face looked smitten, the ripe fruit had turned bitter upon her ruddy lips. The tranquil emptiness of her beauty had filled itself stormily.

Sheila did not answer Hudson's reproachful question. She leaned back, dropped back, rather, into a tired little heap and let the country slide by — the strange, wide, broken country with its circling mesas, its somber grays and browns and dusty greens, its bare purple hills, rocks and sand and golden dirt, and now and then, in the sudden valley bottoms, swaying groves of vivid green and ribbons of emerald meadows. The mountains shifted and opened their cañons, gave a glimpse of their beckoning and forbidding fastnesses and closed them again as though by a whispered Sesame.

IN THE PUBLIC EYE

"What was the row last night?" asked Sylvester in his voice of cracked tenderness. "Carthy says there was a bunch of toughs. Were you scared good and plenty? I'm sorry. It don't happen often, believe *me*.

"I wish you could 'a' heard Carthy talkin' about you, Sheila," went on Sylvester, his eyes, filled with uneasiness, studying her silence and her huddled smallness, hands in the pockets of her light coat, veiled face turned a little away, "Say, that would 'a' set you up all right! Talk about beacons!"

Here she flashed round on him, as though her whole body had been electrified. "Tell me all that again," she begged in a voice that he could not interpret except that there was in it a sound of tears. "Tell me again about a beacon . . ."

He stammered. He was confused. But stumblingly he tried to fulfill her demand. Here was a thirst for something, and he wanted above everything in the world to satisfy it. Sheila listened to him with unsteady, parted lips. He could see them through the veil.

"You still think I am that?" she asked.

He was eager to prove it to her. "Still think? Still think? Why, girl, I don't hev to think. Don't the tillbox speak for itself? Don't Carthy handle a crowd that's growing under his eyes? Don't we sell more booze in a week now than we used to in a — " Suddenly he realized that he was on the wrong tack. It was his first break. He drew in a sharp breath and stopped, his face flushing deeply.

"Yes?" questioned Sheila, melting her syllables like slivers of ice on her tongue. "Go on."

"Er — er, don't we draw a finer lot of fellows than we ever did before? Don't they behave more decent and orderly? Don't they get civilization just for looking at you, Miss Sheila?"

"And — and booze? Jim Greely, for instance, Mr. James Greely, of the Millings National Bank — he never used to patronize The Aura. And now he's there every night till twelve and often later, for he won't obey me any more. I wonder whether Mr. and Mrs. Greely are glad that you are getting a better type of customer! Mrs. Greely almost stopped me on the street the other day — that is, she almost got up courage to speak to me. Before now she's cut me, just as Girlie does, just as your wife does, just as Dickie does — "

"Dickie cut you?" Sylvester threw back his head and laughed uneasily, and with a strained note of alarm. "That's a good one, Miss Sheila. I kinder fancied you did the cuttin' there."

"Dickie hasn't spoken to me since he came to me that day when he heard what I was going to do and tried to talk me out of doing it."

"Yes'm. He came to me first," drawled Sylvester.

They were both silent, busy with the amazing memory of Dickie, of his disheveled fury, of his lashing eloquence. He had burst in upon his family at breakfast that April morning when Millings was

IN THE PUBLIC EYE

humming with the news, had advanced upon his father, stood above him.

"Is it true that you are going to make a barmaid of Sheila?"

Sylvester, in an effort to get to his feet, had been held back by Dickie's thin hand that shot out at him like a sword.

"Sure it's true," Sylvester had said coolly. But he had not felt cool. He had felt shaken and confused. The boy's entire self-forgetfulness, his entire absence of fear, had made Hudson feel that he was talking to a stranger, a not inconsiderable one.

"It's true, then." Dickie had drawn a big breath. "You — you" — he seemed to swallow an epithet — "you'll let that girl go into your filthy saloon and make money for you by her — by her prettiness and her — her ignorance — "

"Say, Dickie," his father had drawled, "you goin' to run for the legislature? Such a lot of classy words!" But anger and alarm were rising in him.

"You've fetched her away out here," went on Dickie, "and kinder got her cornered and you've talked a lot of slush to her and you've — "

Here Girlie came to the rescue.

"Well, anyway, she's a willing victim, Dickie," Girlie had said.

Dickie had flashed her one look. "Is she? I'll see about that. Where's Sheila?"

And then, there was Sheila's memory. Dickie had

come upon her in a confusion of boxes, her little trunk half-unpacked, its treasures scattered over the chairs and floor. Sheila had lifted to him from where she knelt a glowing and excited face. "Oh, Dickie," she had said, her relief at the escape from Mrs. Hudson pouring music into her voice, "have you heard?"

He had sat down on one of the plush chairs of "the suite" as though he felt weak. Then he had got up and had walked to and fro while she described her dream, the beauty of her chosen mission, the glory of the saloon whose high priestess she had become. And Dickie had listened with the bitter and disillusioned and tender face of a father hearing the prattle of a beloved child.

"You honest think all that, Sheila?" he had asked her patiently.

She had started again, standing now to face him and beginning to be angry at his look. This boy whom she had lifted up to be her friend!

"Say," Dickie had drawled, "Poppa's some guardian!" He had advanced upon her as though he wanted to shake her. "You gotta give it right up, Sheila," he had said sternly. "Sooner than immediately. It's not to go through. Say, girl, you don't know much about bars." He had drawn a picture for her, drawing partly upon experience, partly upon his imagination, the gift of vivid metaphor descending upon him. He used words that bit into her memory. Sheila

IN THE PUBLIC EYE 117

had listened and then she had put her hands over her ears. He pulled them down. He went on. Sheila's Irish blood had boiled up into her brain. She stormed back at him.

"It's you, it's your use of The Aura that has been its only shame, Dickie," was the last of all the things she had said.

At which, Dickie standing very still, had answered, "If you go there and stand behind the bar all night with Carthy to keep hands off, I — I swear I'll never set foot inside the place again. You ain't agoin' to be *my* beacon light — "

"Well, then," said Sheila, "I shall have done one good thing at least by being there."

Dickie, going out, had passed a breathless Sylvester on his way in. The two had looked at each other with a look that cut in two the tie between them, and Sheila, running to Sylvester, had burst into tears.

The motor hummed evenly on its way. It began, with a change of tune, to climb the graded side of one of the enormous mesas. Sheila, having lived through again that scene with Dickie, took out a small handkerchief and busied herself with it under her veil. She laughed shakily.

"Perhaps a beacon does more good by warning people away than by attracting them," she said. "Dickie has certainly kept his word. I don't believe he's touched a drop since I've been barmaid, Mr. Hudson. I should think you'd be proud of him."

Sylvester was silent while they climbed the hill. He changed gears and sounded his horn. They passed another motor on a dangerous curve. They began to drop down again.

"Some day," said Sylvester in a quiet voice, "I'll break every bone in Dickie's body." He murmured something more under his breath in too low a tone, fortunately, for Sheila's ear. From her position behind the bar, she had become used to swearing. She had heard a strange variety of language. But when Sylvester drew upon his experience and his fancy, the artist in him was at work.

"Do you suppose," asked his companion in an impersonal tone, "that it was really a hard thing for Dickie to do — to give it up, I mean?"

"By the look of him the last few months," snarled Sylvester, "I should say it had taken out of him what little real feller there ever was in."

Sheila considered this. She remembered Dickie, as he had risen behind the desk half an hour before. She did not contradict Sylvester. She had learned not to contradict him. But Dickie's face with its tight-knit look of battle stood out very clear to refute the accusation of any loss of manliness. He was still a quaint and ruffled Dickie. But he was vastly aged. From twenty to twenty-seven, he seemed to have jumped in a few weeks. A key had turned in the

IN THE PUBLIC EYE 119

formerly open door of his spirit. The indeterminate lips had shut hard, the long-lashed eyes had definitely put a guard upon their dreams. He was shockingly thin and colorless, however. Sheila dwelt painfully upon the sort of devastation she had wrought. Girlie's face, and Dickie's, and Jim's. A grieving pressure squeezed her heart; she lifted her chest with an effort on a stifled breath.

"God! Sheila," said Sylvester harshly. The car wobbled a little. "Ain't you happy, girl?"

Sheila looked up at him. Her veil was wet against her cheeks.

"Last night," she said unevenly, "a man was going to kiss me on my mouth and — and he changed his mind and kissed my hand instead. He left a smear of blood on my fingers from where those — those other men had struck his lips. I don't know why it f-frightens me so to think about that. But it does."

She seemed to collapse before him into a little sobbing child.

"And every day when I wake up," she wailed, "I t-taste whiskey on my tongue and I — I smell cigarette smoke in my hair. And I d-dream about men looking at me — the way Jim looks. And I can't let myself think of Father any more. He used to hold his chin up and walk along as if he looked above every one and everything. I don't believe he'd ever seen a barmaid or a drunken man — not really seen them, Mr. Hudson."

"Then he was n't a real artist after all," Sylvester spoke slowly and carefully. He was pale.

"He l-loved the stars," sobbed Sheila, her broken reserve had let out a flood; "he told me to keep looking at the stars."

"Well, ma'am," Sylvester spoke again, "I never knowed the stars to turn their backs on anything. Barmaids or drunks or kings — they all look about alike to the stars, I reckon. Say, Sheila, maybe you have n't got the pluck for real living. Maybe you're the kind of doll-baby girl that craves sheltering. I reckon I made a big mistake."

Sheila moved slightly as though his speech had pricked her.

"It kind of did n't occur to me," went on Sylvester, "that you'd care a whole lot about being ig-nored by Momma and Mr. and Mrs. Greely and Girlie. Say, Girlie's got to take her chance same's anybody else. Why don't you give Jim a jolt?"

Sheila at this began to laugh. She caught her breath. She laughed and cried together.

Sylvester patted her shoulder. "Poor kid! You're all in. Late hours too much for you, I reckon. Come on now — tell Pap everything. Ease off your heart. It's wonderful what crying does for the nervous system. I laid out on a prairie one night when I was about your age and just naturally bawled. You'd 'a' thought I was a baby steer, hanged if you would n't 'a' thought so. It's the fight scared you plumb to

IN THE PUBLIC EYE 121

pieces. Carthy told me about it and how you let the good-looking kid out by the back. I seen him ride off toward Hidden Creek this morning. He was a real pretty boy too. Say, Sheila, was n't you ever kissed?"

"No," said Sheila. "And I don't want to be."

Sylvester laughed with a little low cackle of intense pleasure and amusement. "Well, you shan't be. No, you shan't. Nobody shall kiss Sheila!"

His method seemed to him successful. Sheila stopped crying and stopped laughing, dried her eyes, murmured, "I'm all right now, thank you, Mr. Hudson," and fell into an abysmal silence.

He talked smoothly, soothingly, skillfully, confident of his power to manage "gels." Once in a while he saw her teeth gleam as though she smiled. As they came back to Millings in the afterglow of a brief Western twilight, she unfastened her veil and showed a quiet, thoughtful face.

She thanked him, gave him her hand. "Don't come up, please, Mr. Hudson," she said with that cool composure of which at times she was surprisingly capable. "I shall have my dinner sent up and take a little rest before I go to work."

"You feel O.K.?" he asked her doubtfully. His brown eyes had an almost doglike wistfulness.

"Quite, thank you." Her easy, effortless smile passed across her face and in and out of her eyes.

Hudson stood beside his wheel tapping his teeth and staring after her. The rockers on the veranda stopped their rocking, stopped their talking, stopped their breathing to see Sheila pass. When she had gone, they fastened their attention upon Sylvester. He was not aware of them. He stood there a full three minutes under the glare of publicity. Then he sighed and climbed into his car.

CHAPTER XII

HUDSON'S QUEEN

THE lobby, empty of its crowd when Sheila passed through it on her way up to her rooms, was filled by a wheezy, bullying voice. In front of the desk a little barrel of a man with piggish eyes was disputing his bill with Dickie. At the sound of Sheila's entrance he turned, stopped his complaint, watched her pass, and spat into a near-by receptacle. Sheila remembered that he had visited the bar early in the evening before, and had guzzled his whiskey and made some wheezy attempts at gallantry. Dickie, flushed, his hair at wild odds with composure, was going over the bill. In the midst of his calculations the man would interrupt him with a plump dirty forefinger pounced upon the paper. "Wassa meanin' of this item, f'rinstance? Highway robbery, thassa meanin' of it. My wife take breakfast in her room? I'd like to see her try it!"

Sheila went upstairs. She took off her things, washed off the dust, and changed into the black-and-white barmaid's costume, fastening the frilly apron, the cuffs, the delicate fichu with mechanical care. She put on the silk stockings and the buckled shoes and the tiny cap. Then she went into her sitting-room, chose the most dignified chair, folded her hands in her lap, and waited for Dickie. Waiting, she looked out through the window and saw the glow fade from the snowy crest of The Hill. The evening star let itself delicately down through the sweeping shadows of the earth from some mysterious fastness of invisibility. The room was dim when Dickie's knock made her turn her head.

"Come in."

He appeared, shut the door without looking at her, then came unwillingly across the carpet and stopped at about three steps from her chair, standing with one hand in his pocket. He had slicked down his hair with a wet brush and changed his suit. It was the dark-blue serge he had worn at the dance five months before. What those five months had been to Dickie, through what abasements and exaltations, furies and despairs he had traveled since he had looked up from Sheila's slippered feet with his heart turned backward like a pilot's wheel, was only faintly indicated in his face. And yet the face gave Sheila a pang. And, unsupported by anger, he was far from formidable, a mere youth. Sheila wondered at her long and sustained persecution of him. She smiled, her lips, her eyes, and her heart.

"Are n't you going to sit down, Dickie? This is n't a school examination."

"If it was," said Dickie, with an uncertain attempt at ease, "I would n't pass." He felt for a chair and got into it. He caught a knee in his hand and looked

HUDSON'S QUEEN

about him. "You've made the room awful pretty, Sheila."

She had spent some of the rather large pay she drew upon coverings of French blue for the plush furniture, upon a dainty yellow porcelain tea-set, upon little oddments of decoration. The wall-paper and carpet were inoffensive, the quietest probably in Millings, so that her efforts had met with some success. There was a lounge with cushions, there were some little volumes, a picture of her father, a bowl of pink wild roses, a vase of vivid cactus flowers. Some sketches in water-color — Marcus's most happy medium — had been tacked up. A piece of tapestry decorated the back of the chair Sheila had chosen. In the dim light it all had an air of quiet richness. It seemed a room transplanted to Millings from some finer soil.

Dickie looked at the tapestry because it was the nearest he dared come to looking at Sheila. His hands and knees shook with the terrible beating of his heart. It was not right, thought Dickie resentfully, that any feeling should take hold of a fellow and shake and terrify him so. He threw himself back suddenly and folded his arms tight across his chest.

"You wanted to see me about something?" he asked.

"Yes. I'll give you some tea first."

Dickie's lips fell apart. He said neither yea nor nay, but watched dazedly her preparations, her concoctions, her advance upon him with a yellow teacup and a wafer. He did not stand up to take it and he knew too late that this was a blunder. He tingled with shame.

Sheila went back to her chair and sipped from her own cup.

"I've been angry with you for three months now, Dickie."

"Yes'm," he said meekly.

"That's the longest I've ever been angry with any one in my life. Once I hated a teacher for two weeks, and it almost killed me. But what I felt about her was — was weakness to the way I've felt about you."

"Yes'm," again said Dickie. His tea was terribly hot and burnt his tongue, so that tears stood in his eyes.

"And I suppose you've been angry with me."

"No, ma'am."

Sheila was not particularly pleased with this gentle reply. "Why, Dickie, you *know* you have!"

"No, ma'am."

"Then why have n't you spoken to me? Why have you looked that way at me?"

"I don't speak to folks that don't speak to me," said Dickie, lifting the wafer as though its extreme lightness was faintly repulsive to him.

"Well," said Sheila bitterly, "you have n't been alone in your attitude. Very few people have been speaking to me. My only loyal friends are Mr. Hudson and Amelia Plecks and Carthy and Jim. Jim made no promises about being my guardian, but — "

"But he *is* your guardian?" Dickie drawled the question slightly. His gift of faint irony and impersonal detachment flicked Sheila's temper as it had always flicked his father's.

"Jim is my friend," Sheila maintained in defiance of a still, small voice. "He has given me a pony and has taken me riding — "

"Yes'm, I've saw you — " Dickie's English was peculiarly fallible in moments of emotion. Now he seemed determined to cut Sheila's description short. "Say, Sheila, did you send for me to tell me about this lovely friendship of yours with Jim?"

Sheila set her cup down on the window-sill. She did not want to lose her temper with Dickie. She brushed a wafer crumb from her knee.

"No, Dickie, I did n't. I sent for you because, after all, though I've been so angry with you, I've known in my heart that — that — you are a loyal friend and that you tell the truth."

This admission was an effort. Sheila's pride suffered to the point of bringing a dim sound of tears into her voice . . .

Dickie did not speak. He too put down his tea-cup and his wafer side by side on the floor near his chair. He put his elbows on his knees and bent his head down as though he were examining his thin, locked hands.

Sheila waited for a long minute; then she said angrily, "Are n't you glad I think that of you?"

"Yes'm." Dickie's voice was indistinct.

"You don't seem glad."

Dickie made some sort of struggle. Sheila could not quite make out its nature. "I'm glad. I'm so glad that it kind of — hurts," he said.

"Oh!" That at least was pleasant intelligence to a wounded pride.

Fortified, Sheila began the real business of the interview. "You are not an artist, Dickie," she said, "and you don't understand why your father asked me to work at The Aura nor why I wanted to work there. It was your entire inability to understand — "

"Entire inability — " whispered Dickie as though he were taking down the phrase with an intention of looking it up later.

This confused Sheila. "Your — your entire inability," she repeated rapidly, "your — your entire inability — "

"Yes'm. I've got that."

"— To understand that made me so angry that day." Sheila was glad to be rid of that obstruction. She had planned this speech rather carefully in the watches of the wakeful, feverish morning which had been her night. "You seemed to be trying to pull your father and me down to some lower spiritual level of your own."

"Lower spiritual level," repeated Dickie.

HUDSON'S QUEEN

"Dickie, stop that, please!"

He looked up, startled by her sharpness. "Stop what, ma'am?"

"Saying things after me. It's insufferable."

"Insufferable — oh, I suppose it is. You're usin' so many words, Sheila. I kind of forgot there was so many words as you're makin' use of this afternoon."

"Oh, Dickie, Dickie! Can't you see how miserable I am! I am so unhappy and — and scared, and you — you are making fun of me."

At that, spoken in a changed and quavering key of helplessness, Dickie hurried to her, knelt down beside her chair, and took her hands.

"Sheila! I'll do anything!"

His presence, his boyish, quivering touch, so withheld from anything but boyishness, even the impulsive humility of his thin, kneeling body, were inexpressibly soothing, inexpressibly comforting. She did not draw away her hands. She let them cling to his.

"Dickie, will you answer me, quite truthfully and simply, without any explaining or softening, please, if I ask you a — a dreadful question?"

"Yes, dear."

"I'm not sure if it is a dreadful question, but — but I'm afraid it is."

"Don't worry. Ask me. Surely, I'll answer you the truth without any fixin's."

Her hands clung a little closer. She was silent, gathering courage. He felt her slim knees quiver.

"What do they mean, Dickie," she whispered with a wan look, "when they call me — 'Hudson's Queen'?"

Dickie bent from her look as though he felt a pain. He took her hands up close to his breast. "Who told you that they called you that?" he asked breathlessly.

"That's what every one calls me — the men over in the Big Horn country — they tell men that are coming to Millings to be sure to look up 'Hudson's Queen.' Do they mean the Hotel, Dickie? They *do* mean the Hotel, don't they, Dickie? — that I am *The* Hudson's Queen?"

The truth sometimes presents itself like a withering flame. Dickie got up, put away her hands, walked up and down, then came back to her. He had heard the epithet and he knew its meaning. He wrestled now with his longing to keep her from such understanding, or, at least, to soften it. She had asked for the clear truth and he had promised it to her. He stood away because he could not trust himself to endure the wincing of her hands and body when she heard the truth. He hoped dimly that she might not understand it.

"They don't mean the Hotel, Sheila," he said harshly. "They mean — Father. You know now what they mean — ?" In her stricken and bewildered eyes he saw that she did know. "I would like to kill them," sobbed Dickie suddenly. "I would like to kill — *him*. No, no, Sheila, don't you cry. Don't you. It's not worth cryin' for. It's jest ignorant folks's ignorant and stupid talk. It's not worth cryin' for.' He sat down on the arm of her chair and fairly gathered her into his arms. He rocked and patted her shoulder and kissed her gently on her hair — all with that boyishness, that brotherliness, that vast restraint so that she could not even guess the strange and unimaginable pangs he suffered from his self-control.

Before Dickie's resolution was burnt away by the young inner fire, Sheila withdrew herself gently from his arms and got up from the chair. She walked over to one of the two large windows — the sunset windows she called them, in contradistinction to the one sunrise window — and stood composing herself, her hands twisted together and lifted to the top of the lower sash, her forehead rested on them.

A rattle of china, a creaking step outside the door, interrupted their tremulous silence in which who knows what mysterious currents were passing between their young minds.

"It's my dinner," said Sheila, and Dickie walked over mechanically and opened the door.

Amelia Plecks came panting into the room, set the tray down on a small table, and looked contempt at Dickie.

"There now, Miss Arundel," she said with breathless tenderness, "I've pro-cured a dandy chop for you. You said you was kind of famished for a lamb chop, and, of course, in a sheep country good mutton's real hard to come by, and this ain't properly speaking — lamb, *but* —! Well, say, it's just dandy meat."

She ignored Dickie as one might ignore the presence of some obnoxious insect in the reception-room of a queen. Her eyes were disgustedly fascinated by his presence, but in her conversation she would not admit this preoccupation of disgust.

"I'll be going," said Dickie.

Amelia nodded as one who applauds the becoming move of an inferior.

"Here's a note for you, Miss Arundel," she said, coming over to Sheila's post at the window, where she was trying to hide the traces of her tears. "Well, say, who's been botherin' you?" Amelia's voice went down a long, threatening octave to a sinister bass note, at the voicing of which she turned to look at Dickie.

"Good-night, Sheila," he said diffidently; and Sheila coming quickly toward him, put out her hand. The note Amelia had handed her fell. Dickie and Amelia both bent to pick it up.

"No, you don't," said Amelia, snatching it and accusing him, by her tone, of inexpressibly base intentions. "Say, Miss Arundel," in a whisper of thrilled confidence, "*Mister Jim!* Uh?"

"Thank you, Dickie," murmured Sheila, half-embarrassed, half-amused by her adoring follower's innuendoes. "Thank you for everything. I shall have to think what I can do . . . Good-night."

Dickie, his eyes forcibly held away from Jim's note, murmured, "Good-night, ma'am," and went out, closing the door with exaggerated gentleness. The quietness of his departure seemed to spare Sheila's sensitiveness.

"Ain't he a worm, though!" exclaimed Amelia, sparing nobody's sensitiveness.

"He's nothing of the sort," Sheila protested indignantly. "He is a dear!"

Amelia opened her prominent eyes and pursed her lips. A reassuring light dawned on her bewilderment. "Oh, say, dearie, I wasn't speakin' of your Mister Jim. I was makin' reference to Dickie."

Sheila thrust the note into her pocket and went over to the table to light her lamp. "I know quite well that you meant Dickie," she said. "Nobody in Millings would ever dream of comparing Mr. James Greely to a worm, even if he came out from the ground just in time for the early bird to peck him. I know that."

"You're ornery to-night, dearie," announced Amelia, and with exemplary tact she creaked and breathed herself to the door. There she had a relapse from tactfulness, however, and planted herself to stare. "Ain't you goin' to read your note?"

Sheila, to be rid of her, unfolded the paper and read. It was quite beautifully penned in green ink on violet paper. Jim had written both wisely and too well.

"My darling — Why not permit me to call you that when it is the simple and sincere truth?" An astonished little voice in Sheila's brain here seemed to counter-question mechanically "Why not, indeed?" — "I cannot think of anything but you and how I love you. These little notes I am going to keep a-sending you are messengers of love. You will never meet with a more tremendous lover than me. . . . Be *my* Queen," Jim had written with a great climatic splash of ink, and he had signed himself, "Your James."

Sheila's face was crimson when she put down the note. She stared straight in front of her for an instant with very large eyes in this scarlet rose of countenance and then she crumpled into mirth. She put her face into her hands and rocked. It seemed as though a giant of laughter had caught her about the ribs.

Amelia stared and felt a wound. She swallowed a lump of balked sentiment as she went out. Her idol was faintly tarnished, her heroine's stature preceptibly diminished. The sort of Madame du Barry atmosphere with which Sheila's image was surrounded in Amelia's fancy lost a little of its rosy glow. The favorite of Kings, the *amorita* of Dukes, does not rock with laughter over scented notes from a High Desirable.

HUDSON'S QUEEN

"She ain't just quite up to it," was Amelia's comment, which she probably could not have explained even to herself.

Sheila presently was done with laughter. She ate a nibble of dinner as soberly as Amelia could have wished, then sat back, her eyes closed with a resolve to think clearly, closely, to some determination of her life. But Jim's note, which had so roused her amusement, began to force itself in another fashion upon her. She discovered that it was an insufferable note. It insinuated everything, it suggested — everything. It was a boastful messenger. It swaggered maleishly. It threw out its chest and smacked its lips. "See what a sad dog my master is," it said; "a regular devil of a fellow." Sheila found her thoughts confused by anger. She found that she was too disturbed for any clear decision. She was terribly weary and full of dread for the long night before her. And a startled look at her clock told her it was time now to go over to the saloon.

She got up, went to her mirror, smoothed her rippled hair with two strokes of a brush, readjusted her cap, and decided that, for once, a little powder on the nose was a necessity. Carthy must not see that she had been crying. As it was, her brilliant color was suspicious, and her eyes, with their deep distended look of tears. She shut them, drew a breath, put out her light, and went down the back stairs to a narrow alley. It led from the hotel to the street that ran back of The Aura . . . the street to which she had taken young Hilliard the night before.

The alley seemed to Sheila, as she stepped into it from the glare of the electric-lighted hotel, a stream of cool and silvery light. Above lay a strip of tender sky in which already the stars shook. In this high atmosphere they were always tremulous, dancing, beating, almost leaping, with a fullness of quick light. They seemed very near to the edges of the alley walls, to be especially visiting it with their detached regard, peering down for some small divine occasion for influence. Sheila prayed to them a desperate prayer of human helplessness.

CHAPTER XIII

SYLVESTER CELEBRATES

"HEY, you girl there! Hi! Hey!"

These exclamations called in a resonant, deep-chested voice succeeded at last in attracting Sheila's attention. She had lingered at the alley's mouth, shirking her entrance into the saloon, and now she saw, halfway down the short, wide street, a gesticulating figure.

At first, as she obeyed the summons, she thought the summoner a man, but on near view it proved itself a woman, of broad, massive hips and shoulders, dressed in a man's flannel shirt and a pair of large corduroy trousers, their legs tucked into high cowboy boots. She wore no hat, and her hair was cut square across her neck and forehead; hair of a dark rusty red, it was, and matched eyes like dark panes of glass before a fire, red-brown and very bright, ruddy eyes in a square, ruddy face, which, with its short, straight, wide-bridged nose, well-shaped lips, square chin, and brilliant teeth, made up a striking and not unattractive countenance.

"I've got a horse here; won't stand," said the woman. "Will you hold his head? Can leaking back here in my wagon, leaking all over my other stuff."

The horse came round the corner. He moved resolutely to meet them. He was the boniest, small horse Sheila had ever seen — a shadow of a horse, one-eyed, morose, embittered. The harness hung loose upon his meagerness; the shafts stuck up like the points of a large collar on a small old man.

"He's not running away," explained the owner superfluously. "It's just that he can't stop. You'd think, to look at him, that stopping would be his favorite sport. But you'd be mistaken. Go he must. He's kind of always crazy to get there — Lord knows where — probably to the end of his life."

Sheila held the horse, and rubbed his nose with her small and gentle hand. The creature drooped under the caress and let its lower lip, with a few stiff white hairs, hang and quiver bitterly. It half-closed its one useful eye, a pale eye of intense, colorless disillusionment.

When the wagon stopped, a dog who was trotting under it stopped too and lay down in the dust, panting. Sheila bent her head a little to see the dog. She had a child's intense interest in animals. Through the dimness she made out a big, wolfish creature with a splendid, clean, gray coat, his pointed nose, short, pointed ears, deep, wild eyes, and scarlet tongue, set in a circular ruff of black. His bushy tail curled up over his back.

"What kind of dog is that?" asked Sheila, thinking the great animal under the wagon better fitted to pull the load than the shadowy little horse in front of it.

SYLVESTER CELEBRATES   139

"Quarter wolf," answered the woman in her casual manner of speech, her resonant voice falling pleasantly on the light coolness of the evening air; "Malamute. This fellow was littered on the body of a dead man."

Sheila had also the child's interest in tales. "Tell me about it," she begged fervently.

The woman stopped in her business of tying down a canvas cover over her load and gave Sheila an amused and searching look. She held an iron spike between her teeth, but spoke around it skillfully.

"Arctic exploration it was. My brother was one of the party. 'T was he brought me home Berg. Berg's mother was one of the sledge dogs. Party was shipwrecked, starved, most of the dogs eaten, one man dead. Berg's mother littered on the body one night. Next morning they were rescued and the new family was saved. Otherwise I guess they'd have had a puppy stew and Berg and his wife and family would n't be earning their living with me."

"How do they earn their living?" asked Sheila, still peering at the hero of the tale.

"They pull my sled about winters, Hidden Creek."

"Oh, you live in the Hidden Creek country?"

"Yes. Got a ranch up not far from the source. Ever been over The Hill?"

She came toward Sheila, gathered the reins into her strong, broad hands, held them in her teeth, and began to pull on her canvas gloves. She talked with the reins between her teeth as she had with the spike, her enunciation triumphantly forceful and distinct.

"Some day, I'm coming over The Hill," said Sheila, less successful with a contraction in her throat.

The woman made a few strides. Now she was looking shrewdly, close into Sheila's face.

"You're a biscuit-shooter at the hotel?"

"No. I work in the saloon."

"In the saloon? Oh, sure. Barmaid. I've heard of you."

Here she put a square finger-tip under Sheila's chin and looked even closer than before. "Not happy, are you?" she said. She moved away abruptly. "Tired of town life. Been crying. Well, when you want to pull out, come over to my ranch. I need a girl. I'm kind of lonesome winters. It's a pretty place if you are n't looking for street-lamps and talking-machines. You don't hear much more than coyotes and the river and the pines and, if you're looking for high lights, you can sure see the stars . . ."

She climbed up to her seat, using the hub of her wheel for a foothold, and springing with surprising agility and strength.

Sheila stepped aside and the horse started instantly. She made a few hurried steps to keep up.

"Thank you," she said, looking up into the ruddy eyes that looked down. "I'll remember that. What is your name?"

"Christina Blake, Miss Blake. I'll make The Hill

SYLVESTER CELEBRATES 141

before morning if I'm lucky. Less dust and heat by night and the horse has loafed since morning. . . . I mean that about coming to my place. Any time. Good-bye to you."

She smiled a smile as casual in its own way as Sheila's own. Berg, under the wagon, trotted silently. He looked neither to right nor left. His wild, deep-set eyes were fastened on the heels of the small horse. He looked as though he were trotting relentlessly toward some wolfish goal of satisfied hunger. A little cloud of dust rose up from the wheels and stood between Sheila and the wagon. She conquered an impulse to run after it, shut her hand tight, and walked in at the back door of the saloon.

A teamster, with a lean, fatherly face, his mouth veiled by a shaggy blond mustache, his eyes as blue as larkspur, smiled at her across the bar.

"Hullo," said he. "How's your pony?"

Sheila had struck up one of her sudden friendships with this man, who visited the saloon at regular intervals. This question warmed her heart. The little pony of Jim's giving was dear. She thought of his soft eyes and snuggling nose almost as often and as fondly as a lover thinks of the face of his lady.

"Tuck's splendid, Mr. Thatcher," she said, leaning her elbows on the bar and cupping her chin in her hands. Her face was bright with its tender, Puckish look. "He's too cute. He can take sugar out of my apron pocket. And he'll shake hands. I'd just love you to see him. Will you be here to-morrow afternoon?"

"No, ma'am. I'm pullin' out about sunup. Round the time you tumble into bed. Got to make The Hill."

"How's your baby?"

A shining smile rewarded her interest in the recent invalid. "Fine and dandy. You ought to see her walk!"

"Isn't that splendid! And how's the little boy? Is he with you?"

"No, ma'am. I kind o' left him to mind the ranch. He's gettin' to be a real rancher, that boy. He was sure sorry not to make Hidden Creek this trip, though. Say, he was sot on seein' you. I told him about you."

Sheila's face flamed and her eyes smarted. Gratitude and shame possessed her. This man, then, did not speak of her as "Hudson's Queen" — not if he told his boy about her. She turned away to hide the flame and smart. When she looked back, Sylvester himself stood at Thatcher's elbow. He very rarely came into the saloon. At sight of him Sheila's heart leaped as though it had been struck.

"Say, Sheila," he murmured, "I'm celebratin' to-night."

She tried to dismiss from her mind its new and ugly consciousness. She tried to smile. The result was an expression strange enough.

Sylvester, however, missed it. He was dressed in

SYLVESTER CELEBRATES 143

one of the brown checked suits, a new one, freshly creased; there was a red wild-rose bud in his buttonhole. The emerald gleamed on his well-kept, sallow hand. He was sipping from his glass and had put a confidential hand on Thatcher's shoulder. He grinned at Carthy.

"Well, sir," he said, "nobody has in-quired as to my celebration. But I'm not proud. I'll tell you. I'm celebratin' to-night the winnin' of a bet."

"That's sure a deservin' cause," said Thatcher.

"Yes, sir. Had a bet with Carthy here. Look at him blush! Carthy sure-ly hates to be wrong. And he's mostly right in his prog-nos-ti-cations. He sure is. You bet yer. That's why I'm so festive."

"What'd he prognosticate?" asked Thatcher obligingly. He had moved his shoulder away from Hudson's hand.

Sylvester wrinkled his upper lip into its smile and looked down into his glass. He turned his emerald.

"Carthy prophesied that about this time a little — er — dream — of mine would go bust," said Hudson. He lifted up his eyes pensively to Sheila, first his eyes and then his glass. "Here's to my dream — you, girl," he said softly.

He drank with his eyes upon her face, drew a deep breath, and looked about the room.

Thatcher glanced from him to Sheila. "Goodnight to you, ma'am," he said with gentleness. "Next time I'll bring the boy."

"Please, please do."

Sheila put her hand in his. He looked down at it as though something had startled him. In fact, her touch was like a flake of snow.

When Thatcher had gone, Sylvester leaned closer to her across the bar. He moved his glass around in his hand and looked up at her humbly.

"The tables kind of turned, eh?" he said.

"What do you mean, Mr. Hudson?" Sheila, by lifting her voice, tried to dissipate the atmosphere of confidence, of secrecy. Carthy had moved away from them, the other occupants of the saloon were very apparently not listening.

"Well, ma'am," Sylvester explained, "six months ago I was kind of layin' claim to gratitude from you, and now it's the other way round."

"Yes," she said. "But I am still grateful." The words came, however, with a certain unwillingness, a certain lack of spontaneity.

"Are you, though?" He put his head on one side so that Sheila was reminded of Dickie. For the first time a sort of shadowy resemblance between father and son was apparent to her. "Well, you've wiped the reckonin' off the slate by what you've done for me. You've given me my Aura. Say, you have been my fairy godmother, all right. Talk about wishes comin' true!"

Again he looked about the room, and that wistfulness of the visionary stole into his face. His eyes came

SYLVESTER CELEBRATES

back to her with an expression that was almost beautiful. "If only that Englishman was here," he sighed. "Yes, ma'am. I'm sure celebratin' to-night!"

It was soon very apparent that he was celebrating. For an hour he stood every newcomer to a drink, and then he withdrew to a table in a shadowy corner, and sitting there, tilted against the wall, he sipped from his glass, smoked and dreamed. Hour after hour of the slow, noisy night went by and still he sat there, watching Sheila through the smoke, seeing in her, more and more glowingly, the body of his dream.

It was after dawn when Sheila touched Carthy's elbow. The big Irishman looked down at her small, drawn face.

"Mr. Carthy," she whispered, "would it be all right if I went home now? It's earlier than usual, but I'm so — awfully tired?"

There was so urgent an air of secrecy in her manner that Carthy muttered his permission out of the corner of his mouth. Sheila melted from his side.

The alley that had been silvery cool with dusk was now even more silvery cool with morning twilight. Small sunrise clouds were winging over it like golden doves. Sheila did not look at them. She ran breathless to her door, opened it, and found herself face to face with Dickie.

CHAPTER XIV
The Light of Dawn

There was a light of dawn in the room and through the open window blew in the keen air of daybreak. Dickie was standing quite still in the middle of the floor. He was more neat and groomed than Sheila had ever seen him. He looked as though he had stepped from a bath; his hair was sleek and wet so that it was dark above the pure pallor of his face; his suit was carefully put on; his cuffs and collar were clean. He did not have the look of a man that has been awake all night, nor did he look as though he had ever been asleep. His face and eyes were alight, his lips firm and delicate with feeling.

Before him Sheila felt old and stained. The smoke and fumes of the bar hung about her. She was shamed by the fresh youthfulness of his slender, eager carriage and of his eyes.

"Dickie," she faltered, and stood against the door, drooping wearily, "what are you doing here at this hour?"

"What does the hour matter?" he asked impatiently. "Come over to the window. I want you to look at this big star. I've been watching it. It's almost gone. It's like a white bird flying straight into the sun."

THE LIGHT OF DAWN 147

He was imperative, laid his cool hand upon hers and drew her to the window. They stood facing the sunrise.

"Why did you come here?" again asked Sheila. The beauty of the sky only deepened her misery and shame.

"Because I could n't wait any longer than one night. It's sure been an awful long night for me, Sheila . . . Sheila — " He drew the hand he still held close to him with a trembling touch and laid his other hand over it. Then she felt the terrible beating of his heart, felt that he was shaking. "Sheila, I love you." She had hidden her face against the curtain, had turned from him. She felt nothing but weariness and shame. She was like a leaden weight tied coldly to his throbbing youth. Her hand under his was hot and lifeless like a scorched rose. "I want you to come away with me from Millings. You can't keep on a-working in that saloon. You can't abear to have folks saying and thinking the fool things they do. And I can't abear it even if you can. I'd go loco, and kill. Sheila, I've been thinking all night, just sitting on the edge of my bed and thinking. Sheila, if you will marry me, I will promise you to take care of you. I won't let you suffer any. I will die" — his voice rocked on the word, spoken with an awful sincerity of young love — "before I let you suffer any. If you could love me a little bit" — he stopped as though that leaping heart had sprung up into his throat — "only a little bit, Sheila," he whispered, "maybe — ?"

"I can't," she said. "I can't love you that way even a little bit. I can't marry you, Dickie. I wish I could. I am *so* tired."

She drew her hand away, or rather it fell from the slackening grasp of his, and hung at her side. She looked up from the curtain to his face. It was still alight and tender and pale.

"You're real sure, Sheila, that you *never* could? — that you'd rather go on with this — ?"

She pressed all the curves and the color out of her lips, still looking at him, and nodded her head.

"I can't stay in Millings," Dickie said, "and work in Poppa's hotel and watch this, Sheila — unless, some way, I can help you."

"Then you'd better go," she said lifelessly, "because I can't see what else there is for me to do. Oh, I shan't go on with it for very long, of course — "

He came an eager half-step nearer. "Then, anyway, you'll let me go away and work, and when I've kind of got a start, you'll let me come back and — and see if — if you feel any sort of — different from what you do now? It would n't be so awful long. I'd work like — like Hell!" His thin hand shot into a fist.

Sheila's lassitude was startled by his word into a faint, unwilling smile.

"Don't laugh at me!" he cried out.

THE LIGHT OF DAWN

"Oh, Dickie, my dear, I'm not laughing. I'm so tired I can hardly stand. And truly you must go now. I'm horrid to you. I always am. And yet I do like you so much. And you are such a dear. And I feel there's something great about you. I should be glad for you to leave Millings. There is a much better chance for you away from Millings. I feel years old to-day. I think I've grown up too old all at once and missed lovely things that I ought to have had. Dickie" — she gave a dry sort of sob — "*you* are one of the lovely things."

His arms drew gently round her. "Let me kiss you, Sheila," he pleaded with tremulous lips. "I want just to kiss you once for good-bye. I'll be so careful. If you knowed how I feel, you'd let me."

She lifted up her mouth like an obedient child. Then, back of Dickie, she saw Sylvester's face.

It was more sallow than usual; its upper lip was drawn away from the teeth and deeply wrinkled; the eyes, half-closed, were very soft; they looked as though there was a veil across their pensiveness. He caught Dickie's elbow in his hand, twisted him about, thrusting a knee into his back, and with his other long, bony hand he struck him brutally across the face. The emerald on his finger caught the light of the rising sun and flashed like a little stream of green fire.

Dickie, caught unawares by superior strength, was utterly defenseless. He writhed and struggled vainly, gasping under the blows. Sylvester forced him across the room, still inflicting punishment. His hand made a great cracking sound at every slap.

Sheila hid her face from the dreadful sight. "Oh, don't, don't, don't!" she wailed again and again.

Then it was over. Dickie was flung out; the door was locked against him and Sylvester came back across the floor.

His collar stood up in a half-moon back of his ears, his hair fell across his forehead, his face was flushed, his lip bled. He had either bitten it himself or Dickie had struck it. But he seemed quite calm, only a little breathless. He was neither snarling nor smiling now. He took Sheila very gently by the wrists, drawing her hands down from her face, and he put her arms at their full length behind her, holding them there.

"You meet Dickie here when you're through work, dream-girl," he said gently. "You kiss Dickie when you leave my Aura, you little beacon light. I've kept my hands off you and my lips off you and my mind off you, because I thought you were too fine and good for anything but my ideal. And all this while you've been sneaking up here to Dickie and Jim and Lord knows who else besides. Now, I am agoin' to kiss you and then you gotta get out of Millings. Do you hear? After I've kissed you, you ain't good enough for my purpose — not for mine."

Gathering both her hands in one of his, he put the hard, long fingers of his free hand back of her head,

THE LIGHT OF DAWN

holding it from wincing or turning and his mouth dropped upon hers and seemed to smother out her life. She tasted whiskey and the blood from his cut lips.

"You won't tell *me*, anyway, that lie again," he panted, keeping his face close, staring into her wide eyes of a horrified childishness — "that you've never been kissed."

Again his lips fastened on her mouth. He let her go, strode to the door, unlocked it, and went out.

She had fallen to the floor, her head against the chair. She beat the chair with her hands, calling softly for her father and for her God. She reproached them both. "You told me it was a good old world," she sobbed. "You told me it was a good old world."

CHAPTER XV
FLAMES

A HOT, dry day followed on the cool dawn. In his room Dickie lay across his bed. The sun blazed in at his single long window; the big flies that had risen from the dirty yard buzzed and bumped against the upper pane and made aimless, endless, mazy circles above and below one another in the stifling, odorous atmosphere. Dickie lay there like an image of Icarus, an eternal symbol of defeated youth; one could almost see about his slenderness the trailing, shattered wings. He had wept out the first shock of his anger and his shame; now he lay in a despairing stupor. His bruised face burned and ached; his chest felt tight with the aching and burning of his heart. Any suspicion of his father's interpretation of his presence in Sheila's room was mercifully spared him, but the knowledge that he had been brutally jerked back from her pure and patient lips, had been ignominiously punished before her eyes and turned out like a whipped boy — this knowledge was a dreadful torture to his pride. Sheila, to be sure, did not love him even a little bit; she had said so. All the longing and the tumult of his heart during these months had made no more impression upon her than a frantic sea makes upon the little bird at the top of the cliff.

FLAMES 153

She had, he must think, hardly been aware of it. And it was such a terrible and frantic actuality. He had fancied that it must have beaten forever, day by day, night by night, at her consciousness. Can a woman live near so turbulent a thing and not even guess at its existence? Her hand against his heart had lain so limp and dead. He had n't hoped, of course, that she loved him the way he loved. Probably no one else could feel what he felt and live — so Dickie in young love's eternal fashion believed in his own miracle; but she might have loved him a little, a very little, in time — if she had n't seen him beaten and shamed and cuffed out of her presence like a dog. Now there was no hope. No hope at all. No hope. Dickie rocked his head against his arm. He had told Sheila that he would take care of her, but he could not even defend himself. He had told her that he would die to save her any suffering, but, before her, he had writhed and gasped helplessly under the weight of another man's hand, his open hand, not even a fist. . . . No after act of his could efface from Sheila's memory that picture of his ignominy. She had seen him twisted and bent and beaten and thrown away. His father had triumphantly returned to reassure and comfort her for the insult of a boy's impertinence. Would Sheila defend him? Would she understand? Or would she not be justified in contemptuous laughter at his pretensions?

Such thoughts — less like thoughts, however, than

like fiery fever fits — twisted and scorched Dickie's mind as he lay there. They burnt into him wounds that for years throbbed slowly into scars.

At noon the heat of his room became even more intolerable than his thoughts. His head beat with pain. He was bathed in sweat, weak and trembling. He dragged himself up, went to his washstand, and dipped his wincing face into the warmish, stale water. His lips felt cracked and dry and swollen. In the wavy mirror he saw a distorted image of his face, with its heavy eyes, scattered hair, and the darkening marks of his father's blows, punctuated by the scarlet scratches of the emerald. He dried his face, loosened his collar, and, gasping for air, came out into the narrow hall.

The hotel was very still. He hurried through it, his face bent, and went by the back way to the saloon. At this hour Sheila was asleep. Carthy would be alone in The Aura and there would be few, if any, customers. Dickie found the place cool and quiet and empty, shuttered from the sun, the air stirred by electric fans. Carthy dozed in his chair behind the bar. He gave Dickie his order, somnambulantly. Dickie took it off to a dim corner and drank with the thirst of a wounded beast.

Three or four hours later he staggered back to his room. A thunderstorm was rumbling and flashing down from the mountains to the north. The window was purple-black, and a storm wind blew the dirty curtains, straight and steady, into the room. The cool wind tasted and smelt of hot dust. Dickie felt his dazed way to the bed and steadied himself into a sitting posture. With infinite difficulty he rolled and lighted a cigarette, drew at it, took it out, tried to put it again between his lips, and fell over on his back, his arm trailing over the edge of the bed. The lighted cigarette slipped from his fingers to the ragged strip of matting. Dickie lay there, breathing heavily and regularly in a drunken and exhausted sleep.

A vivid, flickering pain in his arm woke him. He thought for an instant that he must have died and dropped straight into Hell. The wind still blew in upon him, but it blew fire against him. Above him there was a heavy panoply of smoke. His bedclothes were burning, his sleeve was on fire. The boards of his floor cracked and snapped in regiments of flame. He got up, still in a half stupor, plunged his arm into the water pitcher, saw, with a startled oath, that the woodwork about his door was blazing in long tongues of fire which leaped up into the rafters of the roof. His brain began to telegraph its messages ... the hotel was on fire. He could not imagine what had started it. He remembered Sheila.

He ran along the passage, the roar of that wind-driven fire following him as the draft from his window through his opened door gave a sudden impulse to the flames, and he came to Sheila's sitting-room. He knocked, had no answer, and burst in. He saw instantly that she had gone. Her father's picture had been taken, her little books, her sketches, her workbasket, her small yellow vase. Things were scattered about. As he stood staring, a billow of black smoke rolled into the room. He went quickly through the bedroom and the bath, calling "Sheila" in a low, uncertain voice, returned to the sitting-room to find the air already pungent and hot. There was a paper pinned up on the mantel. Sheila's writing marched across it. Dickie rubbed the smoke from his eyes and read:

I am going away from Millings. And I am not coming back. Amelia may have the things I have left. I don't want them.

This statement was addressed to no one.

"She has gone to New York," thought Dickie. His confused mind became possessed with the immediate purpose of following her. There was an Eastern train in the late afternoon. Only he must have money and it was — most of it — in his room. He dashed back. The passage was ablaze; his room roared like the very heart of a furnace. It was no use to think of getting in there. Well, he had something in his pocket, enough to start him. He plunged, choking, into Sheila's sitting-room again. For some reason this flight of hers had brought back his hope. There was to be a beginning, a fresh start, a chance.

He went over to the chair where Sheila had sat in the comfort of his arms and he touched the piece

FLAMES 157

of tapestry on its back. That was his good-bye to Millings. Then he fastened his collar, smoothed his hair, standing close before Sheila's mirror, peering and blinking through the smoke, and buttoned his coat painstakingly. There would be a hat downstairs. As he turned to go he saw a little brown leather book lying on the floor below the mantel. He picked it up. Here was something he could take to Sheila. With an impulse of tenderness he opened it. His eyes were caught by a stanza —

> "The blessed damozel leaned out
> From the gold bar of Heaven;
> Her eyes were deeper than the depth
> Of waters stilled at even;
> She had three lilies in her hand,
> And the stars in her hair were seven — "

There are people, no doubt, who will not be able to believe this truthful bit of Dickie's history. The smoke was drifting across him, the roar of the nearing fire was in his ears, he was at a great crisis in his affairs, his heart was hot with wounded love, and his brain hot with whiskey and with hope. Nevertheless, he did now, under the spell of those printed words, which did not even remotely resemble any words that he had ever read or heard before, forget the smoke, the roar, the love, the hope, and, standing below Sheila's mirror, he did read "The Blessed Damozel" from end to end. And the love of those lovers, divided by all the space between the shaken worlds, and the beauty of her tears made a great and mystic silence of rapture about him. "O God!" Dickie said twice as he read. He brushed away the smoke to see the last lines, — "And wept — I heard her tears." The ecstatic pain of beauty gripped him to the forgetfulness of all other pain or ecstasy. "O God!"

He came to with a start, shut the book, stuck it into his pocket, and, crooking his arm over his smarting eyes, he plunged out of the room. Millings had become aware of its disaster. Dickie, fleeing by the back way, leaping dangers and beating through fire, knew by the distant commotion that the Fire Brigade, of which he was a member, was gathering its men for the glory of their name. He saw, too, that with a wind like this to aid the fire, there was n't a chance for The Aura, and a queer pang of sympathy for his father stabbed him. "It will kill Pap," thought Dickie. Save for this pang, he ran along the road toward the station with a light, adventurous heart. He did not know that he had started the fire himself. The stupor of his sleep had smothered out all memory of the cigarette he had lighted and let fall. Unwittingly Dickie had killed the beauty of his father's dream, and now, just as unwittingly, he was about to kill the object of his father's passion. When he looked back from the station platform, the roof of The Aura was already in a blaze.

PART TWO
THE STARS

CHAPTER I
THE HILL

THATCHER spoke to his horses, now fatherly, now masterly, now with a professorial sarcasm: "Come on, Monkey, there's a good girl! Get out of that, you Fox! Dern you! You call that pulling? It's my notion of layin' off for the day." Even at its most urgent, his voice was soft, hushed by the great loneliness of this cañon up which he slowly crept. Monkey and Fox had been plodding, foot by foot, the creaking wagon at their heels, since dawn. It was now ten o'clock and they were just beginning to climb. The Hill, that looked so near to the mesa above Hudson's yard, still stood aloof. It had towered there ahead of them as they jerked and toiled across the interminable flat in their accompanying cloud of dust. The great circle of the world had dwarfed them to a bitter insignificance: a team of crickets, they seemed, driven by a gnome. The hushed tone of Thatcher's voice made unconscious tribute to this immensity.

As they came to the opening of the cañon, the high mountain-top disappeared; the immediate foothills closed down and shut it out. The air grew headily light. Even under the blazing July sun, it came cool to the lungs, cool and intensely sweet. Thousands of wild flowers perfumed it and the sun-drawn resin of a thousand firs. All the while the rushing of water accompanied the creaking of Thatcher's progress. Not far from the road, down there below in a tangle of pine branches, willows, and ferns, the frost-white stream fled toward the valley with all the seeming terror of escape. Here the team began their tugging and their panting and their long pauses to get breath. Thatcher would push forward the wooden handle that moved his brake, and at the sound and the grating of the wheel the horses would stop automatically and stand with heaving sides. The wagon shook slightly with their breathing. At such times the stream seemed to shout in the stillness. Below, there began to be an extraordinary view of the golden country with its orange mesas and its dark, purple rim of mountains. Millings was a tiny circle of square pebbles, something built up by children in their play. The awful impersonalities of sky and earth swept away its small human importance. Thatcher's larkspur-colored eyes absorbed serenity. They had drawn their color and their far-sighted clearness from such long contemplations of distant horizon lines.

Now and again, however, Thatcher would glance back and down from his high seat at his load. It consisted, for the most part, of boxes of canned goods, but near the front there was a sort of nest, made from bags of Indian meal. In the middle of the

THE HILL 163

nest lay another bundle of slim, irregular outline. It was covered with a thin blanket and a piece of sacking protected it from the sun. A large, clumsy parcel lay beside it. Each time Thatcher looked at this portion of his load he pulled more anxiously at his mustache. At last, when the noon sun stood straight above the pass and he stopped to water his horses at a trough which caught a trickle of spring water, he bent down and softly raised the piece of sacking, suspended like a tent from one fat sack to another above the object of his uneasiness. There, in the complete relaxation of exhausted sleep, lay Sheila, no child more limp and innocent of aspect; her hair damp and ringed on her smooth forehead, her lips mournful and sweet, sedately closed, her expression at once proud and innocent and wistful, as is the sleeping face of a little, little girl. There was that look of a broken flower, that look of lovely death, that stops the heart of a mother sometimes when she bends over a crib and sees damp curls in a halo about a strange, familiar face.

Thatcher, looking at Sheila, had some of these thoughts. A teamster is either philosopher or clown. One cannot move, day after day, all day for a thousand days, under a changeless, changeful sky, inch by inch, across the surface of a changeless, changeful earth and not come very near to some of the locked doors of the temple where clowns sleep and wise men meditate. And Thatcher was a father, one of the wise and reasonable fathers of the West, whose seven-year-old sons are friends and helpmates and toward whom six-year-old daughters are moved to little acts of motherliness.

The sun blazed for a minute on Sheila's face. She opened her eyes, looked vaguely from some immense distance at Thatcher, and then sat up.

"Oh, gracious!" said Sheila, woman and sprite and adventurer again. "Where the dickens is my hat? Did it fall out?"

"No, ma'am," Thatcher smiled in a relieved fashion. "I put it under the seat."

Sheila scrambled to a perch on one of the sacks and faced the surface of half a world.

"Oh, Mr. Thatcher, is n't it too wonderful! How high are we? Is this the other side? Oh, no, I can see Millings. Poor tiny, tiny Millings! It *is* small, is n't it? How very small it is! What air!" She shut her eyes, drawing in the perfumed tonic. The altitude had intoxicated her. Her heart was beating fast, her blood tingling, her brain electrified. Every sense seemed to be sharpened. She saw and smelt and heard with abnormal vividness.

"The flowers are awfully bright up here, are n't they?" she said. "What's that coral-colored bushy one?"

"Indian paint-brush."

"And that blue one? It *is* blue! I don't believe I ever knew what blueness meant before."

THE HILL

"Lupine. And over yonder's monkshead. That other's larkspur, that poisons cattle in the spring. On the other side you'll see a whole lot more — wild hollyhock and fireweed and columbine — well, say, I learned all them names from a dude I drove over one summer."

"And such a sky!" said Sheila, lifting her head, "and such big pines!" She lost herself for a minute in the azure immensity above. A vast mosque of cloud, dome bubbles great and small, stood ahead of them, dwarfing every human experience of height. "Mr. Thatcher, there is n't any air up here. What is it we're trying to breathe, anyway?"

He smiled patiently, sympathetically, and handed her a tin mug of icy water from the little trickling spring. The bruise of Hudson's kiss ached at the cold touch of the water and a shadow fell over her excitement. She thanked the driver gravely.

"What time is it now?" she asked.

"Past noon. Better eat your sandwich."

She took one from its wrapping pensively, but ate it with absent-minded eagerness. Thatcher's blue eyes twinkled.

"Seems like I recollect a lady that did n't want no food to be put in for her."

"I remember her, too," said Sheila, between bites, "but very, very vaguely."

She stood up after a third sandwich, shook crumbs from her skirt, and stretched her arms. "What a great sleep I've had! Since six o'clock!" She stared down at the lower world. "I've left somebody at Millings."

"Who's that?" asked Thatcher, drawling the words a trifle as a Westerner does when he is conscious of a double meaning.

"Me."

Thatcher laughed. "You're a real funny girl, Miss Arundel," he said.

"Yes, I left one Me when I decided to go into the saloon, and now I've left another Me. I believe people shed their skins like snakes."

"Yes'm, I've had that notion myself. But as you get older, your skin kind of peels off easy and gradual — you don't get them shocks when you sort of come out all new and shiny and admirin' of yourself."

Sheila blushed faintly and looked at him. His face was serene and empty of intention. But she felt that she had been guilty of egotism, as indeed she had. She asked rather meekly for her hat, and having put it on like a shadow above her fairness, she climbed up to Thatcher's side on the driver's seat. The hat was her felt Stetson, and, for the rest, she was clad in her riding-clothes, the boy's shirt, the short corduroy skirt, the high-laced boots. Her youthfulness, rather than her strange beauty, was accentuated by this dress. She had the look of a super-delicate boy, a sort of rose-leaf fairy prince.

"Are we on the road?" asked Sheila presently.

THE HILL

Thatcher gave way to mirth. "Don't it seem like a road to you?"

She lurched against him, then saved herself from falling out at the other side by a frantic clutch.

"Is it a road?" She looked down a dizzy slope of which the horse's foothold seemed to her the most precarious part.

"Yes'm — all the road there is. We call it that. We're kind of po-lite to these little efforts of the Government — kind of want to encourage 'em. Congressmen kind of needs coaxin' and flat'ry. They're right ornery critters. I heard an argyment atween a feller with a hoss and a feller with a mule onct. The mule feller was kind of uppish about hosses; said he did n't see the advantage of the critter. A mule now was steady and easy fed and strong. Well, ma'am, the hoss feller got kind of hot after some of this, so he says, 'Well, sir,' he says, 'there's this about it. When you got a hoss, you got a hoss. You know what you got. He's goin' to act like a hoss. But when you got a mule, why, you can't never tell. All of a sudden one of these days, he's like as not to turn into a Congressman.' Well, ma'am, that's the way we feel about Congressmen. — Ho, there, Monkey! Keep up! I'll just get out an' hang on the wheel while we make this corner. That'll keep us from turnin' over, I reckon."

Sheila sat and held on with both hands. Her eyes were wide and very bright. She held her breath till

Thatcher got in again, the corner safely made. For the next creeping, lurching mile, Sheila found that every muscle in her body had its use in keeping her on that seat. Then they reached the snow and matters grew definitely worse. Here, half the road was four feet of dirty, icy drift and half of abysmal mud. They slipped from drift to mire with awful perils and rackings of the wagon and painful struggles of the team. Sometimes the snow softened and let the horses in up to their necks when Thatcher plied whip and tongue with necessary cruelty. At last there came disaster. They were making one of those heart-stopping turns. Sheila had got out and was adding her mosquito weight to Thatcher's on the upper side, half-walking, half-hanging to the wagon. The outer wheels were deep in mud, the inner wheels hung clear. The horses strained — and slipped.

"Let go!" shouted Thatcher.

Sheila fell back into the snow, and the wagon turned quietly over and began to slide down the slope. Thatcher sprang to his horses' heads. For an instant it seemed that they would be dragged over the edge. Then the wagon stopped, and Thatcher, grim and pale, unhitched his team. He swore fluently under his breath during this entire operation. Afterwards, he turned to the scarlet and astounded passenger and gave her one of his shining smiles.

"Well, ma'am," he said, beginning to roll a cigarette, "what do you think of that?"

THE HILL 169

"Whatever shall we do now?" asked Sheila. She had identified herself utterly with this team, this load, this driver. She brushed the snow from her skirt, climbed down from the drift to the edge of the mire by Thatcher's elbow. The team stood with hanging heads, panting and steaming, glad of the rest and the release.

"Well, ma'am," said Thatcher, looking down at the loyal, anxious face with a certain tenderness, "I'm agoin' to do one of two things. I'm agoin' to lead my team over The Hill and come back with two more horses and a hand to help me or I'm agoin' to set here and wait for the stage."

"How long will it be before the stage comes?"

"Matter of four or five hours."

"Oh, dear! Then I can't possibly overtake my — my friend, Miss Blake!"

"No, ma'am. But you can walk on a quarter-mile; take a rest at Duff's place top of The Hill. I can pick you up when I come by; like as not I'll spend the night at Duff's. By the time I get my load together it'll be along dark — Hullo!" He interrupted himself, lifting his chin. "I hear hosses now."

They both listened. "No wagon," said Thatcher.

Five minutes later, a slouching horseman, cigarette in mouth, shaggy chaps on long legs, spurred and booted and decorated with a red neck-scarf came picturesquely into view. His pony dug sturdy feet into the steep roadside, avoiding the mud of the road itself.

The man led two other horses, saddled, but empty of riders. He stopped and between him and Thatcher took place one of the immensely tranquil, meditative, and deliberate conversations of the Far West.

Sheila's quick, Celtic nerves tormented her. At last she broke in with an inspiration. "Couldn't I hire one of your horses?" she asked, rising from an overturned sack of which she had made a resting-place.

The man looked down at her with grave, considerate eyes.

"Why, yes, ma'am. I reckon you could," he said gently. "They're right gentle ponies," he added.

"Are they yours?"

"One of 'em is. The other belongs to Kearney, dude-wrangler up the valley. But, say, if you're goin' to Rusty you c'd leave my hoss at Lander's and I c'd get him when I come along. I am stoppin' here to help with the load. It would cost you nothin', lady. The hoss has got to go over to Rusty and I'd be pleased to let you ride him. You're no weight."

"How good of you!" said Sheila. "I'll take the best care of him I know how to take. Could I find my way? How far is it?"

"All downhill after a half-mile, lady. You c'd make Rusty afore dark. It's a whole lot easier on hoofs than it is on wheels. You can't miss the road on account of it bein' the only road there is. And Lander's is the only one hotel in Rusty. You'd best stop the night there."

THE HILL

He evidently wanted to ask her her destination, but his courtesy forbade.

Sheila volunteered, "I am going to Miss Blake's ranch up Hidden Creek."

A sort of flash of surprise passed across the reserved, brown, young face. "Yes, ma'am," he said with no expression. "Well, you better leave the rest of your trip until to-morrow."

He slipped from his horse with an effortless ripple, untied a tawny little pony with a thick neck, a round body, and a mild, intelligent face, and led him to Sheila who mounted from her sack. Thatcher carefully adjusted the stirrups, a primitive process that involved the wearisome lacing and unlacing of leather thongs. Sheila bade him a bright and adventurous "Good-bye," thanked the unknown owner of the horse, and started. The pony showed some unwillingness to leave his companions, fretted and tossed his head, and made a few attempts at a right-about face, but Sheila dug in her small spurred heels and spoke beguilingly. At last he settled down to sober climbing. Sheila looked back and waved her hand. The two tall, lean men were gazing after her. They took off their hats and waved. She felt a warmth that was almost loving for their gracefulness and gravity and kindness. Here was another breed of man than that produced by Millings. A few minutes later she came to the top of The Pass and looked down into Hidden Creek.

CHAPTER II

ADVENTURE

SHEILA stood and drew breath. The shadow of the high peak, in the lap of which she stood, poured itself eastward across the warm, lush, narrow land. This was different from the hard, dull gold and alkali dust of the Millings country: here were silvery-green miles of range, and purple-green miles of pine forest, and lovely lighter fringes and groves of cottonwood and aspen trees. Here and there were little dots of ranches, visible more by their vivid oat and alfalfa fields than by their small log cabins. Down the valley the river flickered, lifted by its brightness above the hollow that held it, till it seemed just hung there like a string of jewels. Beyond it the land rose slowly in noble sweeps to the opposite ranges, two chains that sloped across each other in a glorious confusion of heads, round and soft as velvet against the blue sky or blunt and broken with a thundery look of extinct craters. To the north Sheila saw a further serenity of mountains, lying low and soft on the horizon, of another and more wistful blue. Over it all was a sort of magical haze, soft and brilliant as though the air were a melted sapphire. There was still blessedness such as Sheila had never felt. She was filled with a longing to ride on and on until her spirit should pass

ADVENTURE 173

into the wide, tranquil, glowing spirit of the lonely land. It seemed to her that some forgotten medicine man sat cross-legged in a hollow of the hills, blowing, from a great peace pipe, the blue smoke of peace down and along the hollows and the cañons and the level lengths of range. In the mighty breast of the blower there was not even a memory of trouble, only a noble savage serenity too deep for prayer.

She rode for a long while — no sound but her pony's hoofs — her eyes lifted across the valley until a sudden fragrance drew her attention earthwards. She was going through an open glade of aspens and the ground was white with columbine, enormous flowers snowy and crisp as though freshly starched by fairy laundresses. With a cry of delight Sheila jumped off her horse, tied him by his reins to a tree, and began gathering flowers with all the eager concentration of a six-year-old. And, like all the flower-gatherers of fable from Proserpina down, she found herself the victim of disaster. When she came back to the road with a useless, already perishing mass of white, the pony had disappeared. Her knot had been unfaithful. Quietly that mild-nosed, pensive-eyed, round-bodied animal had pulled himself free and tip-toed back to join his friends.

Sheila hurried up the road toward the summit she had so recently crossed, till the altitude forced her to stop with no breath in her body and a pounding redness before her eyes. She stamped her feet with vexation. She longed to cry. She remembered confusedly, but with a certain satisfaction, some of the things Thatcher had said to his team. An entire and sudden lenience toward the gentle art of swearing was born in her. She threw her columbine angrily away. She had come so far on her journey that she could never be able to get back to Thatcher nor even to Duff's shanty before dark. And how far down still the valley lay with that shadow widening and lengthening across it!

Her sudden loneliness descended upon her with an almost audible rush. Dusk at this height — dusk with a keen smell of glaciers and wind-stung pines — dusk with the world nine thousand feet below; and about her this falling-away of mountain-side, where the trees seemed to slant and the very flowers to be outrun by a mysterious sort of flight of rebel earth toward space! The great and heady height was informed with a presence which if not hostile was terrifyingly ignorant of man. There was some one not far away, she felt, just above there behind the rocky ridge, just back there in the confusion of purplish darkness streaked by pine-tree columns, just below in the thicket of the stream — some one to meet whose look meant death.

Her first instinct was to keep to the road. She walked on down toward the valley very rapidly. But going down meant meeting darkness. She began to be unreasonably afraid of the night. She was afflicted by an old, old childish, immemorial dread of bears. In spite of the chill, she was very warm, her tongue dry with rapid breathing of the thin air. She was intolerably thirsty. The sound of water called to her in a lisping, inhuman voice. She resisted till she was ashamed of her cowardice, stepped furtively off the track, scrambled down a slope, parted some branches, and found herself on a rock above a little swirling pool. On the other side a man kneeling over the water lifted a white and startled face.

Through the eerie green twilight up into which the pool threw a shifty leaden brightness, the two stared at each other for a moment. Then the man rose to his feet and smiled. Sheila noticed that he had been bathing a bloody wrist round which he was now wrapping clumsily a handkerchief.

"Don't be frightened," he said in a rather uncertain voice; "I'm not near so desperate as I look. Do you want a drink? Hand me down your cup if you have one and I'll fill it for you."

"I'm not afraid now," Sheila quavered, and drew a big breath. "But I was startled for a minute. I have n't any cup. I — I suppose, in a way — I'm lost."

He was peering at her now, and when she took off her hat and rubbed her damp forehead with a weary, worried gesture, he gave a little exclamation and swung himself across the stream by a branch, and up to her side on the rock.

"The barmaid!" he said. "And I was coming to see you!"

Sheila laughed in the relieved surprise of recognition. "Why, you are the cowboy — the one that fought so — so terribly. Have you been fighting again? Your wrist is hurt. May I tie it up for you?"

He held out his arm silently and she tied the handkerchief — a large, clean, coarse one — neatly about it. What with weariness and the shock of her fright, her fingers were not very steady. He looked down at her during the operation with a contented expression. It seemed that the moment was filled for him with satisfaction to a complete forgetfulness of past or present annoyances.

"This is a big piece of luck for me," he said. "But" — with a sudden thundery change of countenance — "you're not going over to Hidden Creek, are you?"

"I'm trying to go there," said Sheila; "I've been trying ever since five o'clock this morning. But I don't seem to be getting there very fast. I wanted to make Rusty before dark. And my pony got away from me and went back. I know he went back because I saw the marks of his feet and he would have gone back. Would n't he? Do you think I could get to Rusty on foot to-night?"

"No, ma'am. I know you could n't. You could make it easy on horseback, though." He stared meditatively above her head and then said in a tone of

A MAN KNEELING OVER THE WATER LIFTED A WHITE AND
STARTLED FACE

resignation: "I believe I better go back myself. I'll take you."

She had finished her bandage. She looked up at him. "Go back? But you must have just started from there a few hours ago."

"Well, ma'am, I did n't come very direct. I kind of shifted round. But I can go back straight. And I'd really rather. I think I'd better. It was all foolishness my coming over. I can put you up back of me on my horse, if you don't mind, and we'll get to Rusty before it's lit up. I'd rather. You don't mind riding that way, do you? You see, if I put you up and walked, it'd take lots more time."

"I don't mind," said Sheila, but she said it rather proudly so that Hilliard smiled.

"Well, ma'am, we can try it, anyway. If you go back to the road, I'll get my horse."

He seemed to have hidden his horse in a density of trees a mile from the road. Sheila waited till she thought she must have dreamed her meeting with him. He came back, looking a trifle sheepish.

"You see," he said, "I did n't come by the road, ma'am."

The horse was a large, bony animal with a mean eye.

"That is n't the pony you rode when you came to Millings," said Sheila.

He bent to examine his saddle-girth. "No, ma'am," he said gently. "I've been riding quite a variety of horse-flesh lately. I'll get on first if you don't mind and give you a hand up. You put your foot on mine. The horse will stand."

Sheila obeyed, pressing her lips tight, for she was afraid. However, his long, supple fingers closed over her wrist like steel and she got quickly and easily to her perch and clung nervously to him.

"That's right. Put your arms round tight. Are you all fixed?"

"Y—yes."

"And comfortable?"

"Y—yes, I think so."

"We're off, then."

They started on a quick, steady walk down the road. Once, Cosme loosened the six-shooter on his hip. He whistled incessantly through his teeth. Except for this, they were both silent.

"Were you coming to Millings?" asked Sheila at last. She was of the world where silence has a certain oppressive significance. She was getting used to her peculiar physical position and found she did not have to cling so desperately. But in a social sense she was embarrassed. He was quite impersonal about the situation, which made matters easier for her. Now and then she suppressed a frantic impulse to giggle.

"Yes, ma'am. To see you," he answered. "I never rightly thanked you." She saw the back of his neck flush and she blushed too, remembering his quickly diverted kiss which had left a smear of blood across

ADVENTURE

her fingers. That had happened only a few days before, but they were long days. He too must have been well occupied. There was still a bruise on his temple. "I — I was n't quite right in the head after those fellows had beat me up, and I kind of wanted to show you that I am something like a gentleman."

"Have you been in Hidden Creek?"

"Yes, ma'am. I was thinking of prospecting around. I meant to homestead over there. I like the country. But when it comes to settling down I get kind of restless. And usually I get into a mix-up that changes my intentions. So I'd about decided to go back down Arizona way and work. — Where are you going to stay in Hidden Creek?" he asked. "Where's your stuff?"

"Mr. Thatcher has it in his wagon. I'm going to Miss Blake's ranch. She invited me."

"Miss Blake? You mean the lady that wears pants? You don't mean it! Well, that's right amusing." He laughed.

Sheila stirred angrily. "I can't see why it's amusing."

He sobered at once. "Well, ma'am, maybe it is n't. No, I reckon it is n't. How long will you stay?"

Sheila gave a big, sobbing sigh. "I don't know. If she likes me and if I'm happy, I'll stay there always." She added with a queer, dazed realization of the truth: "I've nowhere else to go."

"Have n't you any — folks?" he asked.

"No."

"Got tired of Millings?"

"Yes — very."

"I don't blame you! It's not much of a town. You'll like Hidden Creek. And Miss Blake's ranch is a mighty pretty place, lonesome but wonderfully pretty. Right on a bend of the creek, 'way up the valley, close under the mountains. But can you stand loneliness, Miss — What *is* your name?"

There were curious breaks in his manner of a Western cowboy, breaks that startled Sheila like little echoes from her life abroad and in the East. There was a quickness of voice and manner, an impatience, a hot and nervous something, and his voice and accent suggested training. The abrupt question, for instance, was not in the least characteristic of a Westerner.

"My name is Sheila Arundel. I don't know yours either."

"Do you come from the East?"

"Yes. From New York." He gave an infinitesimal jerk. "But I've lived abroad nearly all my life. I think it would be politer if you would answer my question now."

She felt that he controlled an anxious breath. "My name is Hilliard," he said, and he pronounced the name with a queer bitter accent as though the taste of it was unpleasant to his tongue. "Cosme Hilliard. Don't you think it's a — *nice* name?"

ADVENTURE

For half a second she was silent; then she spoke with careful unconsciousness. "Yes. Very nice and very unusual. Hilliard is an English name, is n't it? Where did the Cosme come from?"

It was well done, so well that she felt a certain tightening of his body relax and his voice sounded fuller. "That's Spanish. I've some Spanish blood. Here's Buffin's ranch. We're getting down."

Sheila was remembering vividly; Sylvester had come into her compartment. She could see the rolling Nebraskan country slipping by the window of the train. She could see his sallow fingers folding the paper so that she could conveniently read a paragraph. She remembered his gentle, pensive speech. "Ain't it funny, though, those things happen in the slums and they happen in the smart set, but they don't happen near so often to just middling folks like you and me! Don't it sound like a Tenderloin tale, though, South American wife and American husband and her getting jealous and up and shooting him? Money sure makes love popular. Now, if it had been poor folks, why, they'd have hardly missed a day's work, but just because these Hilliards have got spondulix they'll run a paragraph about 'em in the papers for a month." — Sheila began to make comparisons: a South American wife and an American husband, and here, this young man with the Spanish-American name and the Spanish-Saxon physique, and a voice that showed training and faltered over the pronouncing of the "Hilliard" as though he expected it to be too well remembered. Had there been some mention in the paper of a son? — a son in the West? — a son under a cloud of some sort? But — she checked her spinning of romance — this youth was too genuine a cowboy, the way he rode, the way he moved, held himself, his phrases, his turn of speech! With all that wealth behind him how had he been allowed to grow up like this? No, her notion was unreasonable, almost impossible. Although dismissed, it hung about her mental presentment of him, however, like a rather baleful aura, not without fascination to a seventeen-year-old imagination. So busy was she with her fabrications that several miles of road slipped by unnoticed. There came a strange confusion in her thoughts. It seemed to her that she was arguing the Hilliard case with some one. Then with a horrible start she saw that the face of her opponent was Sylvester's and she pushed it violently away . . .

"Don't you go to sleep," said Hilliard softly, laughing a little. "You might fall off."

"I — I was asleep," Sheila confessed, in confusion at discovering that her head had dropped against him. "How dark it's getting! We're in the valley, aren't we?"

"Yes, ma'am, we're most there." He hesitated. "Miss Arundel, I think I'd best let you get down just before we get to Rusty."

ADVENTURE 183

"Get down? Why?"

He cleared his throat, half-turning to her. In the dusky twilight, that was now very nearly darkness, his face was troubled and ashamed, like the face of a boy who tries to make little of a scrape. "Well, ma'am, yesterday, the folks in Rusty kind of lost their heads. They had a bad case of Sherlock Holmes. I bought a horse up the valley from a chap who was all-fired anxious to sell him, and before I knew it I was playing the title part in a man-hunt. It seems that I was riding one of a string this chap had rustled from several of the natives. They knew the horse and that was enough for their nervous system. They had never set eyes on me before and they would n't take my word for my blameless past. They told me to keep my story for trial when they took me over to the court. Meanwhile they gave me a free lodging in their pen. Miss Arundel — " Hilliard dropped his ironic tone and spoke in a low, tense voice of child-like horror. His face stiffened and paled. "That was awful. To be locked in. Not to be able to get fresh breath in your lungs. Not to be able to go where you please, when you please. I can't tell you what it's like. . . . I can't stand it! I can't stand a minute of it! I was in that pen six hours. I felt I'd go loco if I was there all night. I guess I am a kind of fool. I broke jail early in the morning and caught up the sheriff's horse. They got a shot or two at me, hit my wrist, but I made my getaway. This horse is not much on looks, but he sure can get over the sagebrush. I was coming over to see you."

There was that in his voice when he said this that touched Sheila's heart, profoundly. This restless, violent young adventurer, homeless, foot-loose, without discipline or duty, had turned to her in his trouble as instinctively as though she had been his mother. This, because she had once served him. Something stirred in Sheila's heart.

"And then," Hilliard went on, "I was going to get down to Arizona. But when I heard you were coming over into Hidden Creek, it seemed like foolishness to cut myself off from the country by running away from nothing. Of course there are ways to prove my identity with those fellows. It only means putting up with a few days of pen." He gave a sigh. "But you can understand, ma'am, that this is n't just the horse that will give you quietest entrance into Rusty and that I'm not just one of the First Citizens."

"But," said Sheila, "if they see you riding in with me, they certainly won't shoot."

He laughed admiringly. "You're game!" he said. "But, Miss Arundel, they're not likely to do any more shooting. It's not a man riding into Rusty that they're after. It's a man riding out of Rusty. They'll know I'm coming to give myself up."

"I'll just stay here," said Sheila firmly.

"I can't let you."

ADVENTURE

"I'm too tired to walk. I'm too sleepy. It'll be all right."

"Then I'll walk." He pulled in his horse, but at the instant stiffened in his saddle and wheeled about on the road. A rattle of galloping hoofs struck the ground behind them; two riders wheeled and stopped. One drew close and held out his hand.

"Say, stranger, shake," he said. "We've been kickin' up the dust to beg your pardon. We got the real rustler this mornin' shortly after you left. I'm plumb disgusted and disheartened with young Tommins for losin' his head an' shootin' off his gun. He's a dern fool, that kid, a regular tenderfoot. Nothin' won't ever cure him short of growin' up. Come from Chicago, anyway. One of them Eastern towns. I see he got you, too."

"Winged me," smiled Hilliard. "Well, I'm right pleased I won't have to spend another night in your pen."

"You're entered for drinks. The sheriff stands 'em." Here he bowed to Sheila, removing his hat.

"This lady" — Hilliard performed the introduction — "lost her horse on The Hill. She's aiming to stop at Rusty for to-night."

The man who had spoken turned to his silent companion. "Ride ahead, Shorty, why don't you?" he said indignantly, "and tell Mrs. Lander there's a lady that'll want to sleep in Number Five."

The other horseman, after a swift, searching look

at Sheila, said "Sure," in a very mild, almost cooing, voice and was off. It looked to Sheila like a runaway. But the men showed no concern.

They jogged companionably on their way. Fifteen minutes later they crossed a bridge and pulled up before a picket fence and a gate.

They were in Rusty.

CHAPTER III

JOURNEY'S END

THE social life of Rusty, already complicated by the necessity it was under to atone for a mistake, was almost unbearably discomposed by the arrival of a strange lady. This was no light matter, be it understood. Hidden Creek was not a resort for ladies: and so signal an event as the appearance of a lady, a young lady, a pretty young lady, demanded considerable effort. But Rusty had five minutes for preparation. By the time Hilliard rode up to Lander's gate a representative group of citizens had gathered there. One contingent took charge of Hilliard — married men, a little unwilling, and a few even more reluctant elders, and led him to the bowl of reparation which was to wash away all memory of his wrongs. The others, far the larger group, escorted Sheila up the twelve feet of board walk to the porch of hospitality filled by the massive person of Mrs. Lander. On that brief walk Sheila was fathered, brothered, grandfathered, husbanded, and befriended and on the porch, all in the person of Mrs. Lander, she was mothered, sistered, and grandmothered. Up the stairs to Number Five she was "eased" — there is no other word to express the process — and down again she was eased to supper, where in a daze of fatigue she ate with surprising relish tough fried meat and large wet potatoes, a bowl of raw canned tomatoes and a huge piece of heavy-crusted preserved-peach pie. She also drank, with no effect upon her drowsiness, an enormous thick cupful of strong coffee, slightly tempered by canned milk. She sat at the foot of the long table, opposite Mr. Lander, a fat, sly-looking man whose eyes twinkled with a look of mysterious inner amusement, caused, probably, by astonishment at his own respectability. He had behind him a career of unprecedented villainy, and that he should end here at Rusty as the solid and well-considered keeper of the roadhouse was, no doubt, a perpetual tickle to his consciousness. Down either side of the table were silent and impressive figures busy with their food. Courteous and quiet they were and beautifully uninquiring, except in the matter of her supplies, The yellow lamplight shone on brown bearded and brown clean-shaven faces, rugged and strong and clean-cut. These bared throats and thickly thatched heads, these faces, lighted by extraordinary, far-seeing brilliant, brooding eyes, reminded Sheila of a master's painting of The Last Supper — so did their coarse clothing melt into the gold-brown shadows of the room and so did their hands and throats and faces pick themselves out in mellow lights and darknesses.

After the meal she dragged herself upstairs to Number Five, made scant use of nicked basin, spout-

JOURNEY'S END

less pitcher, and rough clean towel, blew out her little shadeless lamp, and crept in under an immense, elephantine, grateful weight of blankets and patchwork quilts, none too fresh, probably, though the sheet blankets were evidently newly washed. Of muslin sheeting there was none. The pillow was flat and musty. Sheila cuddled into it as though it had been a mother's shoulder. That instant she was asleep. Once in the night she woke. A dream waked her. It seemed to her that a great white flower had blossomed in the window of her room and that in the heart of it was Dickie's face, tender and as pale as a petal. It drew near to her and bent over her wistfully. She held out her arms with a piteous longing to comfort his wistfulness and woke. Her face was wet with the mystery of dream tears. The flower dwindled to a small white moon standing high in the upper pane of one of the uncurtained windows. The room was full of eager mountain air. She could hear a waterwheel turning with a soft plash in the stream below. There was no other sound. The room smelt of snowy heights and brilliant stars. She breathed deep and, quite as though she had breathed a narcotic, slept suddenly again. This, before any memory of Hudson burned her consciousness.

The next morning she found that her journey had been carefully arranged. Thatcher had come and gone. The responsibility for her further progress had been shifted to the shoulders of a teamster, whose bearded face, except for the immense humor and gallantry of his gray eyes, was startlingly like one of Albrecht Dürer's apostles. Her bundle was in his wagon, half of his front seat was cushioned for her. After breakfast she was again escorted down the board walk to the gate. Mrs. Lander fastened a huge bunch of sweet peas to her coat and kissed her cheek. Sheila bade innumerable good-byes, expressed innumerable thanks. For Hilliard's absence Rusty offered its apologies. They said that he had been much entertained and, after the hurt he had suffered to his wrist, late sleep was a necessity. Sheila understood. The bowl of reparation had been emptied to its last atoning dregs. She mounted to the side of "Saint Mark," she bowed and smiled, made promises, gave thanks again, and waved herself out of Rusty at last. She had never felt so flattered and so warmed at heart.

"I'm agoin'," quoth Saint Mark, "right clost to Miss Blake's. If we don't overtake her — and that hoss of hers sure travels wonderful fast, somethin' wonderful, yes, ma'am, by God — excuse me, lady — it's sure surprisin' the way that skinny little hoss of hers will travel — why, I c'n take you acrost the ford. There ain't no way of gettin' into Miss Blake's exceptin' by the ford. And then I c'n take my team back to the road. From the ford it's a quarter-mile walk to Miss Blake's house. You c'n cache your bundle and she'll likely get it for you in the mornin'.

We had ought to be there by sundown. Her trail from the ford's clear enough. I'm a-takin' this lumber to the Gover'ment bridge forty mile up. Yes, by God — excuse *me*, lady — it's agoin' to be jest a dandy bridge until the river takes it out next spring, by God — you'll have to excuse me again, lady."

He seemed rather mournfully surprised by the frequent need for these apologies. "It was my raisin', lady," he explained. "My father was a Methody preacher. Yes'm, he sure was, by God, yes.— excuse me again, lady. He was always a-prayin'. It kinder got me into bad habits. Yes, ma'am. Those words you learn when you're a kid they do stick in your mind. By God, yes, they do — excuse *me*, lady. That's why I run away. I could n't stand so much prayin' all the time. And bein' licked when I was n't bein' prayed at. He sure licked me, that dern son of a — Oh, by God, lady, you'll just hev to excuse me, please." He wiped his forehead. "I reckon I better keep still."

Sheila struggled, then gave way to mirth. Her companion, after a doubtful look, relaxed into his wide, bearded smile. After that matters were on an easy footing between them and the "excuse me, lady," was, for the most part, left to her understanding.

They drifted like a lurching vessel through the long crystal day. Never before this journey into Hidden Creek had time meant anything to Sheila but a series of incidents, occupations, or emotions; now first she understood the Greek impersonation of the dancing hours. She had watched the varying faces the day turns to those who fold their hands and still their minds to watch its progress. She had seen the gradual heightening of brilliance from dawn to noon, and then the fading-out from that high, white-hot glare, through gold and rose and salmon and purple, to the ashy lavenders of twilight and so into gray and the metallic, glittering coldness of the mountain night. It was the purple hour when she said good-bye to Saint Mark on the far side of a swift and perilous ford. She was left standing in the shadow of a near-by mountain-side while he rode away into the still golden expanse of valley beyond the leafy course of the stream. Hidden Creek had narrowed and deepened. It ran past Sheila now with a loud clapping and knocking at its cobbled bed and with an over-current of noisy murmurs. The hurrying water was purple, with flecks of lavender and gold. The trees on its banks were topped with emerald fire where they caught the light of the sun. The trail to Miss Blake's ranch ran along the river on the edge of a forest of pines. At this hour they looked like a wall into which some magic permitted the wanderer to walk interminably. Sheila was glad that she did not have to make use of this wizard invitation. She "cached" her bundle, as Saint Mark had advised, in a thicket near the stream and walked resolutely forward along the trail. Not even when her pony had left her on The Hill had she felt so desolate or so afraid.

She could not understand why she was here on her way to the ranch of this strange woman. She felt astonished by her loneliness, by her rashness, by the dreadful lack in her life of all the usual protections. Was youth meant so to venture itself? This was what young men had done since the beginning of time. She thought of Hilliard. His life must have been just such a series of disconnected experiments. Danger was in the very pattern of such freedom. But she was a girl, *only* a girl as the familiar phrase expresses it — a seventeen-year-old girl. She was reminded of a pathetic and familiar line, "A woman naturally born to fears . . ." A wholesome reaction to pride followed and, suddenly, an amusing memory of Miss Blake, of her corduroy trousers stuffed into boots, of her broad, strong body, her square face with its firm lips and masterful red-brown eyes; a very heartening memory for such a moment. Here was a woman that had adventured without fear and had quite evidently met with no disaster.

Sheila came to a little tumbling tributary and crossed it on a log. On the farther side the trail broadened, grew more distinct; through an opening in tall, gray, misty cottonwoods she saw the corner of a log house. At the same instant a dreadful tumult broke out. The sound sent Sheila's blood in a slapping wave back upon her heart. All of her body turned cold. She was fastened by stone feet to the ground. It was the laughter of a mob of damned souls, an inhuman, despairing mockery of God. It tore the quiet evening into shreds of fear. This house was a madhouse holding revelry. No — of course, they were wolves, a pack of wolves. Then, with a warmth of returning circulation, Sheila remembered Miss Blake's dogs, the descendants of the wolf-dog that had littered on the body of a dead man. Quarter-wolf, was it? These voices had no hint of the homely barking of a watch-dog, the friend of man's loneliness! But Sheila braced her courage. Miss Blake made good use of her pack. They pulled her sled, winters, in Hidden Creek. They must then be partly civilized by service. If only — she smiled a desperate smile at the uncertainty — they did n't tear her to pieces when she came out from the shelter of the trees. There was very great courage in Sheila's short, lonely march through the little grove of cottonwood trees. She was as white as the mountain columbine. She walked slowly and held her head high. She had taken up a stone for comfort.

At the end of the trees she saw a house, a three-sided, one-storied building of logs very pleasantly set in a circle of aspen trees, backed by taller firs, toppling over which stood a great sharp crest of rocky ledges, nine thousand feet high, edged with the fire of sunset. At one side of the house eight big dogs were leaping at the ends of their chains. They were tied to

JOURNEY'S END

trees or to small kennels at the foot of trees. And, God be thanked! Sheila let fall her stone — they were *all* tied.

The door at the end of the nearest wing of the house opened and Miss Blake stood on the threshold and held up her hands. At sight of her the dogs stopped their howling instantly and cringed on their bellies or sat yawning on their bushy haunches. Miss Blake's resonant, deep voice seemed to pounce upon Sheila above the chatter of the stream which, running about three sides of the glade, was now, at the silence of the dogs, incessantly audible.

"Well, if it is n't the little barmaid!" cried Miss Blake, and advanced, wiping her hand on a white apron tied absurdly over the corduroy trousers and cowboy boots. "Well, if you are n't as welcome as the flowers in May! So you thought you'd leave the street-lamps and come take a look at the stars?"

They met and Sheila took the strong, square hand. She was afflicted by a sudden dizziness.

"That's it," she faltered; "this time I thought I'd try — the stars."

With that she fell against Miss Blake and felt, just before she dropped into blackness, that she had been saved by firm arms from falling to the ground.

CHAPTER IV
BEASTS

THE city rippled into light. It bloomed, blossom on blossom, like some enchanted jungle under the heavy summer sky. Dickie sat on a bench in Washington Square. He sat forward, his hands hanging between his knees, his lips parted, and he watched the night. It seemed to him that it was filled with the clamor of iron-throated beasts running to and fro after their prey. The heat was a humid, solid, breathless weight — a heat unknown to Millings. Dickie wore his threadbare blue serge suit. It felt like a garment of lead.

There were other people on the benches — limp and sodden outlines. Dickie had glanced at them and had glanced away. He did not want to think that he looked like one of these — half-crushed insects, — bruised into immobility. A bus swept round the corner and moved with a sort of topheavy, tipsy dignity under the white arch. It was loaded with humanity, its top black with heads. "It ain't a crowd," thought Dickie; "it's a swarm." His eyes followed the ragged sky-line. "Why is it so horrible?" he asked himself — "horrible and beautiful and sort of poisonous — it plumb scares a fellow — " A diminished moon, battered and dim like a trodden silver coin, stood up above him. By tilting his head he could look directly at it through an opening in the dusty, electric-brightened boughs. The stars were pin-pricks here and there in the dense sky. The city flaunted its easy splendor triumphantly before their pallid insignificance. Tarnished purities, forgotten ecstasies, burned-out inspirations — so the city shouted raucously to its faded firmament.

Dickie's fingers slid into his pocket. The moon had reminded him of his one remaining dime. He might have bought a night's lodging with it, but after one experience of such lodgings he preferred his present quarters. In Dickie's mind there was no association of shame or ignominy with a night spent under the sky. But fear and ignominy tainted and clung to his memory of that other night. He had saved his dime deliberately, going hungry rather than admit to himself that he was absolutely at the end of his resources. To-morrow he would not especially need that dime. He had a job. He would begin to draw pay. In his own phrasing he would "buy him a square meal and rent him a room somewhere." Upon these two prospects his brain fastened with a leech-like persistency. And yet above anything he had faced in his life he dreaded the job and the room. The inspiration of his flight, the impulse that had sped him out of Millings like a fire-tipped arrow, that determination to find Sheila, to rehabilitate himself in her esteem, to serve her, to make a fresh start, had fallen from him like a dead flame. The arrow-flight was spent. He had not found Sheila. He had no way of finding her. She was not at her old address. Her father's friend, the Mr. Hazeldean that had brought Sylvester to Marcus's studio, knew nothing of her. Mrs. Halligan, her former landlady, knew nothing of her. Dickie, having summoned Mrs. Halligan to her doorsill, had looked past her up the narrow, steep staircase. "Did she live away up there?" he had asked. "Yes, sorr. And 't was a climb for the poor little crayture, but there was days when she'd come down it like a burrd to meet her Pa." Dickie had faltered, white and empty-hearted, before the kindly Irishwoman who remembered so vividly Sheila's downward, winged rush of welcome. For several hours after his visit to the studio building he had wandered aimlessly about, then his hunger had bitten at him and he had begun to look for work. It was not difficult to find. A small restaurant displayed a need of waiters. Dickie applied. He had often "helped out" in that capacity, as in most others, at The Aura. He cited his experience, referred to Mr. Hazeldean, and was engaged. The pay seemed to him sufficient to maintain life. So much for that! Then he went to his bench and watched the day pant itself into the night. His loneliness was a pitiful thing; his utter lack of hope or inspiration was a terrible thing.

But as the night went slowly by, he faced this desolation with extraordinary fortitude. It was part of that curious detachment, that strange gift of im-

BEASTS 199

personal observation. Dickie bore no grudges against life. His spirit had a fashion of standing away, tiptoe, on wings. It stood so now like a presence above the miserable, half-starved body that occupied the bench and suffered the sultriness of August and the pains of abstinence. Dickie's wide eyes, that watched the city and found it horrible and beautiful and frightening, were entirely empty of bitterness and of selfpity. They had a sort of wistful patience.

There came at last a cool little wind and under its ministration Dickie let fall his head on his arms and slept. He was blessed by a dream: shallow water clapping over a cobbled bed, the sharp rustle of wind-edged aspen leaves, and two stars, tender and misty, that bent close and smiled. He woke up and stared at the city. He got up and walked about. He was faint now and felt chilled, although the asphalt was still soft underfoot and smelled of hot tar. As he moved listlessly along the pavement, a girl brushed against him, looked up, and murmured to him. She was small and slight. His heart seemed to leap away from the contact and then to leap almost irresistibly to meet it. He turned away and went back quickly toward the Square. It seemed to him that he was followed. He looked over his shoulder furtively. But the girl had disappeared and there was no one in sight but a man who walked unsteadily. Dickie suddenly knew why he had saved that dime. The energy of a definite purpose came to him. He remembered a swinging door back there around a corner, but when he reached the saloon, it was closed. Dickie had a humiliating struggle with tears. He went back to his bench and sat there, trembling and swearing softly to himself. He had not the strength to look farther. He was no longer the Dickie of Millings, a creature possessed of loneliness and vacancy and wandering fancies, he was no longer Sheila's lover, he was a prey to strong desires. In truth, thought Dickie, seeking even now with his deprecatory smile for likenesses and words, the city was full of beasts, silent and stealthy and fanged. That spirit, aloof, maintained its sweet detachment. Beneath its observation Dickie fought with a grim, unreasoning panic that was very like the fear of a man pursued by wolves.

CHAPTER V

NEIGHBOR NEIGHBOR

EVEN in the shadow of after events, those first two months at Miss Blake's ranch swam like a golden galleon through Sheila's memory. Never had she felt such well-being of body, mind, and soul. Never had she known such dawns and days, such dusks, such sapphire nights. Sleep came like a highwayman to hold up an eager traveler, but came irresistibly. It caught her up out of life as it catches up a healthy child. Never before had she worked so heartily: out of doors in the vegetable garden; indoors in the sunny kitchen, its windows and door open to the tonic air; never before had she eaten so heartily. Nothing had tasted like the trout they caught in Hidden Creek, like the juicy, sweet vegetables they picked from their own laborious rows, like the berries they gathered in nervous anticipation of that rival berryer, the brown bear. And Miss Blake's casual treatment of her, half-bluff, half-mocking, her curt, good-humored commands, her cordial bullying, were a rest to nerves more raveled than Sheila knew from her experience in Millings. She grew rosy brown; her hair seemed to sparkle along its crisp ripples; her little throat filled itself out, round and firm; she walked with a spring and a swing; she sang and whistled, no Mrs. Hudson near to scowl at her. Dish-washing was not drudgery, cooking was a positive pleasure. Everything smelt so good. She was always shutting her eyes to enjoy the smell of things, forgetting to listen in order to taste thoroughly, forgetting to look in the delight of listening to such musical silences, and forgetting even to breathe in the rapture of sight . . . Miss Blake and she put up preserves, and Sheila had to invent jests to find some pretext for her laughter, so ridiculous was the look of that broad square back, its hair short above the man's flannel collar, and the apron-strings tied pertly above the very wide, slightly worn corduroy breeches and the big boots. Sheila was always thinking of a certain famous Puss of fairy-tale memory, and biting her tongue to keep it from the epithet. After Hilliard gave her the black horse and she began to explore the mountain game trails, her life seemed as full of pleasantness as it could hold. And yet . . . with just that gift of Hilliard's, the overshadowing of her joy began. No, really before that, with his first visit.

That was in late September when the nights were frosty and Miss Blake had begun to cut and stack her wood for winter, and to use it for a crackling hearth-fire after supper. They were sitting before such a fire when Hilliard came.

Miss Blake sat man-fashion on the middle of her spine, her legs crossed, a magazine in her hands, and on her blunt nose a pair of large, black-rimmed spec-

NEIGHBOR NEIGHBOR

tacles. Her feet and hands and her cropped head, though big for a woman's, looked absurdly small in comparison to the breadth of her hips and shoulders. She was reading the "Popular Science Monthly." This and the "Geographic" and "Current Events" were regularly taken by her and most thoroughly digested. She read with keen intelligence; her comments were as shrewd as a knife-edge. The chair she sat in was made from elk-horns and looked like the throne of some Norse chieftain. Behind her on the wall hung the stuffed head of a huge walrus, his tusks gleaming, the gift of that exploring brother who seemed to be her only living relative. There were other tokens of his wanderings, a polar-bear skin, an ivory Eskimo spear. As a more homelike trophy Miss Blake had hung an elk head which she herself had laid low, a very creditable shot, though out of season. She had been short of meat. In the corner was a pianola topped by piles of record-boxes. At her feet lay Berg, the dog, snoring faintly and as cozy as a kitten.

The firelight made Miss Blake's face and hair ruddier than usual; her eyes, when she raised them for a glance at Sheila, looked as though they were full of red sparks which might at any instant break into flame. Sheila was wearing one of her flimsy little black frocks, recovered from the wrinkles of its journey, and she had decorated her square-cut neck with some yellow flowers. On these Miss Blake's eyes rested every now and then with a sardonic gleam.

Outside Hidden Creek told its interminable chattering tale, centuries long, the little skinny horse cropped getting his difficult meal with his few remaining teeth. They could hear the dogs move with a faint rattle of chains. Sometimes there would be a distant rushing sound, a snow-slide thousands of feet above their heads on the mountain. Above these familiar sounds there came, at about eight o'clock that evening, the rattle of horse's hoofs through the little stream and at the instant broke out the hideous clamor of the dogs, a noise that never failed to whiten Sheila's cheeks.

Miss Blake sat up straight and snatched off her spectacles. She looked at Sheila with a hard look.

"Have you been sending out invitations, Sheila?" she asked.

"No, of course not," Sheila had flushed. She could guess whose horse's hoofs were trotting across the little clearing.

A man's voice spoke to the dogs commandingly. Miss Blake's eyebrows came down over her eyes. A man's step struck the porch. A man's knock rapped sharply at the door.

"Come in!" said Miss Blake. She spoke it like a sentry's challenge.

The door opened and there stood Cosme Hilliard,

hat in hand, his smiling Latin mouth showing the big white Saxon teeth.

Sheila had not before quite realized his good looks. Now, all his lithe, long gracefulness was painted for her against a square of purple night. The clean white silk shirt fitted his broad shoulders, the wide rider's belt clung to his supple waist, the leather chaps were shaped to his Greek hips and thighs. No civilized man's costume could so have revealed and enhanced his beautiful strength. And above the long body his face glowed with its vivid coloring, the liquid golden eyes that moved easily under their lids, the polished black hair sleekly brushed, the red-brown cheeks, the bright lips, flexible and curved, of his Spanish mother.

"Who in God's name are you?" demanded Miss Blake in her deepest voice.

"This is Mr. Hilliard," Sheila came forward. "He is the man that brought me over The Hill, Miss Blake — after I'd lost my horse, you know." There was some urgency in Sheila's tone, a sort of prod to courtesy. Miss Blake settled back on her spine and recrossed her legs.

"Well, come in," she said, "and shut the door. No use frosting us all, is there?" She resumed her spectacles and her reading of the "Popular Science Monthly."

Hilliard, still smiling, bowed to her, took Sheila's hand for an instant, then moved easily across the room and settled on his heels at one corner of the hearth. He had been riding, it would seem, in the thin silk shirt and had found the night air crisp. He rolled a cigarette with the hands that had first drawn Sheila's notice as they held his glass on the bar; gentleman's hands, clever, sensitive, carefully kept. From his occupation, he looked up at Miss Blake audaciously.

"You'd better make friends with me, ma'am," he said, "because we're going to be neighbors."

"How's that?"

"I'm taking up my homestead right down here below you on Hidden Creek a ways. About six miles below your ford."

Miss Blake's face filled with dark blood. She said nothing, put up her magazine.

Sheila, however, exclaimed delightedly, "Taken up a homestead?"

"Yes, ma'am." He turned his floating, glowing look to her and there it stayed almost without deviation during the rest of his visit. "I've built me a log house — a dandy. I had a man up from Rusty to help me. I've bought me a cow. I'm getting my furnishings ready. That's what I've been doing these two months."

"And never rode up to call on us?" Sheila reproached him.

"No, ma'am. I'll tell you the reason for that. I wasn't sure of myself." She opened rather puzzled and astonished eyes at this, but for an instant his

FOR AN INSTANT HIS LOOK WENT BEYOND HER AND
REMEMBERED TROUBLING THINGS

look went beyond her and remembered troubling things. "You see, Miss Arundel, I'm not used to settling down. That's something that I've had no practice in. I'm impatient. I get tired quickly. Damn quickly. I change my mind. It's the worst thing in me — a sort of devil-horse always thirsty for new things. It's touch and go with him. He runs with me. You see, I've always given him his head." His look had come back to her face and dwelt there speaking for him a language headier than that of his tongue. "I thought I'd tie the dern fool down to some good tough work and test him out. Well, ma'am, he has n't quit on me this time. I think he won't. I've got a ball and chain round about that cloven foot." He drew at his cigarette, half-veiling in smoke the ardor of his look. "I'd like to show you my house, Miss Arundel. It's fine. I worked with a builder one season when I was a lad. I've got it peeled inside. The logs shine and I've got a fireplace twice the size of this in my living-room" — he made graceful gestures with the hand that held the cigarette. "Yes, ma'am, a living-room, and a kitchen, and," with a whimsical smile, "a butler's pantry. And, oh, a great big bedroom that gets the morning sun." He paused an instant and flushed from chin to brow, an Anglo-Saxon flush it was, but the bold Latin eyes did not fall. "I've made some furnishings already. And I've sent out an order for kitchen stuff."

Here Miss Blake changed the crossing of her legs.

Sheila was angry with herself because she was consumed with the contagion of his blush. She wished that he would not look as if he had seen the blush and was pleased by it. She wished that his clean young strength and beauty and the ardor of his eyes did not speak quite so eloquently.

"I bought a little black horse about so high" — he held his hand an absurd distance from the floor and laughed — "just the size for a little girl and — do you know who I'm going to give him to?"

Here Miss Blake got up, strode to the pianola, adjusted it, and sat down, broad and solid and unabashed by absence of feminine draperies, upon the stool. She played a comic song.

"I don't like your *family* — "

in some such dreadful way it expressed itself —

"They do *not* look good to me.
I don't think your *Unc*le John
Ever *had* a collar on . . ."

She played it very loud.

Hilliard stood up and came close to Sheila.

"She's mad as a March hare," he whispered, "and she does n't like me a little bit. Come out while I catch up Dusty, won't you, please? It's moonlight. I'll be going." He repeated this very loud for Miss Blake's benefit with no apparent effect upon her enjoyment of the song. She was rocking to its rhythm.

Hilliard was overwhelmed suddenly by the appearance of her. He put his hand to his mouth and bolted. Sheila, following, found him around the corner of the house rocking and gasping with mirth. He looked at her through tears.

"Puss-in-Boots," he gasped, and Sheila ran to the edge of the clearing to be safe in a mighty self-indulgence.

There they crouched like two children till their laughter spent itself. Hilliard was serious first.

"You're a bad, ungrateful girl," he said weakly, "to laugh at a sweet old lady like that."

"Oh, I am!" Sheila took it almost seriously. "She's been wonderful to me."

"I bet she works you," he said jealously.

"Oh, no. Not a bit too hard. I love it."

"Well," he admitted, "you do look pretty fine, that's a fact. Better than you did at Hudson's. What did you quit for?"

Sheila was sober enough now. The moonlight let some of its silver, uncaught by the twinkling aspen leaves, splash down on her face. It seemed to flicker and quiver like the leaves. She shook her head.

He looked a trifle sullen. "Oh, you won't tell me . . . Funny idea, you being a barmaid. Hudson's notion, was n't it?"

Sheila lifted her clear eyes. "I thought asking questions was n't good manners in the West."

"Damn!" he said. "Don't you make me angry! I've got a right to ask you questions."

She put her hand up against the smooth white trunk of the tree near which she stood. She seemed to grow a little taller.

"Oh, have you? I don't think I quite understand how you got any such right. And you like to be questioned yourself?"

She had him there, had him rather cruelly, though he was not aware of the weapon of her suspicion. She felt a little ashamed when she saw him wince. He slapped his gloves against his leather chaps, looking at her with hot, sulky eyes.

"Oh, well . . . I beg your pardon . . . Listen — " He flung his ill-humor aside and was sweet and cool again like the night. "Are you going to take the little horse?"

"I don't know."

His face shadowed and fell so expressively, so utterly, that she melted.

"Oh," he stammered, half-turning from her, "I was sure. I brought him up."

This completed the melting process. "Of course I'll take him!" she cried. "Where is he?"

She inspected the beautiful little animal by the moonlight. She even let Hilliard mount her on the shining glossy back and rode slowly about clinging to his mane, ecstatic over the rippling movement under her.

"He's like a rocking-chair," said Cosme. "You can ride him all day and not feel it." He looked about the silver meadow. "Good feed here, isn't there? I bet he'll stay. If not, I'll get him for you."

Sheila slipped down. They left the horse to graze.

"Yes, it's first-rate feed. Do you think Miss Blake will let me keep him?"

His answer was entirely lost by a sudden outbreak from the dogs.

"Good Lord!" said Cosme, making himself heard, "what a breed! Isn't that awful! Why does she keep the brutes? Isn't she scared they'll eat her?"

Sheila shook her head. Presently the tumult quieted down. "They're afraid of her," she said. "She has a dreadful whip. She likes to bully them. I think she's rather cruel. But she does love Berg; she says he's the only real dog in the pack."

"Was Berg the one on the bearskin inside?"

"Yes."

"He's sure a beauty. But I don't like him. He has wolf eyes. See here — you're shivering. I've kept you out here in the cold. I'll go. Good-night. Thank you for keeping the horse. Will you come down to see my house? I built it " — he drawled the words — "for you" — and added after a tingling moment — "to see, ma'am."

This experiment in words sent Sheila to the house, her hand crushed and aching with his good-bye grasp, her heart jumping with a queer fright.

Miss Blake stood astraddle on the hearth, her hands behind her back.

"You better go to bed, Sheila," she said; "it's eleven o'clock and to-morrow's wash-day."

Her voice was pleasant enough, but its bluffness had a new edge. Sheila found it easy to obey. She climbed up the ladder to the little gabled loft which was her bedroom. Halfway up she paused to assert a belated independence of spirit. "Good-night," she said, "how do you like our neighbor?"

Miss Blake stared up. Her lips were set tight. She made no answer. After an instant she sauntered across the room and out of the door. The whip with which she beat the dogs swung in her hand. A moment later a fearful howling and yelping showed that some culprit had been chosen for condign punishment.

Sheila set down her candle, sat on the edge of her cot, and covered her ears with her hands. When it was over she crept into bed. She felt, though she chided herself for the absurdity, like a naughty child who has been forcibly reminded of the consequences of rebellion.

CHAPTER VI

A HISTORY AND A LETTER

THE next morning, it seemed Miss Blake's humor had completely changed. It showed something like an apologetic softness. She patted Sheila's shoulder when she passed the girl at work. When Hilliard next appeared, a morning visit this time, he was bidden to share their dinner; he was even smiled upon.

"She's not such a bad old girl, is she?" he admitted when Sheila had been given a half-holiday and was riding on the black horse beside Hilliard on his Dusty across one of the mountain meadows.

"*I* think she's a dear," said Sheila, pink with gratitude; then, shadowing, "If only she wouldn't beat the dogs and would give up trapping."

"Why in thunder shouldn't she trap?"

"I loathe trapping. Do you remember how you felt in the pen? It's bad enough to shoot down splendid wild things for food, but, to trap them! — small furry things or even big furry things like bears, why, it's cruel! It's hideously cruel! When a woman does it — "

"Come, now, don't call *her* a woman!"

"Yes, she is. Think of the aprons! And she is so tidy."

"That's not just a woman's virtue."

"Maybe not. I'm not sure. But I've a feeling that it was Eve who first discovered dust."

"Very bad job if she did. Think of all the bother we've been going through ever since."

"There!" Sheila triumphed. "To you it's just bother. You're a man. To me it's a form of sport . . . I wonder what Miss Blake's story is."

"You mean — ?" He turned in his saddle to stare wonderingly at her. "You don't know?"

"No." Sheila blushed confusedly. "I — I don't know anything about her — "

"Good Lord!" He whistled softly. "Sometimes those ventures turn out all right." He looked dubious. "I'm glad I'm here!"

Sheila's smile slipped sweetly across her mouth and eyes. "So am I. But," she added after a thoughtful moment, "I don't know much about your story either, do I?"

"I might say something about asking questions," began Cosme with grimness, but changed his tone quickly with a light, apologetic touch on her arm, "but — but I won't. I ran away from school when I was fourteen and I've been knocking around the West ever since."

"What school?" asked Sheila.

He did not answer for several minutes. They had come to the end of the meadow and were mounting a slope on a narrow trail where the ponies seemed to

A HISTORY AND A LETTER 215

nose their way among the trees. Now and then Sheila had to put out her hand to push her knee away from a threatening trunk. Below were the vivid paint-brush flowers and the blue mountain lupine and all about the nymph-white aspens with leaves turning to restless gold against the sky. The horses moved quietly with a slight creaking of saddles. There was a feeling of stealth, of mystery — that tiptoe breathless expectation of Pan pipes ... At last Cosme turned in his saddle, rested his hand on the cantle, and looked at Sheila from a bent face with troubled eyes.

"It was an Eastern school," he said. "No doubt you've heard of it. It was Groton."

The name here in these Wyoming woods brought a picture as foreign as the artificiality of a drawing-room.

"Groton? You ran away?"

"Yes, ma'am."

Sheila's suspicions were returning forcibly. "I'll have to ask questions, Mr. Hilliard, because it seems so strange — what you are now, and your running away and never having been brought back to the East by — by whoever it was that sent you to Groton."

"I want you to ask questions," he said rather wistfully. "You have the right."

This forced her into something of a dilemma. She ignored it and waited, looking away from him. He would not leave her this loophole, however.

"Why don't you look at me?" he demanded crossly.

She did, and smiled again.

"You have the prettiest smile I ever saw!" he cried; then went on quickly, "I ran away because of something that happened. I'll tell you. My mother" — he flushed and his eyes fell — "came up to see me at school one day. My mother was very beautiful . . . I was mad about her." Curiously enough, every trace of the Western cowboy had gone out of his voice and manner, which were an echo of the voice and manner of the Groton schoolboy whose experience he told. "I was proud of her — you know how a kid is. I kind of paraded her round and showed her off to the other fellows. No other fellow had such a beautiful mother. Then, as we were saying good-bye, a crowd of the boys all round, I did something — trod on her foot or something, I don't quite know what — and she lifted up her hand and slapped me across the face." He was white at the shocking memory. "Right there before them all, when I — I was adoring her. She had the temper of a devil, a sudden Spanish temper — the kind I have, too — and she never made the slightest effort to hold it down. She hit me and she laughed as though it was funny and she got into her carriage. I cut off to my room. I wanted to kill myself. I couldn't face any one. I wanted never to see her again. I guess I was a queer sort of kid . . . I don't know . . ." He drew a big breath, dropped

A HISTORY AND A LETTER 217

back to the present and his vivid color returned. "That's why I ran away from school, Miss Arundel."

"And they never brought you back?"

He laughed. "They never found me. I had quite a lot of money and I lost myself pretty cleverly . . . a boy of fourteen can, you know. It's a very common history. Well, I suppose they did n't break their necks over me either, after the first panic. They were busy people — my parents — remarkably busy going to the devil . . . And they were eternally hard-up. You see, my grandfather had the money — still has it — and he's remarkably tight. I wrote to them after six years, when I was twenty. They wrote back; at least their lawyer did. They tried, not very sincerely, though, I think, to coax me East again . . . told me they'd double my allowance if I did — they've sent me a pittance — " He shuddered suddenly, a violent, primitive shiver. "I'm glad I did n't go," he said.

There was a long stillness. That dreadful climax to the special "business" of the Hilliards was relived in both their memories. But it was something of which neither could speak. Sheila wondered if the beautiful mother was that instant wearing the hideous prison dress. She wished that she had read the result of the trial. She would n't for the world question this pale and silent young man. The rest of their ride was quiet and rather mournful. They rode back at sunset and Hilliard bade her a troubled good-bye.

She wanted to say something comforting, reassuring. She watched him helplessly from where she stood on the porch as he walked across the clearing to his horse. Suddenly he slapped the pocket of his chaps and turned back. "Thunder!" he cried, "I'd forgotten the mail. A fellow left it at the ford. A paper for Miss Blake and a letter for you."

Sheila held out her hand. "A letter for me?" She took it. It was a strange hand, small and rather unsteady. The envelope was fat, the postmark Millings. Her flush of surprise ebbed. She knew whose letter it was — Sylvester Hudson's. He had found her out.

She did not even notice Cosme's departure. She went up to her loft, sat down on her cot and read.

My dear Miss Sheila:
 I don't rightly know how to express myself in this letter because I know what your feelings toward Pap must be like, and they are fierce. But I have got to try to write you a letter just the same, for there are some things that need explaining. At first, when my hotel and my Aura were burned down [here the writing was especially shaky] and I found that you and Dickie had both vamoosed, I thought that you had paid me out and gone off together. You can't blame me for that thought, Miss Sheila, for I had found him in your room at that time of night or morning and I could n't help but see that he was aiming to kiss you and you were waiting for his kiss. So I was angry and I had been drinking and I kissed you myself, taking advantage of you in a way that no gentleman would do. But I thought you were different from the Sheila I had brought to be my barmaid.

Well, ma'am, for a while after the fire, I was pretty near

A HISTORY AND A LETTER 219

crazy. I was about loco. Then I was sick. When I got well again, a fellow who come over from Hidden Creek told me you had gone over to be at a ranch there and that you had come in alone. That sort of got me to thinking about you more and more and studying you out, and I begun to see that I had made a bad mistake. Whatsoever reason brought that damn fool Dickie to your room that morning, it wasn't your doings, and the way you was waiting for his kiss was more a mother's way. I have had some hard moments with myself, Miss Sheila, and I have come to this that I have got to write and tell you how I feel. And ask your forgiveness. You see you were something in my life, different from anything that had ever been there. I don't rightly know — I likely never will know — what you meant in my life. I handled you in my heart like a flower. Before God, I had a religion for you. And that was just why, when I thought you was bad, that it drove me crazy. I wonder if you will understand this. You are awful young and awful ignorant. And I have hurt your pride. You are terrible proud for your years, Miss Sheila. I ache all over when I think that I hurt your pretty mouth. I hope it is smiling now. I am moving out of Millings, — Me and Momma and Babe. But Girlie is agoing to marry Jim. He run right back to her like a little lost lamb the second you was gone. Likely, he'll never touch liquor again. I haven't heard from Dickie. I guess he's gone where the saloons are bigger and where you can get oysters with your drinks. He always was a damn fool. I would dearly like to go over to Hidden Creek and see you, but I feel like I'd better not. It would hurt me if I got a turn-down from you like it will hurt me if you don't answer this letter, which is a mighty poor attempt to tell you my bad reasons for behaving like I did. I am not sorry I thrashed Dickie. He had ought to be thrashed good and plenty. And he has sure paid me off by burning down my Aura. That was a saloon in a million, Miss Sheila, and the picture of you standing there back of my bar, looking so dainty and sweet and fine in your black dress and your frills — well, ma'am, I'll sure try to be thinking of that when I cash in.

Well, Miss Sheila, I wish you good fortune in whatever you do, and I hope that if you ever need a friend you will overlook my bad break and remember the artist that tried to put you in his big work and — failed.

This extraordinary document was signed — "Sylvester." Sheila was left bewildered with strange tears in her throat.

CHAPTER VII
Sanctuary

THERE came to the restaurant where Dickie worked, a certain sallow and irritable man, no longer in his early youth. He came daily for one of his three meals: it might be lunch or dinner or even breakfast, Dickie was always in haste to serve him. For some reason, the man's clever and nervous personality intrigued his interest. And this, although his customer never threw him a glance, scowled at a newspaper, barked out an order, gulped his food, stuck a fair-sized tip under the edge of his plate, and jerked himself away.

On a certain sluggish noon hour in August, Dickie, as far as the kitchen door with a tray balanced on his palm, realized that he had forgotten this man's order. He hesitated to go back. "Like as not," reasoned Dickie, "he did n't rightly know what the order was. He never does look at his food. I'll fetch him a Spanish omelette and a salad and a glass of iced tea. It's a whole lot better order than he'd have thought of himself."

Nevertheless, it was with some trepidation that he set the omelette down before that lined and averted countenance. Its owner was screwed into his chair as usual, eyes, with a sharp cleft between their brows, bent on his folded newspaper, and he put his right hand blindly on the fork. But as it pricked the contents of the plate a savory fragrance rose and the reader looked.

"Here, you damn fool — that's not my order," he snapped out.

Dickie tasted a homely memory — "Dickie damn fool." He stood silent a moment looking down with one of his quaint, impersonal looks.

"Well, sir," then he said slowly, "it ain't your order, but you look a whole lot more like a feller that would order Spanish omelette than like a feller that would order Hamburger steak."

For the first time the man turned about, flung his arm over his chair-back, and looked up at Dickie. In fact, he stared. His thin lips, enclosed in an ill-tempered parenthesis of double lines, twisted themselves slightly.

"I'll be derned!" he said. "But, look here, my man, I didn't order Hamburger steak. I ordered chicken."

Dickie deliberately smoothed down the cowlick on his head. He wore his look of a seven-year-old with which he was wont to face the extremity of Sylvester's exasperation.

"I reckon I clean forgot your order, sir," he said. "I figured out that you would n't be caring what was on your plate. This heat," he added, "sure puts a blinder on a feller's memory."

The man laughed shortly. "It's all right," he said. "This 'll go down."

He ate in silence. Then he glanced up again. "What are you waiting for, anyway?"

SANCTUARY

Dickie flushed faintly. "I was sort of wishful to see how it would go down."

"Oh, I don't mean that kind of waiting. I mean — why are you a waiter in this — hash-hole?"

Dickie meditated. "There ain't no answer to that," he said. "I don't know why — " He added — "Why anything. It's a sort of extry word in the dictionary — don't mean much any way you look at it."

He gathered up the dishes. The man watched him, tilting back a little in his chair, his eyes twinkling under brows drawn together. A moment afterwards he left the restaurant.

It was a few nights later when Dickie saw him again — or rather when Dickie was again seen by him. This time Dickie was not in the restaurant. He was at a table in a small Free Library near Greenwich Avenue, and he was copying painstakingly with one hand from a fat volume which he held down with the other. The strong, heavily-shaded light made a circle of brilliance about him; his fair hair shone silvery bright, his face had a sort of seraphic pallor. The orderer of chicken, striding away from the desk with a hastily obtained book of reference, stopped short and stared at him; then came close and touched the thin, shiny shoulder of the blue serge coat.

"This the way you take your pleasure?" he asked abruptly.

Dickie looked up slowly, and his consciousness seemed to travel even more slowly back from the fairy doings of a midsummer night. Under the observant eyes bent upon it, his face changed extraordinarily from the face of untroubled, almost immortal childhood to the face of struggling and reserved manhood.

"Hullo," he said with a smile of recognition. "Well — yes — not always."

"What are you reading?" The man slipped into the chair beside Dickie, put on his glasses, and looked at the fat book. "Poetry? Hmp! What are you copying it for? — letter to your girl?"

Dickie had all the Westerner's prejudice against questions, but he felt drawn to this patron of the "hash-hole," so, though he drawled his answer slightly, it was an honest answer.

"It ain't my book," he said. "That's why I'm copying it."

"Why in thunder don't you take it out, you young idiot?"

Dickie colored. "Well, sir, I don't rightly understand the workings of this place. I come by it on the way home and I kep' a-seein' folks goin' in with books and comin' out with books. I figured it was a kind of exchange proposition. I've only got one book — and that ain't rightly mine — " the man looking at him wondered why his face flamed — "so, when I came in, I just watched and I figured you could read here if you had the notion to take down a book and fetch it over to the table and copy from it and return it. So I've been doin' that."

SANCTUARY

"Why did n't you go to the desk, youngster, and ask questions?"

"Where I come from" — Dickie was drawling again — "folks don't deal so much in questions as they do here."

"Where you came from! You came from Mars! Come along to the desk and I'll fix you up with a card and you can take an armful of poetry home with you."

Dickie went to the desk and signed his name. The stranger signed his — Augustus Lorrimer. The librarian stamped a bit of cardboard and stuck it into the fat volume. She handed it to Dickie wearily.

"Thank *you*, ma'am," he said with such respectful fervor that she looked up at him and smiled.

"Now, where's your diggings," asked Lorrimer, who had taken no hints about asking questions, "east or west?" He was a newspaper reporter.

"Would you be carin' to walk home with me?" asked Dickie. There was a great deal of dignity in his tone, more in his carriage.

"Yes. I'd be caring to! Lead on, Martian!" And Lorrimer felt, after he said that, that he was a vulgarian — a long-forgotten sensation. "In Mars," he commented to himself, "this young man was some kind of a prince."

"What do you look over your shoulder that way for, Dick?" he asked aloud, a few blocks on their way. "Scared the police will take away your book?"

Dickie blinked at him with a startled air. "Did I? I reckon a feller gets into queer ways when he's alone a whole lot. I get kind of feelin' like somebody was following me in this town — so many folks goin' to and fro does it to me most likely."

"Yes, a fellow does get into queer ways when he's alone a whole lot," said Lorrimer slowly. His mind went back a dozen years to his own first winter in New York. He looked with keenness at Dickie's face. It was a curiously charming face, he thought, but it was tight-knit with a harried, struggling sort of look, and this in spite of its quaint detachment.

"Know any one in this city?"

"No, sir, not rightly. I've made acquaintance with some of the waiters. They've asked me to join a club. But I have n't got the cash."

"What pay do you draw?"

Dickie named a sum.

"Not much, eh? But you've got your tips."

"Yes, sir. I pay my board with my pay and live on the tips."

"Must be uncertain kind of living! Where do you live, anyway? What? Here?"

They had crossed Washington Square and were entering a tall studio building to the south and east. Dickie climbed lightly up the stairs. Lorrimer followed with a feeling of bewilderment. On the top landing, dimly lighted, Dickie unlocked a door and stood aside.

SANCTUARY

"Just step in and look up," he said, "afore I light the light. You'll see something."

Lorrimer obeyed. A swarm of golden bees glimmered before his eyes.

"Stars," said Dickie. "Down below you would n't hardly know you had 'em, would you?"

Lorrimer did not answer. A moment later an asthmatic gas-jet caught its breath and he saw a bare studio room almost vacant of furniture. There was a bed and a screen and a few chairs, one window facing an alley wall. The stars had vanished.

"Pretty palatial quarters for a fellow on your job," Lorrimer remarked. "How did you happen to get here?"

"Some — people I knowed of once lived here." Dickie's voice had taken on a certain remoteness, and even Lorrimer knew that here questions stopped. He accepted a chair, declined "the makings," proffered a cigarette. During these amenities his eyes flew about the room.

"Good Lord!" he ejaculated, "is all that stuff your copying?"

There was a pile of loose and scattered manuscript upon the table under the gas-jet.

"Yes, sir," Dickie smiled. "I was plumb foolish to go to all that labor."

Lorrimer drew near to the table and coolly looked over the papers. Dickie watched him with rather a startled air and a flush that might have seemed one of resentment if his eyes had not worn their impersonal, observing look.

"All poetry," muttered Lorrimer. "But some of it only a line — or a word." He read aloud, — "'Close to the sun in lonely lands —' what's that from, anyway?"

"A poem about an eagle by a man named Alfred Tennyson. Ain't it the way a feller feels, though, up on the top of a rocky peak?"

"Never been on the top of a rocky peak — kind of a sky-scraper sensation, is n't it? What's all this — 'An' I have been faithful to thee, Cynara, after my fashion'?"

Dickie's face again flamed in spite of himself. "It's a love poem. The feller could n't forget. He could n't keep himself from loving that-away because he loved so much the other way — well, sir, you better read it for yourself. It's a mighty real sort of a poem — if you were that sort of a feller, I mean."

"And this is 'The Ballad of Reading Gaol.' And here's a sonnet, 'It was not like your great and gracious ways' — ? Coventry Patmore. Well, young man, you've a catholic taste."

"I don't rightly belong to any church," said Dickie gravely. "My mother is a Methodist."

Lorrimer moved abruptly away and moved abruptly back.

"Where were you educated, Dick?"

"I was raised in Millings" — Dickie named the

Western State — "I did n't get only to grammar school. My father needed me to work in his hotel."

"Too bad!" sighed Lorrimer. "Well, I'll bid you good-night. And many thanks. You've got a fine place here." Again he sighed. "I dare say — one of these days — "

He was absent and irritable again. Dickie accompanied him down the three long, narrow flights and climbed back to his loneliness. He was, however, very much excited by his adventure, excited and disturbed. He felt restless. He walked about and whistled to himself.

Until now he had had but one companion — the thought of Sheila. It was extraordinary how immediate she was. During the first dreadful weeks of his drudgery in the stifling confusions of the restaurant, when even the memory of Sylvester's tongue-lashings faded under the acute reality of the head waiter's sarcasms, that love of his for Sheila had fled away and left him dull and leaden and empty of his soul. And his tiny third-story bedroom had seemed like a coffin when he laid himself down in it and tried to remember her. It had come to him like a mountain wind, overwhelmingly, irresistibly, the desire to live where she lived: the first wish he had had since he had learned that she was not to be found by him. And the miracle had accomplished itself. Mrs. Halligan had been instructed to get a lodger at almost any price for the long-vacant studio room. She lowered the rent to the exact limit of Dickie's wages. She had never bargained with so bright-eyed a hungry-looking applicant for lodgings. And that night he lay awake under Sheila's stars. From then on he lived always in her presence. And here in the room that had known her he kept himself fastidious and clean. He shut out the wolf-pack of his shrewd desires. The room was sanctuary. It was to rescue Sheila rather than himself that Dickie fled up to the stars. So deeply, so intimately had she become a part of him that he seemed to carry her soul in his hands. So had the young dreamer wedded his dream. He lived with Sheila as truly, as loyally, as though he knew that she would welcome him with one of those downward rushes or give him Godspeed on sultry, feverish dawns with a cool kiss. Dickie lay sometimes across his bed and drew her cheek in trembling fancy close to his until the anguish wet his pillow with mute tears.

Now to this dual loneliness Lorrimer had climbed, and Dickie felt, rather gratefully, that life had reached up to the aching unrealities of his existence. His tight and painful life had opened like the first fold of a fan. He built upon the promise of a friendship with this questioning, impertinent, mocking, keenly sympathetic visitor.

But a fortnight passed without Lorrimer's appearing at the restaurant and, when at last he did come, Dickie, flying to his chair, was greeted by a cold, unsmiling word, and a businesslike quotation from the menu. He felt as though he had been struck. His face burned. In the West, a fellow could n't do that and get away with it! He tightened an impotent, thin fist. He filled the order and kept his distance, and, absurdly enough, gave Lorrimer's tip to another waiter and went without his own dinner. For the first time in his life a sense of social inferiority, of humiliation concerning the nature of his work, came to him. He felt the pang of servitude, a pang unknown to the inhabitants of frontier towns. When Sheila washed dishes for Mrs. Hudson she was "the young lady from Noo York who helps round at Hudson's house." Dickie fought this shame sturdily, but it seemed to cling, to have a sticky pervasiveness. Try as he might he could n't brush it off his mind. Nevertheless, it was on the very heels of this embittering experience that life plucked him up from his slough. One of the leveling public catastrophes came to Dickie's aid — not that he knew he was a dumb prayer for aid. He knew only that every day was harder to face than the last, that every night the stars up there through Sheila's skylight seemed to glimmer more dully with less inspiration on his fagged spirit.

The sluggish monotony of the restaurant's existence was stirred that September night by a big neighboring fire. Waiters and guests tumbled out to the call of fire-engines and running feet. Dickie found himself beside Lorrimer, who caught him by the elbow.

"Keep by me, kid," he said, and there was something in his tone that softened injury. "If you want a good look-in, I can get through the ropes."

He showed his card to a policeman, pulled Dickie after him, and they found themselves in an inner circle of the inferno. Before them a tall, hideous warehouse broke forth into a horrible beauty. It was as though a tortured soul had burst bars. It roared and glowed and sent up petals of smoky rose and seeds of fire against the blue-black sky. The crowds pressed against the ropes and turned up their faces to drink in the terror of the spectacle.

Lorrimer had out his notebook. "Damn fires!" he said. "They bore me. Does all this look like anything to you? That fire and those people and their silly faces all tilted up and turned red and blue and purple — "

He was talking to himself, and so, really, was Dickie when he made his own statement in a queer tone of frightened awe. "They look like a flower garden in Hell," he whispered.

Lorrimer threw up his chin. "Say that again, will you?" he snapped out. "Go on! Don't stop! Tell me everything that comes into your damn young head of a wandering Martian! Fly at it! I'll take you down."

"You mean," said Dickie, "tell you what I think this looks like?"

"That's what I mean, bo."

Dickie smiled a queer sort of smile. He had found a listener at last. A moment later Lorrimer's pencil was in rapid motion. And the reporter's eyes shot little stabbing looks at Dickie's unself-conscious face. When it was over he snapped an elastic round his notebook, returned it to his pocket, and laid his hand on Dickie's thin, tense arm.

"Come along with me, Dick," said Lorrimer. "You've won. I've been fighting you and my duty to my neighbor for a fortnight. Your waiter days are over. I've adopted you. I'm my brother's keeper all right. We'll both go hungry now and then probably, but what's the odds! I need you. I have n't been able to hand in a story like that for years. I'm a burnt-out candle and you're the divine fire. I'm going to educate the life out of you. I'm going to train you till you wish you'd died young and ungrammatical in Millings. I may not be much good myself," he added solemnly, "but God gave me the sense to know the real thing when I see it. I've been fighting you, calling myself a fool for weeks. Come along, young fellow, don't hang back, and for your credit's sake close your lips so you won't look like a case of arrested development. First we'll say good-bye to the hash-hole and the white apron and then I'll take you up to your sky parlor and we'll talk things over."

"God!" said Dickie faintly. It was a prayer for some enlightenment.

CHAPTER VIII

DESERTION

HILLIARD rode up along Hidden Creek on a frosty October morning. Everywhere now the aspens were torches of gold, the cottonwood trees smoky and gaunt, the ground bright with fallen leaves. He had the look of a man who has swept his heart clean of devils . . . his face was keen with his desire. He sang as he rode — sweetly an old sentimental Spanish song, something his mother had taught him; but it was not of his mother he thought, or only, perhaps, deep down in his subconsciousness, of that early mother-worship, age-old and most mysterious, which now he had translated and transferred.

> "Sweet, sweet is the jasmine flower —
> Let its stars guide thee.
> Sweet is the heart of a rose . . .
> Sweet is the thought of thee . . .
> Deep in my heart . . ."

The dogs were off coursing the woods that afternoon, and the little clearing lay as still as a green lake under the threatening crest of the mountain. Cosme slipped from his horse, pulled the reins over his head, and left him to graze at will.

Miss Blake opened the ranch-house door at his knock. She greeted him with a sardonic smile. "I

DESERTION 235

don't know whether you'll see your girl or not," she said. "Give her time to get over her tantrums."

Cosme turned a lightning look upon her. "Tantrums? Sheila?"

"Oh, my friend, she has a devil of her own, that little angel-face! Make yourself comfortable." Miss Blake pointed him to a chair. "I'll tell her you're here."

She went to the foot of the ladder, which rose from the middle of the living-room floor, and called heartily, an indulgent laugh in her voice, "You, Sheila! Better come down! Here's your beau."

There was no answer.

"Hear me, Sheila? Mis-ter Cos-me Hill-iard."

This time some brief and muffled answer was returned. Miss Blake smiled and went over to her elk-horn throne. There she sat and sewed — an incongruous occupation it looked.

Cosme was leaning forward, elbows on knees, his face a study of impatience, anger, and suspicion.

"What made her mad?" he asked bluntly.

"O-oh! She'll get over it. She'll be down. Sheila can't resist a young man. You'll see."

"What did you do?" insisted the stern, crisp, unwestern voice. When Cosme was angry he reverted rapidly to type.

"Why," drawled Miss Blake, "I crept up when she was drying her hair and I cut it off." She laughed loudly at his fierce start.

"Cut off her hair! What right — ?"

"No right at all, my friend, but common sense. What's the good of all that fluffy stuff hanging about and taking hours of her time to brush and wash and what-not. Besides" — she shot a look at him — "it's part of the cure."

"By the Lord," said Cosme, "I'd like you to explain."

The woman crossed her legs calmly. She was still indulgently amused.

"Don't lose your head, young man," she advised. "Better smoke."

After an instant Cosme rolled and lighted a cigarette and leaned back in his chair. His anger had settled to a sort of patient contempt.

"I've put her into breeches, too," said Miss Blake.

"What the devil! What do you mean? She has a will of her own, has n't she?"

"Oh, yes. But you see I've got Miss Sheila just about where I want her. She's grateful enough for her food and the roof over her head and for the chance I'm giving her."

"Chance?" He laughed shortly. "Chance to do all your heavy work?"

"Why not say *honest* work? It's something new to her."

There was a brief, thunderous silence. Cosme's cigarette burned between his stiff fingers. "What do you mean?" he asked, hoarse with the effort of his self-control.

DESERTION

She looked at him sharply now. "Are you Paul Carey Hilliard's son — the son of Roxana Hilliard?" she asked. She pointed a finger at him.

"Yes," he answered with thin lips. His eyes narrowed. His face was all Latin, all cruel.

"Well" — Miss Blake slid her hands reflectively back and forth on the bone arms of her chair. She had put down her work. "I was just thinking," she said slowly and kindly, "that the son of your mother would be rather extra careful in choosing the mother of his sons."

"I shall be very careful," he answered between the thin lips. "I *am* being careful."

She fell back with an air of relief. "Oh," she said, as though illuminated. "O-oh! I understand. Then it's all right. I did n't read your game."

His face caught fire at her apparent misunderstanding.

"I don't read yours," he said.

"Gamé? Bless you, I've no game to play. I'm giving Sheila her chance. But I'm not going to give her a chance at the cost of your happiness. You're too good a lad for that. I thought you were going to ask her to be your wife. And I was n't going to allow you to do it — blind. I was going to advise you to come back three years from now and see her again. Maybe this fine clean air and this life and this honest work and the training she gets from me will make her straight. My God! Cosme Hilliard, have you set eyes on Hudson? What kind of girl travels West from New York at Sylvester Hudson's expense and in his company and queens it in the suite at his hotel?"

"Miss Blake," he muttered, "do you *know* this?"

The cigarette had burnt itself out. Cosme's face was no longer cruel. It was dazed.

She laughed shortly. "Why, of course, I know Sheila. I know her whole history — and it's some history! She's twice the age she looks. Do you think I'd have her here with me this way without knowing the girl? I tell you, I want to give her a chance. I don't care if you try to test her out. I'd like to see if two months has done anything for her. She was real set on being a good girl when she quit Hudson. I don't *know*, but I'm willing to bet that she'll turn you down."

From far away up the mountain-side came the fierce baying of the dog pack. Cosme pulled himself together and stood up. His face had an ignorant, baffled look, the look of an unskilled and simple mind caught in a web.

"I reckon she — she is n't coming down," he said slowly, without lifting his eyes from the floor. "I reckon I'll be going. I won't wait."

He walked to the door, his steps falling without spring, and went out and so across the porch and the clearing to his horse.

At the sound of the closing door there came a flurry of movement in the loft. The trap was raised.

DESERTION

Sheila came quickly down the ladder. She was dressed in a pair of riding-breeches and her hair was cropped like Miss Blake's just below the ears. The quaintest rose-leaf of a Rosalind she looked, just a wisp of grace, utterly unlike a boy. All the soft, slim litheness with its quick turns revealed — a little figure of unconscious sweet enchantment. But the face was flushed and tear-stained, the eyes distressed. She stood, hands on her belt, at the foot of the ladder.

"Why has he gone? Why did n't he wait?"

Miss Blake turned a frank, indulgent face. But it was deeply flushed. "Oh, shucks!" she said, "I suppose he got tired. Why did n't you come down?"

Sheila sent a look down her slim legs. "Oh, because I *am* a fool. Miss Blake — did you *really* burn my two frocks — both of them?" Her eyes coaxed and filled.

"It's all they're fit for, my dear. You can make yourself new ones. You know it's more sensible and comfortable, too, to work and ride in breeches. I know what I'm doing, child. — I've lived this way quite a number of years. You look real nice. I can't abide female floppery, anyhow. What's it a sign of? Rotten slavery." She set her very even teeth together hard as she said this.

But Sheila was neither looking nor listening. She had heard horse's hoofs. Her cheeks flamed. She ran to the door. She stood on the porch and called.

"Cosme Hilliard! Come back!"

There was no answer. A few minutes later she came in, pale and puzzled.

"He didn't even wave," she said. "He turned back in his saddle and stared at me. He rode away staring at me. Miss Blake — what did you say to him? You were talking a long time."

"We were talking," said Miss Blake, "about dogs and how to raise 'em. And then he up and said good-bye. Oh, Sheila, it's all right. He'll be back when he's got over being miffed. Why, he expected you to come tumblin' down the ladder head over heels to see him — a handsome fellow like that! Shucks! Have n't you ever dealt with the vanity of a young male before? It's as jumpy as a rabbit. Get to work."

And, as though to justify Miss Blake's prophecy, just ten days later, Hilliard did come again. It was a Sunday and Sheila had packed her lunch and gone off on "Nigger Baby" for the day. The ostensible object of her ride was a visit to the source of Hidden Creek. Really she was climbing away from a hurt. She felt Hilliard's wordless departure and prolonged absence keenly. She had not — to put it euphemistically — many friends. Her remedy was successful. Impossible, on such a ride, to cherish minor or major pangs. She rode into the smoky dimness of pine-woods where the sunlight burned in flecks and out again across the little open mountain meadows, jeweled with white and gold, blue and coral-colored flowers, a stained-glass window scattered across the ground.

From these glades she could see the forest, an army of tall pilgrims, very grave, going up, with long staves in their hands, to worship at a high shrine. The rocks above were very grave, too, and grim and still against the even blue sky. Across their purplish gray a waterfall streaked down struck crystal by the sun. An eagle turned in great, swinging circles. Sheila had an exquisite lifting of heart, a sense of entire fusion, body blessed by spirit, spirit blessed by body. She felt a distinct pleasure in the flapping of her short, sun-filled hair against her neck, at the pony's motion between her unhampered legs, at the moist warmth of his neck under her hand — and this physical pleasure seemed akin to the ecstasy of prayer.

She came at last to a difficult, narrow, cañon trail, where the pony hopped skillfully over fallen trees, until, for very weariness of his choppy, determined efforts, she dismounted, tied him securely, and made the rest of her climb on foot. Hidden Creek tumbled near her and its voice swelled. All at once, round the corner of a great wall of rock, she came upon the head. It gushed out of the mountain-side in a tumult of life, not in a single stream, but in many frothy, writhing earth-snakes of foam. She sat for an hour and watched this mysterious birth from the mountain-side, watched till the pretty confusion of the water, with its half-interpreted voices, had dizzied and dazed her to the point of complete forgetfulness of self. She had entered into a sort of a trance, a

Nirvana... She shook herself out of it, ate her lunch and scrambled quickly back to "Nigger Baby." It was late afternoon when she crossed the mountain glades. Their look had mysteriously changed. There was something almost uncanny now about their brilliance in the sunset light, and when she rode into the streaked darkness of the woods, they were full of ghostly, unintelligible sounds. To rest her muscles she was riding with her right leg thrown over the horn as though on a side saddle — a great mass of flowers was tied in front of her. She had opened her shirt at the neck and her head was bare. She was singing to keep up her heart. Then, suddenly, she had no more need of singing. She saw Cosme walking toward her up the trail.

His face lacked all its vivid color. It was rather haggard and stern. The devils he had swept out of his heart a fortnight earlier had, since then, been violently entertained. He stepped out of the path and waited for her, his hands on his hips. But, as she rode down, she saw this look melt. The blood crept up to his cheeks, the light to his eyes. It was like a rock taking the sun. She had smiled at him with all the usual exquisite grace and simplicity. When she came beside him, she drew rein, and at the same instant he put his hand on the pony's bridle. He looked up at her dumbly, and for some reason she, too, found it impossible to speak. She could see that he was breathing fast through parted lips and that

DESERTION

the lips were both cruel and sensitive. His hand slid back along "Nigger Baby's" neck, paused, and rested on her knee. Then, suddenly, he came a big step closer, threw both his arms, tightening with a python's strength, about her and hid his face against her knees.

"Sheila," he said thickly. He looked up with a sort of anguish into her face. "Sheila, if you are not fit to be the mother of my children, you are *sure* fit for any man to love."

Her soft, slim body hardened against him even before her face. They stared at each other for a minute.

"Let me get down," said Sheila.

He stepped back, not quite understanding. She dropped off the horse, dragging her flowers with her, and faced him. She did not feel small or slender. She felt as high as a hill, although she had to look up at him so far. Her anger had its head against the sky.

"Why do you talk about a man's love?" she asked him with a queer sort of patience. "I think — I hope — that you don't know anything about a man's love, oh, the *way* men love!" She thought with swift pain of Jim, of Sylvester. "Oh, the *way* they love!" And she found that, under her breath, she was sobbing, "Dickie! Dickie!" as though her heart had called.

"Will you take back your horse, please?" she said, choking over these sobs which hurt her more at the moment than he had hurt her. "I'll never ride on him again. Don't come back here. Don't try to see me any more. I suppose it — it — the way you love me — is because I was a barmaid, because you heard people speak of me as 'Hudson's Queen.'" She conquered one of the sobs. "I thought that after you'd looked into my face so hard that night and stopped yourself from — from — my lips, that you had understood." She shook her head from side to side so violently, so childishly, that the short hair lashed across her eyes. "No one ever will understand!" She ran away from him and cried under her breath, "Dickie! Dickie!"

She ran straight into the living-room and stopped in the middle of the floor. Her arms were full of the flowers she had pulled down from "Nigger Baby's" neck.

"What did you want to bring in all that truck —?" Miss Blake began, rising from the pianola, then stopped. "What's the matter with you?" she asked. "Did your young man find you? I sent him up the trail." Her red eyes sparkled.

"He insulted me!" gasped Sheila. "He dared to insult me!" She was dramatic with her helpless young rage. "He said I was n't fit to — to be the mother of his children. And" — she laughed angrily, handling behind Cosme's back the weapon that she had been too merciful to use — "and *his* mother is a murderess, found guilty of murder — and of worse!"

A sort of ripple of sound behind made her turn.

DESERTION 245

Cosme had followed her, was standing in the open door, and had heard her speech. The weapon had struck home, and she saw how it had poisoned all his blood.

He vanished without a word. Sheila turned back to Miss Blake a paler face. She let fall all her flowers.

"Now he'll never come back," she said.

She climbed up the ladder to her loft.

There she sat for an hour, listening to the silence. Her mind busied itself with trivial memories. She thought of Amelia Plecks . . . It would have comforted her to hear that knock and the rattle of her dinner tray. The little sitting-room at Hudson's Hotel, with its bit of tapestry and its yellow tea-set and its vases filled with flowers, seemed to her memory as elaborate and artificial as the boudoir of a French princess. Farther than Millings had seemed from her old life did this dark little gabled attic seem from Millings. What was to be the end of this strange wandering, this withdrawing of herself farther and farther into the lonely places! She longed for the noise of Babe's hearty, irrepressible voice with its smack of chewing, of her step coming up the stairs to that little bedroom under Hudson's gaudy roof. Could it be possible that she was homesick for Millings? For the bar with its lights and its visitors and its big-aproned guardian? Her lids were actually smarting with tears at the recollection of Carthy's big Irish face . . . He had been such a good, faithful watch-dog. Were men always like that — either watch-dogs or wolves? The simile brought her back to Hidden Creek. It grew darker and darker, a heavy darkness; the night had a new soft weight. There began to be a sort of whisper in the stillness — not the motion of pines, for there was no wind. Perhaps it was more a sensation than a sound, of innumerable soft numb fingers working against the silence . . . Sheila got up, shivering, lighted her candle, and went over to the small, four-paned window under the eaves. She pressed her face against it and started back. Things were flying toward her. She opened the sash and a whirling scarf of stars flung itself into the room. It was snowing. The night was blind with snow.

CHAPTER IX

Work and a Song

On the studio skylight the misty autumn rain fell that night, as the snow fell against Sheila's windowpanes, with a light tapping. Below it Dickie worked. He had very little leisure now for stars or dreams. For the first time in his neglected and mismanaged life he knew the pleasure of congenial work; and this, although Lorrimer worked him like a slave. He dragged him over the city and set his picture-painting faculty to labor in dark corners. Dickie, every sense keen and clean, was not allowed to flinch. No, his freshness was his value. And the power that was in him, driven with whip and spur, throve and grew and fairly took the bit in its teeth and ran away with its trainer.

"Look here, my lad," Lorrimer had said that morning, "you keep on laying hands on the English language the way you've been doing lately and I'll have to get a job for you on the staff. Then my plagiarism that has been paying us both so well comes to an end. I won't have the face to edit stuff like this much longer." Lorrimer did not realize in his amazement that Dickie's mind had always busied itself with this exciting and nerve-racking matter of choosing words. From his childhood, in the face of ridicule and outrage, he had fumbled with the tools of Lorrimer's trade. No wonder that now knowledge and practice, and the sort of intensive training he was under, magically fitted all the jumbled odds and ends into place. Dickie had stopped looking over his shoulder. The pursuing pack, the stealthy-footed beasts of the city, had dropped utterly from his flying imagination. There was only one that remained faithful — that craving for beauty — half-god, half-beast. Against him Dickie still pressed his door shut. Lorrimer's gift of work had not quieted the leader of the pack. But it had brought Dickie something that was nearly happiness. The very look of him had changed: he looked driven rather than harried, keen rather than harassed, eager instead of vague, hungry rather than wistful. Only, sometimes, Dickie's brain would suddenly turn blank and blind from sheer exhaustion. This happened to him now. The printed lines he was studying lost all their meaning. He put his forehead on his hands. Then he heard that eerie, light tapping above him on the skylight. But he was too tired to look up.

It was on that very afternoon when Sheila rode down the trail with her flowers tied before her on the saddle, singing to keep up her heart. It was that very afternoon when she had cried out half-consciously for "Dickie — Dickie — Dickie" — and now it was, as though the cry had traveled, that a memory of her leapt upon his mind; a memory of Sheila singing.

WORK AND A SONG

She had come into the chocolate-colored lobby from one of her rides with Jim Greely. She had held a handful of cactus flowers. She had stopped over there by one of the windows to put them in a glass. And to show Dickie, a prisoner at his desk, that she did not consider his presence — it was during the period of their estrangement — she had sung softly as a girl sings when she knows herself to be alone: a little tender, sad chanting song, that seemed made to fit her mouth. The pain her singing had given him that afternoon had cut a picture of her on Dickie's brain. Just because he had tried so hard not to look at her. Now it jumped out at him against his closed, wet lids. The very motions of her mouth came back, the positive dear curve of her chin, the throat there slim against the light. Hard work had driven her image a little from his mind lately; it returned now to revenge his self-absorption — returned with a song.

Dickie got up and wandered about the room. He tried to hum the air, but his throat contracted. He tried to whistle, but his lips turned stiff. He bent over his book — no use, she still sang. All night he was tormented by that chanting, hurting song. He sobbed with the hurt of it. He tossed about on his bed. He could not but remember how little she had loved him. All at once there came to him a mysterious and beautiful release. It seemed that the cool spirit, detached, winged, drew him to itself or became itself entirely possessed of him. He was taken out of his pain and yet he understood it. And he began suddenly, easily, to put it into words. The misery was ecstasy, the hurt was inspiration, the song sang sweetly as though it had been sung to soothe and not to make him suffer.

"Oh, little song you sang to me" —

Ah, yes, at heart she had been singing to him —

> "A hundred, hundred days ago,
> Oh, little song, whose melody
> Walks in my heart and stumbles so;
> I cannot bear the level nights,
> And all the days are over-long,
> And all the hours from dark to dark
> Turn to a little song . . ."

Dickie, not knowing how he got there, was at his table again. He was writing. He was happy beyond any conception he had ever had of happiness. That there was agony in his happiness only intensified it. The leader of the wolf-pack, beast with a god's face, the noblest of man's desires, that passionate and humble craving for beauty, had him by the throat.

So it was that Dickie wrote his first poem.

CHAPTER X
WINTER

WINTER snapped at Hidden Creek as a wolf snaps, but held its grip as a bulldog holds his. There came a few November days when all the air and sky and tree-tops were filled with summer again, but the snow that had poured itself down so steadily in that October storm did not give way. It sank a trifle at noon and covered itself at night with a glare of ice. It was impossible to go anywhere except on snow-shoes. Sheila quickly learned the trick and plodded with bent knees, limber ankles, and wide-apart feet through the winter miracle of the woods. It was another revelation of pure beauty, but her heart was too sore to hold the splendor as it had held the gentler beauty of summer and autumn. Besides, little by little she was aware of a vague, encompassing uneasiness. Since the winter jaws had snapped them in, setting its teeth between them and all other life, Miss Blake had subtly and gradually changed. It was as though her stature had increased, her color deepened. Sometimes to Sheila that square, strong body seemed to fill the world. She was more and more masterful, quicker with her orders, charier of her smiles, shorter of speech and temper. Her eyes seemed to grow redder, the sparks closer to flame, as though the intense cold fanned them.

Once they harnessed the dogs to the sled and rode down the country for the mail. The trip they made together. Sheila sat wrapped in furs in front of the broad figure of her companion, who stood at the back of the sledge, used a long whip, and shouted to the dogs by name in her great musical voice of which the mountain echo made fine use. They sped close to the frozen whiteness of the world, streaked down the slopes, and were drawn soundlessly through the columned vistas of the woods. Here, there, and everywhere were tracks, of coyotes, fox, rabbit, martin, and the little pointed patteran of winter birds, yet they saw nothing living. "What's got the elk and moose this season?" muttered Miss Blake. Nothing stirred except the soft plop of shaken snow or the little flurry of drifting flakes. These frost-flakes lay two inches deep on the surface of the snow, dry and distinct all day in the cold so that they could be blown apart at a breath. Miss Blake was cheerful on this journey. She sang songs, she told brief stories of other sled trips. At the post-office an old, lonely man delivered them some parcels and a vast bagful of magazines. There was a brief passage of arms between him and Miss Blake. She accused him of withholding a box of cartridges, and would not be content till she had poked about his office in dark corners. She came out swearing at the failure of

WINTER

her search. "I needed that shot," she said. "My supply is short. I made sure it'd be here to-day." There were no letters for either of them, and Sheila felt again that queer shiver of her loneliness. But, on the whole, it was a wonderful day, and, under a world of most amazing stars, the small, valiant ranch-house, with its glowing stove and its hot mess of supper, felt like home.... Not long after that came the first stroke of fate.

The little old horse left them and, though they shoed patiently for miles following his track, it was only to find his bones gnawed clean by coyotes or by wolves. Sheila's tears froze to her lashes, but Miss Blake's face went a little pale. She said nothing, and in her steps Sheila plodded home in silence. That evening Miss Blake laid hands on her.... They had washed up their dishes. Sheila was putting a log on the fire. It rolled out of her grasp to the bearskin rug and struck Miss Blake's foot. Before Sheila could even say her quick "I'm sorry," the woman had come at her with a sort of spring, had gripped her by the shoulders, had shaken her with ferocity, and let her go. Sheila fell back, her own hands raised to her bruised shoulders, her eyes phosphorescent in a pale face.

"Miss Blake, how dare you touch me!"

The woman kicked back the log, turned a red face, and laughed.

"Dare! You little silly! What's to scare me of you?"

An awful conviction of helplessness depressed Sheila's heart, but she kept her eyes leveled on Miss Blake's.

"Do you suppose I will stay here with you one hour, if you treat me like this?"

That brought another laugh. But Miss Blake was evidently trying to make light of her outbreak. "Scared you, did n't I?" she said. "I guess you never got much training, eh!"

"I am not a dog," said Sheila shortly.

"Well, if you are n't" — Miss Blake returned to her chair and took up a magazine. She put the spectacles on her nose with shaking hands. "You're my girl, are n't you? You can't expect to get nothing but petting from me, Sheila."

If she had not been icy with rage, Sheila might have smiled at this. "I don't know what you mean, Miss Blake, by my being your girl. I work for you, to be sure. I know that. But I know, too, that you will have to apologize to me for this."

Miss Blake swung one leg across the other and stared above her glasses.

"Apologize to *you!*"

"Yes. I will allow nobody to touch me."

"Shucks! Go tell that to the marines! You've never been touched, have you? Sweet sixteen!"

Hudson's kiss again scorched Sheila's mouth and her whole body burned. Miss Blake watched that fire consume her, and again she laughed.

WINTER

"I'm waiting for you to apologize," said Sheila again, this time between small set teeth.

"Well, my girl, wait. That'll cool you off."

Sheila stood and felt the violent beating of her heart. A log in the wall snapped from the bitter frost.

"Miss Blake," she said presently, a pitiful young quaver in her voice, "if you don't beg my pardon I'll go to-morrow."

Miss Blake flung her book down with a gesture of impatience. "Oh, quit your nonsense, Sheila!" she said. "What's a shaking! You know you can't get out of here. It'd take you a week to get anywhere at all except into a frozen supper for the coyotes. Your beau's left the country — Madder told me at the post-office. Make the best of it, Sheila. Lucky if you don't get worse than that before spring. You'll get used to me in time, get broken in and learn my ways. I'm not half bad, but I've got to be obeyed. I've got to be master. That's me. What do you think I've come 'way out here to the wilderness for, if not because I can't stand anything less than being master? Here I've got my place and my dogs and a world that don't talk back. And now I've got you for company and to do my work. You've got to fall into line, Sheila, right in the ranks. Once, some one out there in the world" — she made a gesture, dropped her chin on her big chest, and looked out under her short, dense, rust-colored eyelashes — "tried to break *me*. I won't tell you what he got. That's where I quit the ways of women — yes, ma'am, and the ways of men." She stood up and walked over to the window and looked out. The dogs were sleeping in their kennels, but a chain rattled. "I've broke the wolf-pack. You've seen them wriggle on their bellies for me, have n't you? Well, my girl, do you think I can't break you?" She wheeled back and stood with her hands on her hips. It was at that moment that she seemed to fill the world. Her ruddy eyes glowed like blood. They were not quite sane. That was it. Sheila went suddenly weak. They were not *quite* sane — those red eyes filled with sparks.

The girl stepped back and sat down in her chair. She bent forward, pressed her hands flat together, palm to palm between her knees, and stared fixedly down at them. She made no secret of her desperate preoccupation.

Miss Blake's face softened a little at this withdrawal. She came back to her place and resumed her spectacles.

"I'll tell you why I'm snappy," she said presently. "I'm scared."

This startled Sheila into a look. Miss Blake was moistening her lips. "That horse — you know — the coyotes got him. I guess he went down and they fell upon him. Well, he was to feed the dogs with until I could get my winter meat."

"What do you mean?"

"That's what I buy 'em for. Little old horses, for a

WINTER

couple of bits, and work 'em out and shoot 'em for dog-feed. Well, Sheila, when they're fed, they're dogs. But when they're starved — they're wolves ... And I can't think what's come to the elk this year. To-morrow I'll take out my little old gun."

To-morrow and the next day and the next she took her gun and strapped on her shoes and went out for all day long into the cold. Each time she came back more exhausted and more fierce. Sheila would have her supper ready and waiting sometimes for hours.

"The dogs have scared 'em off," said Miss Blake. "That must be the truth." She let the pack hunt for itself at night, and they came back sometimes with bloody jaws. But the prey must have been small, for they were not satisfied. They grew more and more gaunt and wolfish. They would howl for hours, wailing and yelping in ragged cadence to the stars. Table-scraps and brews of Indian meal vanished and left their bellies almost as empty as before.

"And," said Miss Blake, "we got to eat, ourselves."

"Had n't we better go down to the post-office or to Rusty?" Sheila asked nervously.

Miss Blake snapped at her. "Harness that team now? As much as your life is worth, Sheila! And we can't make it on foot. We'd drop in our tracks and freeze. If it comes to the worst we may have to try it, but — oh, I'll get something to-morrow."

But to-morrow brought no better luck. During the

hunting the dogs were left on their chains, and Sheila, through the lonely hours, would watch them through the window and could almost see the wolfishness grow in their deep, wild eyes. She would try to talk to them, pat them, coax them into doggy-ness. But day by day they responded more unwillingly. All but Berg: Berg stayed with her in the house, lay on her feet, leaned against her knee. He shared her meals. He was beginning to swing his heart from Miss Blake to her, and this was the second cause for strife.

Since that one outbreak, Sheila had gone carefully. She was dignified, aloof, very still. She obeyed and slaved as she had never done in the summer days. The dread of physical violence hung on her brain like a cloud. She encouraged Berg's affection, and wondered, if it came to a struggle, whether he would side with her. She was given the opportunity to put this matter to the test.

Miss Blake was very late that night. It was midnight, a stark midnight of stars and biting cold, when Berg stood up from his sleep and barked his low, short bark of welcome. Outside the other dogs broke into their clamor, drowning all other sound, and in the midst of it the door flew rudely open. Miss Blake stood and clung to the side of the door. Her face was bluish-white. She put out her hand toward Sheila, clutching the air. Sheila ran over to her.

"You're hurt?"

"Twisted my blamed ankle. God!" She hobbled

over, a heavy arm round Sheila, to her chair and sat there while the girl gave her some brandy, removed the snowshoes, and cut away the boot from a swollen and discolored leg.

"That's the end of my hunting," grunted the patient, who bore the agony of rubbing and bathing stoically. "And, I reckon, I could n't have stood much more." She clenched her hand in Berg's mane. "God! Those dogs! I'll have to shoot them — next." Sheila looked up to her with a sort of horrified hope. There was then a way out from that fear.

"I'd rather die, I think," said the woman hoarsely. "I love those dogs." Sheila looked up into a tender and quivering face — the face of a mother. "They mean something to me — those brutes. I guess I kind of centered my heart on 'em — out here alone. I raised 'em up, from puppies, all but Berg and the mother. They were the cutest little fellows. I remember when Wreck got porcupine quills in his nose and came to me and lay on his back and whined to me. It was as if he said, 'Help me, momma.' Sure it was. And he pretty near died. Oh, damn! If I have to shoot 'em I might just as well shoot myself and be done with it . . . Thanks, Sheila. I'll eat my supper here and then you can help me to bed. When my ankle's all well, we can have a try for the post-office, perhaps." She leaned back and drew Berg roughly up against her. She caressed him. He made little soft, throaty sounds of tenderness.

Sheila came back with a tray and, as she came, Berg pulled himself away from his mistress and went wagging over to greet her.

"Come here!" snapped Miss Blake. Berg hesitated, cuddled close to Sheila, and kept step beside her.

Miss Blake's eyes went red. "Come here!" she said again. Berg did not cringe or hasten. He reached Miss Blake's chair at the same instant as Sheila, not a moment earlier.

Miss Blake pulled herself up. The tray went shattering to the floor. She hobbled over to the fire, white with the anguish, took down the whip from its nail. At that Berg cringed and whined. The woman fell upon him with her terrible lash. She held herself with one hand on the mantel-shelf, while with the other she scored the howling victim. His fur came off his back under the dreadful, knife-edge blows.

"Oh, stop!" cried Sheila. "Stop! You're killing him!" She ran over and caught Miss Blake's arm.

"Damn you!" said the woman fiercely. She stood breathing fast. Sweat of pain and rage and exertion stood out on her face. "Do *you* want that whip?"

She half-turned, lifting her lash, and at that, with a snarl, Berg crouched himself and bared his teeth.

Miss Blake started and stared at him. Suddenly she gave in. Pain and anger twisted her spirit.

"You'd turn my Berg against me!" she choked, and fell heavily down on the rug in a dead faint.

WINTER

When she came to she was grim and silent. She got herself with scant help to bed, her big bed in the corner of the living-room, and for a week she was kept there with fever and much pain. Berg lay beside her or followed Sheila about her work, and the woman watched them both with ruddy eyes.

CHAPTER XI
THE PACK

IN January a wind blew steadily from the east and snow came as if to bury them alive. The cabin turned to a cave, a small square of warmth under a mountain of impenetrable white; one door and one window only, opening to a space of sun. Against the others the blank white lids of winter pressed. Sheila shoveled this space cut sometimes twice a day. The dog kennels were moved into it, and stood against the side of a snow-bank eight feet high, up which, when they were unchained, the gaunt, wolfish animals leapt in a loosely formed pack, the great mother, Brenda, at their head, and padded off into the silent woods in their hungry search for food.

But, one day, they refused to go. Miss Blake, her whip in her hand, limped out. The snow had stopped. The day was still and bright again above the snowy firs, the mountain scraped against the blue sky like a cliff of broken ice. The dogs had crept out of their houses and were squatted or huddled in the sun. As she came out they rose and strained at their tethers. One of them whined. Brenda, the mother, bared her teeth. One by one, as they were freed, they slunk close to Miss Blake, looking up into her face. They crowded close at her heels as she went back to the

THE PACK 263

house. She had to push the door to in their very jaws and they pressed against it, their heads hung low, sniffing the odor of food. Presently a long-drawn, hideous howling rose from them. Time and again Miss Blake drove them away with lash and voice. Time and again they came back. They scratched at the threshold, whimpered, and whined.

Sheila and Miss Blake gave them what food they would have eaten themselves that day. It served only to excite their restlessness, to hold them there at the crack of the door, snuffling and slobbering. The outer circle slept, the inner watched. Then they would shift, like sentries. They had a horrible sort of system. Most of that dreadful afternoon Miss Blake paced the floor, trying to strengthen her ankle for the trip to the post-office. At sunset, when the small snow-banked room was nearly dark, she stopped, threw up her head, and looked at Sheila. The girl was sitting on the lowest step of the ladder washing some dried apples. Her face had thinned to a silvery wedge between the thick square masses of her hair. There was a haunted look in her clear eyes. The soft mouth had tightened.

"How in God's name," said Miss Blake, "shall I get 'em on their chains again?"

Sheila stopped her work, and her lips fell helplessly apart. She looked up at the older woman and shook her head.

Miss Blake's fear snapped into a sort of frenzy.

She gritted her teeth and stamped. "You simpleton!" she said. "You never have a notion in your head."

Sheila stood up quickly. Something told her that she had better be on her feet. She kept very still. "You will know better than I could what to do about the dogs," she said quietly. "They'll go back on their chains for you, I should think. They're afraid of you."

"Are n't you?" Miss Blake asked roughly.

"No. Of course not."

"You little liar! You're scared half out of your wits. You're scared of the whole thing — scared of the snow, scared of the cold, scared of the dogs, and scared sick of me. Come, now. Tell me the truth."

It was almost her old bluff, bullying tone, but back of it was a disorder of stretched nerves. Sheila weighed her words and tried to weigh her thoughts.

"I don't think I am afraid, Miss Blake. Why should I be afraid of the dogs, if you are n't? And why should I be afraid of you? You have been good to me. You are a good woman."

At this Miss Blake threw back her head and laughed. She was terribly like one of the dogs howling. There was something wild and wolfish in her broad neck and in the sound she made. And she snapped back into silence with wolfish suddenness.

"If you're not scared, then," she scoffed, "go and chain up the dogs yourself."

THE PACK 265

For an instant Sheila quite calmly balanced the danger out of doors against the danger within.

"I think," she said — and managed one of her drifting smiles — "I think I am a great deal more afraid of the dogs than I am of you, Miss Blake."

The woman studied her for a minute in silence, then she walked over to her elk-horn throne and sat down on it.

She leaned back in a royal way and spread her dark broad hands across the arms.

"Well," she said coolly, "did you hear what I said? Go out and chain up the dogs!"

Sheila held herself like a slim little cavalier. "If I go out," she said coolly, "I will not take a whip. I'll take a gun."

"And shoot my dogs?"

"Miss Blake, what else is left for us to do? We can't let them claw down the door and tear us into bits, can we?"

"You'd shoot my dogs?"

"You said yourself that we might have to shoot them."

Miss Blake gave her a stealthy and cunning look. "Take my gun, then" — her voice rose to a key that was both crafty and triumphant — "and much good it will do you! There's shot enough to kill one if you are a first-rate shot. I lost what was left of my ammunition the day I hurt my ankle. The new stuff is down at the post-office by now, I guess."

The long silence was filled by the shifting of the dog-watch outside the door.

"We must chain them up at any cost," said Sheila. Her lips were dry and felt cold to her tongue.

"Go out and do it, then." The mistress of the house leaned back and crossed her ankles.

"Miss Blake, be reasonable. You have a great deal of control over the dogs and I have none. I *am* afraid of them and they will know it. Animals always know when you're afraid . . ." Again she managed a smile. "I shall begin to think you are a coward," she said.

At that Miss Blake stood up from her chair. Her face was red with a violent rush of blood and the sparks in her eyes seemed to have broken into flame.

"Very good, Miss," she said brutally. "I'll go out and chain 'em up and then I'll come back and thrash you to a frazzle. Then you'll know how to obey my orders next time."

She caught up her whip, swung it in her hand, and strode to the door.

"And mind you, Sheila, you won't be able to hide yourself from me. Nor make a getaway. I'll lock this door outside and winter's locked the other. You wait. You'll see what you'll get for calling me a coward. Your friend Berg's gone off on a long hunt . . . he's left his friends outside there and he's left you . . . Understand?"

She shouted roughly to the dogs, snapped her whip, threw open the door, and stepped out boldly. She

THE PACK 267

shut the door behind her and shot a bolt. It creaked as though it had grown rusty with disuse.

In the stillness — for, except for a quick shuffling of paws, there was no sound at first — Sheila chose her weapon of defense. She took down from its place the Eskimo ivory spear, and, holding it short in her hand, she put herself behind the great elk-horn chair. Her Celtic blood was pounding gloriously now. She was not afraid; though if there had been time to notice it, she would have confessed to an abysmal sense of horror and despair. And again she wondered at her own loneliness and youth and the astounding danger that she faced. Yes, it was more astonishment than any other emotion that possessed her consciousness. The horror was below the threshold practicing its part.

Then anger, astonishment, horror itself were suddenly thrown out of her. She was left like an empty vessel waiting to be filled with fear. Miss Blake had cried aloud, "Help, Sheila! Help!" This was followed by a dreadful screaming. Sheila dropped her spear and leapt to the door. On it, outside, Miss Blake beat and screamed, "Open, for God's sake!"

Sheila shouted in as dreadful a key. "On your side — the bolt! Miss Blake — the bolt!"

Fingers clawed at the bolt, but it would not slip. Through all the horrible sounds the woman made, Sheila could hear the snarling and leaping and snapping of the dogs. She dashed to the small, tight window, broke a pane with her fist, and thrust out her arm. She meant to reach the bolt, but what she saw took the warm life out of her. Miss Blake had gone down under the whirling, slobbering pack. The screaming had stopped. In that one awful look the poor child saw that no human help could save. She dropped down on the floor and lay there moaning, her hands pressed over her ears . . .

So she lay, shuddering and gasping, the great part of the night. At last the intense cold drove her to the fire. She heaped up the logs high and hung close above them. Her very heart was cold. Liquid ice moved sluggishly along her veins. The morning brought no comfort or courage to her, only a freshening of horror and of fear. The dogs had gone, and all the winter world lay still about the house.

She was shaken by a regular pulse of nervous sobbing. But, driven by a sort of restlessness, she made herself coffee and forced some food down her contracted throat. Then she put on her coat, took down Miss Blake's six-shooter and cartridge belt, and saw, with a slight relaxing of the cramp about her heart, that there were four shots in the chamber. Four shots and eight dogs, but — at least — she could save herself from *that* death! She strapped the gun round her slim hips, filled her pockets with supplies — a box of dried raisins, some hard bread, a cake of chocolate, some matches — pulled her cap down over her ears, and took her snowshoes from the wall. With closed eyes she put her arm out through the broken pane, and, after a short struggle, slipped the rusty bolt. Then she went over to the door and, leaning against it, prayed. Even with the mysterious strength she drew from that sense of kinship with a superhuman Power, it was a long time before she could force herself to open. At last, with a big gasp, she flung the door wide, skirted the house, her hands against the logs, her eyes shut, ran across the open space, scrambled up the drift, tied on her snowshoes, and fled away under the snow-laden pines. There moved in all the wilderness that day no more hunted and fearful a thing.

The fresh snow sunk a little under her webs, but she was a featherweight of girlhood, and made quicker and easier progress than would have been possible to any one else but a child. And her fear gave her both strength and speed. Sometimes she looked back over her shoulder; always she strained her ears for the pad of following feet. It was a day of rainbows and of diamond spray, where the sun struck the shaken snow sifted from overweighted branches. Sheila remembered well enough the route to the post-office. It meant miles of weary plodding, but she thought that she could do it before night. If not, she would travel by starlight and the wan reflection of the snow. There was no darkness in these clear, keen nights. She would not tell herself what gave her strength such impetus. She thought resolutely of the post-office, of the old, friendly man, of his stove, of his chairs and his picture of the President, of his gun laid across two nails against his kitchen wall — all this, not more than eighteen miles away! And she thought of Hilliard, too; of his young strength and the bold young glitter of his eyes.

She stopped for a minute at noon to drink some water from Hidden Creek and to eat a bite or so of bread. She was pulling on her gloves again when a distant baying first reached her ears. She turned faint, seemed to stand in a mist; then, with her teeth set defiantly, she started again, faster and steadier, her body bent forward, her head turned back. Before her now lay a great stretch of undulating, unbroken white. At its farther edge the line of blue-black pines began again. She strained her steps to reach this shelter. The baying had been very faint and far away — it might have been sounded for some other hunting. She would make the woods, take off her webs, climb up into a tree and, perhaps, attracted by those four shots — no, three, she must save one — some trapper, some unimaginable wanderer in the winter forest, would come to her and rescue her before the end. So her mind twisted itself with hope. But, an hour later, with the pines not very far away, the baying rose so close behind that it stopped her heart. Twenty minutes had passed when above a rise of ground she saw the shaggy, trotting black-gray body of Brenda, the leader of the pack. She was running slowly, her nose close to the snow, casting a little right and left over the tracks. Sheila counted eight — Berg, then, had joined them. She thought that she could distinguish him in the rear. It was now late afternoon, and the sun slanted driving back the shadows of the nearing trees, of Sheila, of the dogs. It all seemed fantastic — the weird beauty of the scene, the weird horror of it. Sheila reckoned the distance before her, reckoned the speed of the dogs. She knew now that there was no hope. Ahead of her rose a sharp, sudden slope — she could never make it. There came to her quite suddenly, like a gift, a complete release from fear. She stopped and wheeled. It seemed that the brutes had not yet seen her. They were nose down at the scent. One by one they vanished in a little dip of ground, one by one they reappeared, two yards away. Sheila pulled out her gun, deliberately aimed and fired.

A spurt of snow showed that she had aimed short. But the loud, sudden report made Brenda swerve. All the dogs stopped and slunk together circling, their haunches lowered. Wreck squatted, threw up his head, and howled. Sheila spoke to them, clear and loud, her young voice ringing out into that loneliness.

"You Berg! Good dog! Come here."

One of the shaggy animals moved toward her timidly, looking back, pausing. Brenda snarled.

"Berg, come here, boy!"

Sheila patted her knee. At this the big dog whined,

cringed, and began to swarm up the slope toward her on his belly. His eyes shifted, the struggle of his mind was pitifully visible — pack-law, pack-power, the wolf-heart and the wolf-belly, and against them that queer hunger for the love and the touch of man. Sheila could not tell if it were hunger or loyalty that was creeping up to her in the body of the beast. She kept her gun leveled on him. When he had come to within two feet of her, he paused. Then, from behind him rose the starved baying of his brothers. Sheila looked up. They were bounding toward her, all wolf these — but more dangerous after their taste of human blood than wolves — to the bristling hair along their backs and the bared fangs. Again she fired. This time she struck Wreck's paw. He lifted it and howled. She fired again. Brenda snapped sideways at her shoulder, but was not checked. There was one shot left. Sheila knew how it must be used. Quickly she turned the muzzle up toward her own head.

Then behind her came a sharp, loud explosion. Brenda leapt high into the air and fell at Sheila's feet. At that first rifle-shot, Berg fled with shadow swiftness through the trees. For the rest, it was as though a magic wall had stopped them, as though, at a certain point, they fell upon death. Crack, crack, crack — one after another, they came up, leapt, and dropped, choking and bleeding on the snow. At the end Sheila turned blindly. A yard behind her and slightly above her there under the pines stood Hilliard, very pale, his gun tucked under his arm, the smoking muzzle lowered. Weakly she felt her way up toward him, groping with her hands.

He slid down noiselessly on his long skis and she stood clinging to his arm, looking up dumbly into his strained face.

"I heard your shots," he said breathlessly. "You're within a hundred yards of my house . . . For months I've been trying to make up my mind to come to you. God forgive me, Sheila, for not coming before!"

Swinging his gun on its strap across his shoulder, he lifted her in his arms, and, like a child, she was carried through the silence of the woods, all barred with blood-red glimmers from a setting sun.

CHAPTER XII
The Good Old World Again

HILLIARD carried Sheila into the house that he had built for her and laid her down in that big bedroom that "got the morning sun." For a while it seemed to him that she would never open her eyes again, and when she did regain consciousness she was so prostrate with her long fear and the shock of Miss Blake's death that she lay there too weak to smile or speak, too weak almost to breathe. Hilliard turned nurse, a puzzled, anxious nurse. He would sit up in his living-room half the night, and when sleep overpowered his anxiety he would fall prone on the elk-hide rug before his fire.

At last Sheila pulled herself up and crept about the house. She spent a day in the big log chair before Hilliard's hearth, looking very wan, shrinking from speech, her soft mouth gray and drawn.

"Are n't you ever going to smile for me again?" he asked her, after a long half-hour during which he had stood as still as stone, his arm along the pine mantel-shelf, looking at her from the shelter of a propping hand.

She lifted her face to him and made a pitiful effort enough. But it brought tears. They ran down her cheeks, and she leaned back and closed her lids, but the crystal drops forced themselves out, clung to her lashes, and fell down on her clenched hands. Hilliard went over to her and took the small, cold hands in both of his.

"Tell me about what happened, Sheila," he begged her. "It will help."

Word by difficult word, he still holding fast to her hands, she sobbed and gasped out her story, to which he listened with a whitening face. He gripped her hands tighter, then, toward the end, he rose with a sharp oath, lit his cigarette, paced to and fro.

"God!" he said at the last. "And she told you I had gone from the country! The devil! I can't help saying it, Sheila — she tortured you. She deserved what God sent her."

"Oh, no!" — Sheila rocked to and fro — "no one could deserve such dreadful terror and pain. She — she was n't sane. I was — foolish to trust her . . . I am so foolish — I think I must be too young or too stupid for — for all this. I thought the world would be a much safer place." She looked up again, and speech had given her tormented nerves relief, for her eyes were much more like her own, clear and young again. "Mr. Hilliard — what shall I do with my life, I wonder? I've lost my faith and trustingness. I'm horribly afraid."

He stood before her and spoke in a gentle and reasonable tone. "I'll tell you the answer to that, ma'am," he said. "I've thought that all out while I've been taking care of you."

She waited anxiously with parted lips.

"Well, ma'am, you see — it's like this. I'm plumb ashamed of myself through and through for the way I have acted toward you. I was a fool to listen to that dern lunatic. She told me — lies about you."

"Miss Blake did?"

"Yes, ma'am." His face crimsoned under her look.

Sheila closed her eyes and frowned. A faint pink stole up into her face. She lifted her lids again and he saw the brightness of anger. "And, of course, you took her lies for the truth?"

"Oh, damn! Now you're mad with me and you won't listen to my plan!"

He was so childish in this outbreak that Sheila was moved to dim amusement. "I'm too beaten to be angry at anything," she said. "Just tell me your plan."

"No," he said sullenly. "I'll wait. I'm scared to tell you now!"

She did not urge him, and it was not till the next morning that he spoke about his plan. She had got out to her chair again and had made a pretense of eating an ill-cooked mess of canned stuff which he had brought to her on a tray. It was after he had taken this breakfast away that he broke out as though his excitement had forced a lock.

"I'm going down to Rusty to-day," he said. His

THE GOOD OLD WORLD AGAIN 277

eyes were shining. He looked at her boldly enough now.

"And take me?" Sheila half-started up. "And take me?"

"No, ma'am. You're to stay here safe and snug." She dropped back. "I'll leave everything handy for you. There's enough food here for an army and enough fuel . . . You're as safe here as though you were at the foot of God's throne. Don't look like that, girl. I can't take you. You're not strong enough to make the journey in this cold, even on a sled. And we can't" — his voice sunk and his eyes fell — "we can't go on like this, I reckon."

"N-no." Sheila's forehead was puckered. Her fingers trembled on the arms of her chair. "N-no . . ." Then, with a sort of quaver, she added, "Oh, why can't we go on like this? — till the snow goes and I can travel with you!"

"Because," he said roughly, "we can't. You take my word for it." After a pause he went on in his former decisive tone. "I'll be back in two or three days. I'll fetch the parson."

Sheila sat up straight.

His eyes held hers. "Yes, ma'am. The parson. I'm going to marry you, Sheila."

She repeated this like a lesson. "You are going to marry me . . ."

"Yes, ma'am. You'll have three days to think it over. If you don't want to marry me when the parson

comes, why, you can just go back to Rusty with him."
He laughed a little, came over to her, put a hand on
each arm of her chair, and bent down. She shrank
back before him. His eyes had the glitter of a hawk's,
and his red and beautiful lips were soft and eager and
— again — a little cruel.

"No," he said, "I won't kiss you till I come back
— not even for good-bye. Then you'll know how I
feel about you. You'll know that I believe that you're
a good girl and, Sheila" — here he seemed to melt
and falter before her: he slipped down with one of his
graceful Latin movements and hid his forehead on
her knees — "Sheila, my *darling* — that I know you
are fit — oh, so much more than fit — to be the
mother of my children . . ."

In half an hour, during which they were both profoundly silent, he came to her again. He was ready
for his journey. She was sitting far back in her chair,
her slim legs stretched out. She raised inscrutable
eyes wide to his.

"Good-bye," he said softly. "It's hard to leave
you. Good-bye."

She said good-bye even more softly with no change
in her look. And he went out, looking at her over his
shoulder till the last second. She heard the voice of
his skis, hissing across the hard crust of the snow.
She sat there stiff and still till the great, wordless
silence settled down again. Then she started up from
her chair, ran across to the window, and saw that he

was indeed gone. She came storming back and threw herself down upon the hide. She cried like a deserted child.

"Oh, Cosme, I'm afraid to be alone! I'm afraid! Why did I let you go? Come back! Oh, please come back!"

It was late that night when Hilliard reached Rusty, traveling with all his young strength across the easy, polished surface of the world. He was dog-tired. He went first to the saloon. Then to the post-office. To his astonishment he found a letter. It was postmarked New York and he recognized the small, cramped hand of the family lawyer. He took the letter up to his bedroom in the Lander Hotel and sat on the bed, turning the square envelope about in his hands. At last, he opened it.

MY DEAR COSME [the lawyer had written ... he had known Hilliard as a child], It is my strong hope that this letter will reach you promptly and safely at the address you sent me. Your grandfather's death, on the fifteenth instant, leaves you, as you are no doubt aware, heir to his fortune, reckoned at about thirty millions. If you will wire on receipt of this and follow wire in person as soon as convenient, it will greatly facilitate arrangements. It is extremely important that you should come at once. Every day makes things more complicated ... in the management of the estate. I remain, with congratulations,
Sincerely your friend, ...

The young man sat there, dazed.

He had always known about those millions; the

expectation of them had always vaguely dazzled his imagination, tampered more than he was aware with the sincerity of his feelings, with the reality of his life; but now the shower of gold had fallen all about him and his fancy stretched its eyes to take in the immediate glitter.

Why, thought Hilliard, this turns life upside down . . . I can begin to live . . . I can go East. He saw that the world and its gifts were as truly his as though he were a fairy prince. A sort of confusion of highly colored pictures danced through his quick and ignorant brain. The blood pounded in his ears. He got up and prowled about the little room. It was oppressively small. He felt caged. The widest prairie would have given him scant elbow-room. He was planning his trip to the East when the thought of Sheila first struck him like a cold wave . . . or rather it was as if the wave of his selfish excitement had crashed against the wave of his desire for her. All was foam and confusion in his spirit. He was quite incapable of self-sacrifice — a virtue in which his free life and his temperament had given him little training. It was simply a war of impulses. His instinct was to give up nothing — to keep hold of every gift. He wanted, as he had never in his life wanted anything before, to have his fling. He wanted his birthright of experience. He had cut himself off from all the gentle ways of his inheritance and lived like a very Ishmael through no fault of his own. Now, it seemed to him that before he settled down to the soberness of marriage, he must take one hasty, heady, compensating draft of life, of the sort of life he might have had. He would go East, go at once; he would fling himself into a tumultuous bath of pleasure, and then he would come back to Sheila and lay a great gift of gold at her feet. He thought over his plans, reconstructing them. He got pen and ink and wrote a letter to Sheila. He wrote badly — a schoolboy's inexpressive letter. But he told his story and his astounding news and drew a vivid enough picture of the havoc it had wrought in his simplicity. He used a lover's language, but his letter was as cold and lumpish as a golden ingot. And yet the writer was not cold. He was throbbing and distraught, confused and overthrown, a boy of fourteen beside himself at the prospect of a holiday ... It was a stolen holiday, to be sure, a sort of truancy from manliness, but none the less intoxicating for that. Cosme's Latin nature was on top; Saxon loyalty and conscience overthrown. He was an egoist to his finger-tips that night. He did not sleep a wink, did not even try, but lay on his back across the bed, hands locked over his hair while "visions of sugar plums danced through his head." In the morning he went down and made his arrangements for Sheila, a little less complete, perhaps, than he had intended, for he met a worthy citizen of Rusty starting up the country with a sled to visit his traps and to him he gave the letter and confided his perplexities. It was a hasty interview, for the stage was about to start.

"My wife will sure take your girl and welcome; don't even have to ask her," the kind-eyed old fellow assured Hilliard. "We'll be glad to have her for a couple of months. She'll like the kids. It'll be home for her. Yes, sir" — he patted the excited traveler on the shoulder — "you pile into the stage and don't you worry any. I'll be up at your place before night and bring the lady down on my sled. Yes, sir. Pile in and don't you worry any."

Cosme wrung his hand, avoided his clear eye, and climbed up beside the driver on the stage. He did not look after the trapper. He stared ahead beyond the horses to the high white hill against a low and heavy sky of clouds.

"There's a big snowstorm a comin' down," growled the driver. "Lucky if we make The Hill to-day. A reg'lar oldtimer it's agoin' to be. And cold — ugh!"

Cosme hardly heard this speech. The gray world was a golden ball for him to spin at his will. Midas had touched the snow. The sleigh started with a jerk and a jingle. In a moment it was running lightly with a crisp, cutting noise. Cosme's thoughts outran it, leaping toward their gaudy goal . . . a journey out to life and a journey back to love — no wonder his golden eyes shone and his cheeks flushed.

"You look almighty glad to be going out of here," the driver made comment.

THE GOOD OLD WORLD AGAIN 283

Hilliard laughed an explosive and excited laugh. "No almighty gladder than I shall be to be coming back again," he prophesied.

But to prophesy is a mistake. One should leave the future humbly on the knees of the gods. That night, when Hilliard was lying wakeful in his berth listening to the click of rails, the old trapper lay under the driving snow. But he was not wakeful. He slept with no visions of gold or love, a frozen and untroubled sleep. He had caught his foot in a trap, and the blizzard had found him there and had taken mercy on his pain. They did not find his body until spring, and then Cosme's letter to Sheila lay wet and withered in his pocket.

CHAPTER XIII

LONELINESS

THE first misery of loneliness takes the form of a restless inability to concentrate. It is as if the victim wanted to escape from himself. After Cosme's departure Sheila prowled about the silent cabin, began this bit of work and that, dropped it, found herself staring vaguely, listening, waiting, and nervously shook herself into activity again. She tried to whistle, but it seemed like somebody else's music and frightened her ears. At dusk she fastened sacking across the uncurtained windows, lighted both Cosme's lamps, bringing the second from her bedroom, and heaped up a dancing and jubilant fire upon the hearth. In the midst of this illumination she sat, very stiff and still, in the angular elk-hide-covered chair, and knitted her hands together on her knee. Her mind was now intensely active; memories, thoughts, plans, fancies racing fast and furious like screen pictures across her brain. And they seemed to describe themselves in loud whispers. She had difficulty in keeping these voices from taking possession of her tongue.

"I don't want to talk to myself," she murmured, and glanced over her shoulder.

A man has need of his fellows for a shield. Man is

man's shelter from all the storm of unanswered questions. Where am I? What am I? Why am I? — No reply. No reassuring double to take away the ghost-sense of self, that unseen, intangible aura of personality in which each of us moves as in a cloud. In the souls of some there is an ever-present Man God who will forever save them from this supreme experience. Sheila's religion, vague, conventional, childish, faltered away from her soul. Except for her fire, which had a sort of sympathy of life and warmth and motion, she was unutterably alone. And she was beginning to suffer from the second misery of solitude — a sense of being many personalities instead of one. She seemed to be entertaining a little crowd of confused and argumentative Sheilas. To silence them she fixed her mind on her immediate problem.

She tried to draw Hilliard close to her heart. She had an honest hunger for his warm and graceful beauty, for his young strength, but this natural hunger continually shocked her. She tried not to remember the smoothness of his neck as her half-conscious hands had slipped away from it that afternoon when he raised her from the snow. It seemed to her that her desire for him was centered somewhere in her body. Her mind remained cool, detached, critical, even hostile. She disliked the manner of his wooing — not that there should have been any insult to the pride of a nameless little adventurer, Hudson's barmaid, a waif, in being told that she was a "good girl" and fit to be the mother of this young man's children. But Sheila knew instinctively that these things could not be said, could not even be thought of by such a man as Marcus Arundel. She remembered his words about her mother . . . Sheila wanted with a great longing to be loved like that, to be so spoken of, so exquisitely entreated. A phrase in Hudson's letter came to her mind, "I handled you in my heart like a flower". . . Unconsciously she pressed her hand against her lips, remembered the taste of whiskey and of blood. If only it had been Dickie's lips that had first touched her own. Blinding tears fell. The memory of Dickie's comfort, of Dickie's tremulous restraint, had a strange poignancy . . . Why was he so different from all the rest? So much more like her father? What was there in this pale little hotel clerk who drank too much that lifted him out and up into a sort of radiance? Her memory of Dickie was always white — the whiteness of that moonlight of their first, of that dawn of their last, meeting. He had had no chance in his short, unhappy, and restricted life — not half the chance that young Hilliard's life had given him — to learn such delicate appreciations, such tenderness, such reserves. Where had he got his delightful, gentle whimsicalities, that sweet, impersonal detachment that refused to yield to stupid angers and disgusts? He was like — in Dickie's own fashion she fumbled for a simile. But there was no word. She thought of a star, that morning star he had drawn her over to look at from the window of her sitting-room. Perhaps the artist in Sylvester had expressed itself in this son he so despised; perhaps Dickie was, after all, Hudson's great work . . . All sorts of meanings and symbols pelted Sheila's brain as she sat there, exciting and fevering her nerves.

In three days Hilliard would be coming back. His warm youth would again fill the house, pour itself over her heart. After the silence, his voice would be terribly persuasive, after the loneliness, his eager, golden eyes would be terribly compelling! He was going to "fetch the parson" . . . Sheila actually wrung her hands. Only three days for this decision and, without a decision, that awful, helpless wandering, those dangers, those rash confidences of hers. "O God, where are you? Why don't you help me now?" That was Sheila's prayer. It gave her little comfort, but she did fall asleep from the mental exhaustion to which it brought at least the relief of expression.

When she woke, she found the world a horrible confusion of storm. It could hardly be called morning — a heavy, flying darkness of drift, a wind filled with icy edges that stung the face and cut the eyes, a wind with the voice of a driven saw. The little cabin was caught in the whirling heart of a snow spout twenty feet high. The firs bent and groaned. There is a storm-fear, one of the inherited instinctive fears. Sheila's little face looked out of the whipped windows with a pinched and shrinking stare. She went from window to hearth, looking and listening, all day. A drift was blown in under the door and hardly melted for all the blazing fire. That night she could n't go to bed. She wrapped herself in blankets and curled herself up in the chair, nodding and starting in the circle of the firelight.

For three terrible days the world was lost in snow. Before the end of that time Sheila was talking to herself and glad of the sound of her own hurried little voice. Then, like God, came a beautiful stillness and the sun. She opened the door on the fourth morning and saw, above the fresh, soft, ascending dazzle of the drift, a sky that laughed in azure, the green, snow-laden firs, a white and purple peak. She spread out her hands to feel the sun and found it warm. She held it like a friendly hand. She forced herself that day to shovel, to sweep, even to eat. Perhaps Cosme would be back before night. He and the parson would have waited for the storm to be over before they made their start. She believed in her own excuses for five uneasy days, and then she believed in the worst of all her fears. She had a hundred to choose from — Cosme's desertion, Cosme's death . . . One day she spent walking to and fro with her nails driven into her palms.

Late that night the white world dipped into the still influence of a full white moon. Before Hilliard's cabin the great firs caught the light with a deepening flush of green, their shadows fell in even lavender tracery delicate and soft across the snow, across the drifted roof. The smoke from the half-buried chimney turned to a moving silver plume across the blue of the winter night sky — intense and warm as though it reflected an August lake.

The door of the cabin opened with a sharp thrust and Sheila stepped out. She walked quickly through the firs and stood on the edge of the open range-land, beyond and below which began the dark ridge of the primeval woods. She stood perfectly still and lifted her face to the sky. For all the blaze of the moon the greater stars danced in radiance. Their constellations sloped nobly across her dazzled vision. She had come very close to madness, and now her brain was dumb and dark as though it had been shut into a blank-walled cell. She stood with her hands hanging. She had no will nor wish to pray. The knowledge had come to her that if she went out and looked this winter Pan in the face, her brain would snap, either to life or death. It would burst its prison ... She stared, wide-eyed, dry-eyed, through the immense cold height of air up at the stars.

All at once a door flew open in her soul and she knew God ... no visible presence and yet an enveloping reality, the God of the savage earth, of the immense sky, of the stars, the God unsullied and untempted by man's worship, no God that she had ever known, had ever dreamed of, had ever prayed to before. She did not pray to Him now. She let her soul stand open till it was filled as were the stars and the earth with light . . .

The next day Sheila found her voice and sang at her work. She gave herself an overwhelming task of cleaning and scrubbing. She was on her knees like a charwoman, sniffing the strong reek of suds, when there came a knocking at her door. She leapt up with pounding heart. But the knocking was more like a scraping and it was followed by a low whine. For a second Sheila's head filled with a fog of terror and then came a homely little begging bark, just the throaty, snuffling sob of a homeless puppy. Sheila took Cosme's six-shooter, saw that it was loaded, and, standing in the shelter of the door, she slowly opened it. A few moments later the gun lay a yard away on the soapy, steaming floor and Berg was held tight in her arms. His ecstasy of greeting was no greater than her ecstasy of welcome. She cried and laughed and hugged and kissed him. That night, after a mighty supper, he slept on her bed across her feet. Two or three times she woke and reached her hand down to caress his rough thick coat. The warmth of his body mounted from her feet to her heart. She thought that he had been sent to her by that new God. As for Berg, he had found his God again, the taming touch of a small human hand.

It was in May, one morning in May — she had

LONELINESS

long ago lost count of her days — when Sheila stepped across her sill and saw the ground. Just a patch it was, no bigger than a tablecloth, but it made her catch her breath. She knelt down and ran her hands across it, sifted some gravel through her fingers. How strange and various and colorful were the atoms of stone, rare as jewels to her eyes so long used to the white and violet monotony of snow. Beyond the gravel, at the very edge of the drift, a slender crescent of green startled her eyes and — yes — there were a dozen valorous little golden flowers, as flat and round as fairy doubloons.

Attracted by her cry, Berg came out, threw up his nose, and snuffed. Spring spoke loudly to his nostrils. There was sap, rabbits were about — all of it no news to him. Sheila sat down on the sill and hugged him close. The sun was warm on his back, on her hands, on the boards beneath her.

"May — May — May —" she whispered, and up in the firs quite suddenly, as though he had thrown reserve to the four winds, a bluebird repeated her "May — May — May" on three notes, high, low, and high again, a little musical stumble of delight. It had begun again — that whistling-away of winter fear and winter hopelessness.

The birds sang and built and the May flies crept up through the snow and spun silver in the air for a brief dazzle of life.

The sun was so warm that Berg and Sheila dozed

on their doorsill. They did little else, these days, but dream and doze and wait.

The snow melted from underneath, sinking with audible groans of collapse and running off across the frozen ground to swell Hidden Creek. The river roared into a yellow flood, tripped its trees, sliced at its banks. Sheila snowshoed down twice a day to look at it. It was a sufficient barrier, she thought, between her and the world. And now, she had attained to the savage joy of loneliness. She dreaded change. Above all she dreaded Hilliard. That warmth of his beauty had faded utterly from her senses. It seemed as faint as a fresco on a long-buried wall. Intrusion must bring anxiety and pain, it might bring fear. She had had long communion with her stars and the God whose name they signaled. She, with her dog friend under her hand, had come to something very like content.

The roar of Hidden Creek swelled and swelled. After the snow had shrunk into patches here and there under the pines and against hilly slopes, there was still the melting of the mountain glaciers.

"Nobody can possibly cross!" Sheila exulted. "A man would have to risk his life." And it was in one of those very moments of her savage self-congratulation when there came the sound of nearing hoofs.

She was sitting on her threshold, watching the slow darkness, a sifting-down of ashes through the still air. It was so very still that the little new moon hung

LONELINESS

there above the firs like faint music. Silver and gray, and silver and green, and violet — Sheila named the delicacies of dappled light. The stars had begun to shake little shivers of radiance through the firs. They were softer than the winter stars — their keenness melted by the warm blue of the air. Sheila sat and held her knees and smiled. The distant, increasing tumult of the river, so part of the silence that it seemed no sound at all, lulled her — Then — above it — the beat of horse's hoofs.

At first she just sat empty of sensation except for the shock of those faint thuds of sound. Then her heart began to beat to bursting; with dread, with a suffocation of suspense. She got up, quiet as a thief. The horse stopped. There came a step, rapid and eager. She fled like a furtive shadow into the house, fell on her knees there by the hearth, and hid her face against the big hide-covered chair. Her eyes were full of cold tears. Her finger-tips were ice. She was shaking — shuddering, rather — from head to foot. The steps had come close, had struck the threshold. There they stopped. After a pause, which her pulses filled with shaken rhythm, her name was spoken — So long it had been since she had heard it that it fell on her ear like a foreign speech.

"Sheila! Sheila!"

She lifted her head sharply. It was not Hilliard's voice.

"Sheila —" There was such an agony of fear in

the softly spoken syllables, there was such a weight of dread on the breath of the speaker, that, for very pity, Sheila forgot herself. She got up from the floor and moved dazedly to meet the figure on the threshold. It was dimly outlined against the violet evening light. Sheila came up quite close and put her hands on the tense, hanging arms. They caught her. Then she sobbed and laughed aloud, calling out in her astonishment again and again, softly, incredulously —

"*You*, Dickie? Oh, Dickie, Dickie, it's — *you?*"

CHAPTER XIV

SHEILA AND THE STARS

HILLIARD'S first messenger had been hindered by death. Several times it seemed that his second messenger would suffer the same grim prevention. But this second messenger was young and set like steel to his purpose. He left the railroad at Millings, hired a horse, crossed the great plain above the town and braved the Pass, dangerous with overbalanced weights of melting snow. There, on the lonely Hill, he had his first encounter with that Arch-Hinderer. A snow-slide caught him and he left his horse buried, struggling out himself from the cold smother like a maimed insect to lie for hours by the road till breath and life came back to him. He got himself on foot to the nearest ranch, and there he hired a fresh horse and reached Rusty, at the end of the third day.

Rusty was overshadowed by a tragedy. The body of the trapper, Hilliard's first messenger, had been found under the melting snow, a few days before, and to the white-faced young stranger was given that stained and withered letter in which Hilliard had excused and explained his desertion.

Nothing, at Rusty, had been heard of Sheila. No one knew even that she had ever left Miss Blake's ranch — the history of such lonely places is a sealed book from snowfall until spring. Their tragedies are as dumb as the tragedies of animal life. No one had ever connected Sheila's name with Hilliard's. No one knew of his plans for her. The trapper had set off without delay, not even going back to his house, some little distance outside of Rusty, to tell his wife that he would be bringing home a lodger with him. There was, to be sure, at the office a small bundle of letters all in the same hand addressed to Miss Arundel. They had to wait, perforce, till the snow-bound country was released.

"It's not likely even now," sly and twinkling Lander of the hotel told Dickie, "that you can make it to Miss Blake's place. No, sir, nor to Hilliard's neither. Hidden Creek's up. She's sure some flood this time of the year. It's as much as your life's good for, stranger."

But Dickie merely smiled and got for himself a horse that was "good in deep water." And he rode away from Rusty without looking back.

He rode along a lush, wet land of roaring streams, and, on the bank of Hidden Creek, there was a roaring that drowned even the beating of his heart. The flood straddled across his path like Apollyon.

A dozen times the horse refused the ford — at last with a desperate toss of his head he made a plunge for it. Almost at once he was swept from the cobbled bed. He swam sturdily, but the current whirled him down like a straw — Dickie slipped from the saddle

SHEILA AND THE STARS

on the upper side so that the water pressed him close to the horse, and, even when they both went under, he held to the animal with hands like iron. This saved his life. Five blind, black, gasping minutes later, the horse pulled him up on the farther bank and they stood trembling together, dazed by life and the warmth of the air.

It was growing dark. The heavy shadow of the mountain fell across them and across the swollen yellow river they had just escaped. There began to be a dappling light — the faint shining of that slim young moon. She was just a silver curl there above the edge of the hill. In an hour she would set. Her brightness was as shy and subtle as the brightness of a smile. The messenger pulled his trembling body to the wet saddle and, looking about for landmarks that had been described to him, he found the faint trail to Hilliard's ranch. Presently he made out the low building under its firs. He dropped down, freed the good swimmer and turned him loose, then moved rapidly across the little clearing. It was all so still. Hidden Creek alone made a threatening tumult. Dickie stopped before he came to the door. He stood with his hands clenched at his sides and his chin lifted. He seemed to be speaking to the sky. Then he stumbled to the door and called,

"Sheila —"

She seemed to rise up from the floor and stand before him and put her hands on his arms.

A sort of insanity of joy, of childish excitement came upon Sheila when she had recognized her visitor. She flitted about the room, she laughed, she talked half-wildly — it had been such a long silence — in broken, ejaculatory sentences. It was Dickie's dumbness, as he leaned against the door, looking at her, that sobered her at last. She came close to him again and saw that he was shivering and that streams of water were running from his clothes to the floor.

"Why, Dickie! How wet you are!" — Again she put her hands on his arms — he was indeed drenched. She looked up into his face. It was gray and drawn in the uncertain light.

"That dreadful river! How did you cross it!"

Dickie smiled.

"It would have taken more than a river to stop me," he said in his old, half-demure, half-ironical fashion. And that was all Sheila ever heard of that brief epic of his journey. He drew away from her now and went over to the fire.

"Dickie" — she followed him — "tell me how you came here. How you knew where I was. Wait — I'll get you some of Cosme's clothes — and a cup of tea."

This time, exhausted as he was, Dickie did not fail to stand up to take the cup she brought him. He shook his head at the dry clothes. He did n't want Hilliard's things, thank you; he was drying out nicely by the fire. He was n't a bit cold. He sat and drank the tea, leaning forward, his elbows on his knees. He was, after all, just the same, she decided — only more so. His Dickie-ness had increased a hundredfold. There was still that quaint look of having come in from the fairy doings of a midsummer night. Only, now that his color had come back and the light of her lamp shone on him, he had a firmer and more vital look. His sickly pallor had gone, and the blue marks under his eyes — the eyes were fuller, deeper, more brilliant. He was steadier, firmer. He had definitely shed the pitifulness of his childhood. And Sheila did not remember that his mouth had so sweet a firm line from sensitive end to end of the lips.

Her impatience was driving her heart faster at every beat.

"You *must*, please, tell me everything now, Dickie," she pleaded, sitting on the arm of Hilliard's second chair. Her cheeks burned; her hair, grown to an awkward length, had come loose from a ribbon and fallen about her face and shoulders. She had made herself a frock of orange-colored cotton stuff — something that Hilliard had bought for curtains. It was a startling color enough, but it could not dim her gypsy beauty of wild dark hair and browned skin with which the misty and spiritual eyes and the slightly straightened and saddened lips made exquisite disharmony.

Dickie looked up at her a minute. He put down his cup and got to his feet. He went to stand by the shelf, half-turned from her.

"Tell me, at least," she begged in a cracked key of suspense, "do you know anything about — *Hilliard?*"

At that Dickie was vividly a victim of remorse.

"Oh — Sheila — damn! I *am* a beast. Of course — he's all right. Only, you see, he's been hurt and is in the hospital. That's why I came."

"You? — Hilliard? — Dickie. I can't really understand." She pushed back her hair with the same gesture she had used in the studio when Sylvester Hudson's offer of "a job" had set her brain whirling.

"No, of course. You would n't." Dickie spoke slowly again, looking at the rug. "I went East —"

"But — Hilliard?"

He looked up at her and flashed a queer, pained sort of smile. "I am coming to him, Sheila. I've got to tell you *some* about myself before I get around to him or else you would n't savvy —"

"Oh." She could n't meet the look that went with the queer smile, for it was even queerer and more pained, and was, somehow, too old a look for Dickie. So she said, "Oh," again, childishly, and waited, staring at her fingers.

"I went to New York because I thought I'd find you there, Sheila. Pap's hotel was on fire."

"Did you really burn it down, Dickie?"

He started violently. "*I* burned it down? Good Lord! No. What made you think such a thing?"

"Never mind. Your father thought so."

SHEILA AND THE STARS

Dickie's face flushed. "I suppose he would." He thought it over, then shrugged his shoulders. "I did n't. I don't know how it started ... I went to New York and to that place you used to live in — the garret. I had the address from the man who took Pap there."

"The studio? *Our* studio? — *You* there, Dickie?"

"Yes, ma'am. I lived there. I thought, at first, you might come ... Well" — Dickie hurried as though he wanted to pass quickly over this necessary history of his own experience — "I got a job at a hotel." He smiled faintly. "I was a waiter. One night I went to look at a fire. It was a big fire. I was trying to think out what it was like — you know the way I always did. It used to drive Pap loco — I must have been talking to myself. Anyway, there was a fellow standing near me with a notebook and a pencil and he spoke up suddenly — kind of sharp, and said: 'Say that again, will you?' — He was a newspaper reporter, Sheila ... That's how I got into the job. But I'm only telling you because —"

Sheila hit the rung of her chair with an impatient foot. "Oh, Dickie! How silly you are! As if I were n't *dying* to hear all about it. How did you get 'into the job'? What job?"

"Reporting," said Dickie. He was troubled by this urgency of hers. He began to stammer a little. "Of course, the — the fellow helped me a lot. He got me on the staff. He went round with me. He — he took down what I said and later he — he kind of edited my copy before I handed it in. He — he was almighty good to me. And I — I worked awfully hard. Like Hell. Night classes when I was n't on night duty, and books. Then, Sheila, I began to get kind of crazy over words." His eyes kindled. And his face. He straightened. He forgot himself, whatever it was that weighed upon him. "Are n't they wonderful? They're like polished stones — each one a different shape and color and feel. You fit 'em this way and that and turn 'em and — all at once, they shine and sing. God! I never knowed what was the matter with me till I began to work with words — and that *is* work. Sheila! Lord! How you hate them, and love them, and curse them, and worship them. I used to think I wanted *whiskey*." He laughed scorn at that old desire; then came to self-consciousness again and was shamefaced — "I guess you think I am plumb out of my head," he apologized. "You see, it was because I was a — a reporter, Sheila, that I happened to be there when Hilliard was hurt. I was coming home from the night courts. It was downtown. At a street-corner there was a crowd. Somebody told me; 'Young Hilliard's car ran into a milk cart; turned turtle. He's hurt.' Well, of course, I knew it'd be a good story — all that about Hilliard and his millions and his coming from the West to get his inheritance — it had just come out a couple of months before . . ."

"His millions?" repeated Sheila. She slipped off the arm of her chair without turning her wide look from Dickie and sat down with an air of deliberate sobriety. "His inheritance?" she repeated.

"Yes, ma'am. That's what took him East. He had news at Rusty. He wrote you a letter and sent it by a man who was to fetch you to Rusty. You were to stay there with his wife till Hilliard would be coming back for you. But, Sheila, the man was caught in a trap and buried by a blizzard. They found him only about a week ago — with Hilliard's letter in his pocket." Dickie fumbled in his own steaming coat. "Here it is. I've got it."

"Don't give it to me yet," she said. "Go on."

"Well," Dickie turned the shriveled and stained paper lightly in restless fingers. "That morning in New York I got up close to the car and had my notebook out. Hilliard was waiting for the ambulance. His ribs were smashed and his arm broken. He was conscious. He was laughing and talking and smoking cigarettes. I asked him some questions and he took a notion to question *me*. 'You're from the West,' he said; and when I told him 'Millings,' he kind of gasped and sat up. That turned him faint. But when they were carrying him off, he got a-holt of my hand and whispered, 'Come see me at the hospital.' I was willing enough — I went. And they took me to him — private room. And a nice-looking nurse. And flowers. He has lots of friends in New York — Hilliard, you bet you — " It was irony again and Sheila stirred nervously. That changed his tone. He moved abruptly and came and sat down near her, locking his hands and bending his head to study them in the old way. "He found out who I was and he told me about you, Sheila, and, because he was too much hurt to travel or even to write, he asked me to go out and carry a message for him. Nothing would have kept me from going, anyway," Dickie added quaintly. "When I learned what had been happening and how you were left and no letters coming from Rusty to answer his — well, sir, I could hardly sit still to hear about all that, Sheila. But, anyway — " Dickie moved his hands. They sought the arms of his chair and the fingers tightened. He looked past Sheila. "He told me then how it was with you and him. That you were planning to be married. And I promised to find you and tell you what he said."

"What did he say?"

Dickie spoke carefully, using his strange gift. With every word his face grew a trifle whiter, but that had no effect upon his eloquence. He painted a vivid and touching picture of the shattered and wistful youth. He repeated the shaken words of remorse and love. "I want her to come East and marry me. I love her. Tell her I love her. Tell her I can give her everything she wants in all the world. Tell her to come — " And far more skillfully than ever Hilliard himself could have done, Dickie pleaded the intoxication of that

SHEILA AND THE STARS 305

sudden shower of gold, the bewildering change in the young waif's life, the necessity he was under to go and see and touch the miracle. There was a long silence after Dickie had delivered himself of the burden of his promise. The fire leapt and crackled on Hilliard's forsaken hearth. It threw shadows and gleams across Dickie's thin, exhausted face and Sheila's inscrutably thoughtful one.

She held out her hand.

"Give me the letters now, Dickie."

He handed her the bundle that had accumulated in Rusty and the little withered one taken from the body of the trapper. Sheila took them and held them on her knee. She pressed both her hands against her eyes; then, leaning toward the fire, she read the letters, beginning with that one that had spent so many months under the dumb snow.

Berg, who had investigated Dickie, leaned against her knee while she read, his eyes fixed upon her. She read and laid the pile by on the table behind her. She sat for a long while, elbows on the arms of her chair, fingers laced beneath her chin. She seemed to be looking at the fire, but she was watching Dickie through her eyelashes. There was no ease in his attitude. He had his arms folded, his hands gripped the damp sleeves of his coat. When she spoke, he jumped as though she had fired a gun.

"It is not true, Dickie, that things were — were that way between Cosme and me ... We had not settled to be married . . ." She paused and saw that he forced himself to sit quiet. "Do you really think," she said, "that the man that wrote those letters, loves me?" Dickie was silent. He would not meet her look. "So you promised Hilliard that you would take me back to marry him?" There was an edge to her voice.

Dickie's face burned cruelly. "No," he said with shortness. "I was going to take you to the train and then come back here. I am going to take up this claim of Hilliard's — he's through with it. He likes the East. You see, Sheila, he's got the whole world to play with. It's quite true." He said this gravely, insistently. "He can give you everything —"

"And you?"

Dickie stared at her with parted lips. He seemed afraid to breathe lest he startle away some hesitant hope. "I?" he whispered.

"I mean — *you* don't like the East? — You will give up your work?"

"Oh — " He dropped back. The hope had flown and he was able to breathe again, though breathing seemed to hurt. "Yes, ma'am. I'll give up newspaper reporting. I don't like New York."

"But, Dickie — your — words? I'd like to see something you've written."

Dickie's hand went to an inner pocket.

"I wanted you to see this, Sheila." His eyes were lowered to hide a flaming pride. "My *poems*."

Sheila felt a shock of dread. Dickie's *poems!* She

was afraid to read them. She could not help but think of his life at Millings, of that sordid hotel lobby . . . Newspaper stories — yes — that was imaginable. But — poetry? Sheila had been brought up on verse. There was hardly a beautiful line that had not sung itself into the fabric of her brain.

"Poems?" she repeated, just a trifle blankly; then, seeing the hurt in his face, about the sensitive and delicate lips, she put out a quick, penitent hand. "Let me see them — at once!"

He handed a few folded papers to her. They were damp. He put his face down to his hands and looked at the floor as though he could not bear to watch her face. Sheila saw that he was shaking. It meant so much to him, then —? She unfolded the papers shrinkingly and read. As she read, the blood rushed to her cheeks for shame. She ought never to have doubted him. Never after the first look into his face, never after hearing him speak of the "cold, white flame" of an unforgotten winter night. Dickie's words, so greatly loved and groped for, so tirelessly pursued in the face of his world's scorn and injury, came to him, when they did come, on wings. In the four short poems, there was not a word outside of his inner experience, and yet she felt that those words had blown through him mysteriously on a wind — the wind that fans such flame —

> "Oh, little song you sang to me
> A hundred, hundred days ago,

> Oh, little song whose melody
> Walks in my heart and stumbles so;
> I cannot bear the level nights,
> And all the days are over-long,
> And all the hours from dark to dark
> Turn to a little song — "

"Like the beat of the falling rain,
 Until there seems no roof at all,
 And my heart is washed with pain — "

"Why is a woman's throat a bird,
 White in the thicket of the years? — "

Sheila suddenly thrust back the leaves at him, hid her face, and fell to crying bitterly. Dickie let fall his poems; he hovered over her, utterly bewildered, utterly distressed.

"Sheila — h-how could they possibly hurt you so? It was your song — your song — Are you angry with me —? I could n't help it. It kept singing in me — It — it hurt."

She thrust his hand away.

"Don't be kind to me! Oh — I am ashamed! I've treated you *so!* And — and snubbed you. And — and condescended to you, Dickie. And shamed you. You —! And you can write such lines — and you are great — you will be very great — a poet! Dickie, why could n't I see? Father would have seen. Don't touch me, please! I can't bear it. Oh, my dear, you must have been through such long, long misery — there in Millings, behind that desk — all stifled and cramped and shut in. And when I came, I might have helped

SHEILA AND THE STARS

you. I might have understood . . . But I hurt you more."

"Please don't, Sheila — it is n't true. Oh, — *damn* my poems!"

This made her laugh a little, and she got up and dried her eyes and sat before him like a humbled child. It was quite terrible for Dickie. His face was drawn with the discomfort of it. He moved about the room, miserable and restless.

Sheila recovered herself and looked up at him with a sort of wan resolution.

"And you will stay here and work the ranch and write, Dickie?"

"Yes, ma'am." He managed a smile. "If you think a fellow can push a plough and write poetry with the same hand."

"It's been done before. And — and you will send me back to Hilliard and — the good old world?"

Dickie's artificial smile left him. He stood, white and stiff, looking down at her. He tried to speak and put his hand to his throat.

"And I must leave you here," Sheila went on softly, "with my stars?"

She got up and walked over to the door and stood, half-turned from him, her fingers playing with the latch.

Dickie found part of his voice.

"What do you mean, Sheila, about your stars?"

"You told me," she said carefully, "that you

would go and work and then come back — But, I suppose —"

That was as far as she got. Dickie flung himself across the room. A chair crashed. He had his arms about her. He was shaking. That pale and tender light was in his face. The whiteness of a full moon, the whiteness of a dawn seemed to fall over Sheila.

"He — he can give you everything —" Dickie said shakily.

"I've been waiting" — she said — "I did n't know it until lately. But I've been waiting, so long now, for — for —" She closed her eyes and lifted her soft sad mouth. It was no longer patient.

That night Dickie and Berg lay together on the hide before the fire, wrapped in a blanket. Dickie did not sleep. He looked through the uncurtained, horizontal window, at the stars.

"You've got everything else, Hilliard," he muttered. "You've got the whole world to play with. After all, it was your own choice. I told you how it was with me. I promised I'd play fair. I did play fair." He sighed deeply and turned with his head on his arm and looked toward the door of the inner room. "It's like sleeping just outside the gate of Heaven, Berg," he said. "I never thought I'd get as close as that —" He listened to the roar of Hidden Creek. "It won't be long, old fellow, before we take her down to Rusty and bring her back." Tears stood on Dickie's eyelashes. "Then we'll walk straight into Heaven." He played with the dog's rough mane. "She'll keep on looking at the stars," he murmured. "But I'll keep on looking at her — *Sheila*."

But Sheila, having made her choice, had shut her eyes to the world and to the stars and slept like a good and happy child.

THE END

The Riverside Press
CAMBRIDGE · MASSACHUSETTS
U · S · A